the summer
of no regrets

the summer
of no regrets

KATHERINE GRACE BOND

sourcebooks
fire

Published by Sourcebooks Fire, an imprint of Sourcebooks, Inc.
P.O. Box 4410, Naperville, Illinois 60567-4410
(630) 961-3900
Fax: (630) 961-2168
teenfire.sourcebooks.com

Library of Congress Cataloging-in-Publication data is on file with the publisher.

Printed and bound in the United States of America.
BG 10 9 8 7 6 5 4 3 2 1

For my Nana, Grace Elizabeth Willey, beyond the veil

IS BAD BOY TRENT OUT OF CONTROL?

Hot teen actor Trent Yves erupted from his mangled Mini Cooper ready for a fight Saturday, after ramming a wall at the LA Equestrian Center. Asked if he'd been chug-a-lugging at the wheel, chick-magnet Trent gave reporters the one-fingered salute and threatened to smash a photographer's camera.

Trent's crazy mom Wendy Burke, a passenger in the car, was unhurt. Rumor has it that Mom's even more wacko than we thought, spending thousands on outlandish protection systems for her clothing and shoes. "Totally paranoid," said a source close to the family. "She'd drive anyone to drink."

"Trent was careening through the parking lot like he had rocket boosters," said a shaken onlooker. "Jumping curbs, horn blaring. He nearly ran over my grandma!"

Trent, who recently snagged Best Actor at the Cannes Film Festival for *Rocket,* certainly doesn't need an ego boost. While Europe and Japan go Trent-crazy, gobbling up Trent films and Trent TV, the former child wonder is his own number one fan.

Celeb' caught up with him Monday to congratulate him on being voted our Readers' Choice Hot Teen Actor of the Month. Trent's reply (to a reporter twice his age)? "I'm surprised you can keep your hands off me."

Trent's manager had no comment.

chapter ONE

"Touch him," Natalie whispered. "Go put your hands on his shoulders."

I slid my chair back into the shadows of Earl's Country Burger Arcade. "Are you kidding?"

"No, I'm not kidding, Brigitta. Boys love it when you touch them. Don't you want him back?"

Devon sat by himself playing Darkstalkers. A curl of hair fell across his cheek, and he brushed it back, revealing a constellation of freckles. "I don't do massages," I hissed. "And I didn't come here for Devon."

It hurt to look at him: Devon, who made raspberry sandwiches for me when we were five. Devon, who knew our twenty acres better than Natalie. Devon, who won us the homeschool science fair prize in third grade for our project on animal scat (it *is* what you're thinking). Devon, the first friend I let in our tree house, even though my sister Mallory said, "Girls only." Devon, who started putting his arm around me last summer and saying things like, "I'd rather be with you than anyone." Devon, who now found Jazmina_of_the_Night in his stupid sci-fi/ fantasy forum more interesting than me.

It was Natalie's craving for French fries that had brought us into charming downtown Kwahnesum (that's Kwa-NEE-sum, rustic Washington hamlet, population 1,054). It was supposed to be a blissful stroll through the shelves of the Dusty Cover New and Used. Just books. Quiet and reliable. No drama. No friends who betray you. No Devon.

His wiry arms flexed as he punched the buttons, concentrating the way he used to when he was helping me with a physics problem. I missed that. Natalie didn't need to know how much.

The arcade was crowded. It was midsummer hot, and we were blockaded by sweaty gaming bodies. The bottom book in my stack stuck to the table. Natalie's pile of romances was topped by *Makeup Secrets: Twenty Strokes to a Great New You.* She'd been giving it a try in the restroom, so now her L'Oreal Smoldering Dark Auburn curls were caught up in a silver barrette, and she'd added extra glam liner to her eyes.

I am the complete opposite of Natalie—hair: longish, blondish, straightish; eyes: non-glam; goal: to find the meaning of life. Natalie wants to "ditch this two-cow town and make it big in LA." Honest to God. But she was my best friend from the time we believed our Barbies came to life at night, and if I still have a best friend, I guess it would be her.

"By the way"—Natalie sneaked a peek toward the food counter—"that new guy they have scooping ice cream? Josh Hutcherson."

On the other hand, maybe she *still* believed dolls came to life. It would be at least as weird as her "sightings." Natalie spotted celebrity look-alikes everywhere: Nick Jonas making lattes at Starbucks, Taylor Lautner taking tickets at the Space Needle.

"Why would Josh Hutcherson take a job *here*?"

Natalie rolled her eyes. "Research," she explained patiently. "Actors are always going undercover to explore some new role. And they come to the Northwest *all the time*."

My Hollywood education started with Natalie—since my family doesn't own a TV. When Natalie saw my pop-culture ineptitude the year I went to Kwahnesum High School, she instituted "Media Night." It had cured me of saying homeschoolish things like "What's *American Idol*?" and depleting her social points.

At the Darkstalkers' console, Devon leaned toward the screen, where a nearly topless succubus was fighting a pharaoh in a giant headdress.

I shifted my body away from him. Couldn't Natalie just finish her fries?

"You should totally let me do your makeup." Natalie opened her bag.

I shook my head. "My face wouldn't know what to do with makeup."

She rummaged in her lipsticks and brushes. "Just maybe a little bronzer? I could so bring out your cheekbones."

It would be so completely Natalie to try to make me over and then present me to Devon like her 4-H project. I shook my head again. "They test that stuff on defenseless bunnies—doesn't that bother you?"

Had I heard him turn? Was he staring at my back?

Natalie poked at my books. "What did you get?" She scrutinized the top title with one of her upside-down smiles. "*The Complete Poems of John Donne*? You're hopeless, Brigitta." She offered me a fry.

"Donne was the greatest of the metaphysical poets."

"Ooh! How exciting!" She touched the second book. "And what's that? *Sound the Shofar: A High Holy Days Handbook*? You're going Jewish now?"

"Mom and Dad have a kosher group staying with us at The Center. They're biking for a sustainable planet. We're one of their stops."

"Wasn't it the alien abduction victims last weekend? Why weren't you studying them?"

"'Abductees.' And I don't consider them a religion."

For Natalie, religion is something that runs in your family—or not. If I asked her whether she likes being Jewish, she'd say it was the same as asking whether she likes having brown eyes. I can't talk to her about how I want the Great Cosmic Mystery to let me climb on its back.

I slid the books into my lap before Natalie could look closer. Fortunately, she hadn't noticed the item folded between them: the

3

literary equivalent of fried pork rinds. Poetry and religion were not enough to redeem it. And I'd die if Devon saw it.

"You can't just *become* Jewish, Brigitta." Natalie licked some ketchup off her thumb. "You have to either be born Jewish or convert."

I took another French fry. (I hoped they weren't cooked in animal fat.) "I'm only reading up, okay?"

"Whatever," said Natalie. "I like it better than your Baptist phase." She peered over my head. "He's still heeere," she singsonged.

"What's he doing?" I whispered, hating myself for giving in.

Natalie patted my hand. "Sweet Brigitta." She stood up. "You'll just have to turn around, won't you?" She wiggled her eyebrows. "Do you want some ice cream?"

I shook my head. Natalie headed for Josh Hutcherson. I would so *not* turn around.

Devon's parents stopped homeschooling and stuck him in Kwahnesum High School in ninth grade because it had a chess club. A *chess club*. Why *my* parents decided Kwahnesum High School was a good idea after they'd carefully cultivated counterculture children, I'll never know. Mallory begged to go when she was a freshman and stayed through graduation. I lasted (barely) through one awe-inspiring year. Then I went back to the woods.

In September Devon was back at KHS and I wasn't. In October he quit chess club. And as fall moved into winter we were (I think) a couple. On Valentine's Day he gave me a card, but it didn't say "I love you" or anything. It didn't even have hearts on it. It had a picture of Arthur Schopenhauer with a quote that said, "Religion is the master-piece of the art of animal training."

He never did get around to kissing me.

I shifted, ever so slightly, in my chair.

Did his head whip back to the screen? I peeked furtively. The pharaoh turned the succubus into a mummy. Had Devon fumbled the joystick?

I had a rush of sympathy. I could make it easier on him. I could walk over there. I'd smile and in that smile would be Divine Forgiveness. He wouldn't have to speak. He'd take my hand, and…

Devon's cell phone rang. "Hey!" His face broke into a grin. "Nothing much." He laughed a goofy, unDevonlike laugh and leaned back in his seat. Beneath the pharaoh flashed the words, "You misbegotten spawn of a jackal! Crawl back to your hole."

"I've got all the time in the world," said Devon. "For you."

Thoughts of saintliness vanished.

Natalie zipped over with a bowl of Cherry Garcia. "I gave Josh my phone number." She shivered. "God, he's beautiful. I have a good feeling about this."

Devon closed his phone like he'd just been named Beefcake of the Year. Natalie glanced at him. "So," she said, still flushed with her own victory, "why are you still huddled over your books, Brigitta?"

Before I could run, she was beside him. "Devon!" she trilled. "Guess who's here?"

There was no way to hide.

"Brigitta Schopenhauer," he said as if I was a distant acquaintance.

"Hey." I felt wobbly. Did I have big wet spots under my arms? Why did I care?

Devon slid his phone into his pocket. "I meant to come by," he said. Was that, just maybe, regret in his eyes?

Natalie seized her matchmaking opportunity. "You should come by. Tonight. We're getting together in the tree house, and you haven't been in forever."

His irises had little gold flecks in them. He'd said he meant to come by. "Coming by" had meaning for him: it meant—

"I left my jacket the last time," he said.

I imagined strangling him with said jacket.

"There'll be pizza," said Natalie while I stood there like an idiot.

"Um, okay," said Devon. He looked caught. He pulled on his hoodie. "See you around." He beat it fast out the door.

"Huh." Natalie frowned. "Don't worry, Brigitta. He's just nervous around you. It's obvious he still likes you. We just need to—"

I didn't stick around to hear what "we" needed to do. I made for the cave in the back. No one played the '80s games. Space Invaders faced the wall, making a phone booth–sized hidey-hole. I threw myself in.

I landed, hard, in someone's lap. "Hey!" he yelled.

I jumped off him as my books hit his feet and his third life dematerialized on the screen. He sprang up, his hands in fists. "What the hell?" Clearly, I'd invaded *his* space.

He looked a little older than me—dark hair, scowling eyebrows. And better looking than I wanted to notice. Maybe *I* could dematerialize.

He bent and began gathering my books. He smelled good. He had very broad shoulders. He handed me the Donne, the Jewish festivals…

Too late, I dove for the floor. I groped for the rest in a last-ditch attempt to save my dignity, but it was useless. The boy reached under the console and retrieved the last item: the *National Enquirer*, flopped open to shout, "Pamela's New Boy Toy Needs Penis Implants." He slapped it on my stack with an expression of pure disgust.

He offered me a hand, but I ignored it. Fake gallantry I could do without. I straightened as loftily as possible and pitched the *Enquirer* into a garbage can.

The boy's scorn melted into amusement. "Who are you?"

"Never mind," I said as Natalie sailed in calling, "Brigitta!"

She stopped as soon as she saw him. "God," she said, "you look just like Trent Yves."

Maybe a hole would open up in the floor.

The boy shoved his hands in his pockets. "I'm Luke," he said.

"Did you see Trent in *Rocket*?" Natalie babbled. "He should win a Golden Globe, I think."

"I don't follow movies," said Luke.

"Really?" Natalie flashed her pearly whites at him. "What are you into? Music? Football?"

He smirked and looked at me. "Tabloids," he said. "Love those tabloids."

I wanted to brain him with my Donne.

He glanced at the clock. "I have to go," he said. He edged past the still-chattering Natalie.

I squeezed my books tight so my arms wouldn't shake. Natalie didn't notice. "What was that about?" she said when he was gone.

"Let's just leave." I scanned tables for my purse. Mom wanted me home. Mallory was coming back from college so she could help us with The Center for the rest of the summer.

"He's so hot," said Natalie. "God, those muscles. And the long lashes? Didn't you think he looked like Trent Yves?"

I shrugged. Trent Yves was definitely not a star I kept track of.

"What is wrong with you?" said Natalie. "Did you look at that face? That gorgeous, gorgeous face?"

I had looked at that face, and it had looked back at me, and seen— what? Poet-and-violinist Brigitta? Seeker-after-truth Brigitta? Brigitta-who-knows-the-origins-of-hundreds-of-words? No. He'd seen vapid Brigitta. Easily entertained Brigitta. Sellout Brigitta.

Seeing Starzz ★ Celebrities Find Their Deep Space
Hollywood's Hidden Spiritual Quest

····································· *June 30*

Why Am I Writing About Trent Yves?

Trent Yves (Pronounced "Eve." I *still* hear people saying the *s* sometimes.)

Real name: Michael Boeglin

Film: *A Capella, Quitclaim, Sparrowtree, Imlandria, Le Petit Chose, Rocket*

Television: *Laser Boy, Presto!*

(see full list on <u>IMDB</u>)

Birthday: October 7

Age: 17

Born in: Trent, England

Spirituality: None.

So today, Starlet, the ever watchful, was sure she spotted Trent Yves in the Burger Arcade. I swear, any time I'm with Starlet, celebrities are swinging from the trees. ("Trent" by the way sounded exactly like an American. You'd think he'd have that telltale British accent when he's not play-ing a deaf Appalachian child or a kid from Milwaukee. But Starlet didn't notice.)

I apologize for wasting valuable blog

space on someone like Trent Yves, but hey, why don't we talk about the *opposite* of the spiritual quest? Trent: A pretty boy *Celeb'* magazine cover decoration who doesn't even try for meaning.

Here's a direct quote from the May 2 *Celeb'*: "I've been accused of having 'reckless good looks.' Makes me afraid I'll cause an accident." 'Nuff said.

Whitley Sandstone has met with the Dalai Lama. Timothy Castle raises money for orphans in Haiti.

Trent flips off photographers and shows off his pecs on Malibu beach.

Wake up, Trent! There's a whole wide universe out there beyond your bathroom mirror.

Trentsbabe responds:

trent is varry misunderstood & how can u dis him? hav u even seen *Rocket*? he is ½ french and that is why he is so sexy. so what if he knows it? i dont care if he dosent have a religion. who cares? thats personal anyway's. and he flipped off those reporters b-cuz they where bothering him. I LOVE U TRENTY!!!!!!!!! I AM URS 4EVER!!!!!

Mystic responds:

Rocket? No, I did not race out to see it. A runaway living on the streets with a reformed hit man isn't sure whether to stop a murder plot against his rich father? Puh-leeze. First of all, that's a pure Hollywood-obvious script. Second—Trent Yves? The smart-alecky magician's son from *Presto!*? The one who's always strutting around with his shirt off? Truly, I'd go see it if Trent's conceited slimeballness didn't take over everything he's in.

Xombiemistress responds:

Hey, Mystic! I agree with you. He might have wowed the critics in *Sparrowtree,* but since he's grown up, Trent is nothing but hype.

Loved your Whitley Sandstone post. I didn't know he was a Buddhist. Did you see my post on the Dalai Lama? I got to hear him speak! So awesome! Haven't heard from you in a while, girl.

Aquarius0210 responds:

Mystic, will you hate me if I admit I'm a Trent fan? You have GOT to give *Rocket* a chance. He's not just the cute kid from *Sparrowtree* anymore.

Elfmaiden36 responds:

trent iz so hottt!

Girrlpowr10 responds:

women need to be empowered by goddess energy—not worship at the altar of outmoded male supremacist hollywood culture.

Kitty_earz12 responds:

sexee sexee trent. mmmmm.

Natalie was planted on the tree house rug when I climbed through the trapdoor. I swung my feet onto the porch and went inside. No Devon. Not that I expected him.

Natalie scrambled up before I could even say hello. "Oh. My. God, Brigitta. I just talked to Ruby Chavez from the post office. Why didn't you tell me?"

"Tell you what?" I brushed some dirt off the rug and sat.

Natalie rested against the ladder to the loft and folded her arms. "About who bought the Hansen mansion."

Dad called the Hansen place an "eco-monstrosity": a sprawling estate built by a software millionaire, complete with fountains, a theater, and a heated driveway.

"Trent Yves is living right next door to you!"

My heart started to beat faster. The Trent Yves guy? Fifteen acres from my bedroom?

"Ruby Chavez said it was Trent Yves? Really, Natalie?"

Natalie sighed loudly. "Well, okay, no. She says their name is Geoffrey. Luke and Ann Geoffrey. But it's a boy and his mom. And didn't Trent's parents have a vicious divorce?"

My stomach twisted. Next door! The arcade boy lived next door! It was one thing to be humiliated in town; it was another to face repeated humiliation from now until college. The fact that he looked like a movie star only made it worse. Now Natalie would never leave it alone.

so hot!" Natalie plunked herself on the rug. "We should go see
, Brigitta. We should go over there right now!"

I propped a cushion against the cedar trunk that grew through the
floor. What could derail this train?

A sudden yank on the pulley rope brought Natalie back to her feet.
"That'll be Cheryl."

"Cheryl?" Cheryl Thompson was a friend of Natalie's. I couldn't
think why she'd be coming to the tree house. She'd hardly known I
existed when I was at KHS.

"She's bringing the pizza." Natalie hauled on the rope to pull up the
wooden "stuff" bin. The tree house is twenty feet up and at the edge of
a clearing. It's surrounded by enough cedar boughs that it's practically
invisible from the ground.

Cheryl's fishnet arm gloves emerged through the trapdoor, followed
by her green and purple striped head. "Hey"—she glanced at me as
Natalie lifted two pizzas out of the bin—"I heard Mallory's back."

Mallory was always with us in the tree house even when she wasn't
in the tree house, especially since I had been her senior project: the
Tree House Club (her name) was supposed to be a gathering where her
pathetic little sister could find friends. We would discuss self-esteem
and peer pressure. We would reject tobacco and say no to drugs. We
would be a Community of Trust.

Mallory had scoured the KHS freshman class for members. A scat-
tering of drama girls and brainiacs had rotated through. Being associ-
ated with Mallory Schopenhauer was never a bad move. Cheryl had
come once or twice. Tarah, who lived on the property behind ours,
had come a few times, but once The Center was completed, her mom
thought it would make her demon-possessed and forbade her to come
back. Eventually the "club" had dwindled to me, Natalie, and sometimes Devon.

So why was Cheryl here now?

"Okay," said Natalie. "Let's eat quick, so we can go next door."

Great. Natalie had invited her so she'd have backup for her Celebrity Ambush. I would chain myself here if I had to. I was not going to see "Trent." "Hansen Manor's probably guarded by rottweilers," I said.

"So, we'll bring hamburger." Natalie passed me a Veggie Bonanza, but I waved it away. Thoughts of re-humiliation had killed my appetite.

Cheryl rolled her eyes. "Nat, are you still going on about that new guy?" She sat.

"Cheryl, he is so Trent Yves, it's unbelievable." Natalie folded a slice of Hawaiian Heaven in half and began taking rapid bites.

"Yeah"—Cheryl wound some cheese around her finger—"like that guy in Pioneer Square you thought was Robert Pattinson? The one who later asked us for change?"

Suddenly, I had a new appreciation for Cheryl Thompson.

Natalie pulled out her sunglasses and stuck them on top of her head. "All we have to do is knock on the door. We'll speak French—and he'll answer in French before he knows what he's doing. And then, bang! We'll have him!" She stood up.

"You mean you'll speak French," said Cheryl. "And he'll wonder what the hell you're talking about."

"My French is good!" Natalie looked hurt. "I get As!"

Cheryl picked off her pineapple bits and ate them all at once.

Natalie sat back down. "All right, you nonbelievers"—she pulled a DVD case out of her backpack—"this is the perfect time for a TRENT MARATHON! Voilà! All three seasons of *Presto!* Compare Fox to Hansen Manor Hottie, and you will be a convert." Natalie slid her laptop out of her pack.

Cheryl perked up. "I'm so bummed that show was canceled. Do you have the 'locked in the workroom' one?"

It was better than being dragged next door.

Dad calls television the "domain of the mindless." Because I don't relish being mindless, I've never let on how media-hooked I've become. More than once I've tried to quit cold turkey: no gossip mags, no movie blogs. I've lasted an average of three and a half days. Nobody knows about the fansites I've bookmarked or the stack of *Celeb'* magazines under my bed (along with a *tiny* number of *National Enquirers*). Nobody knows about my blog.

The fact is, nobody knows me. Not really. I am a secret.

It didn't start out that way. I used to be *The Brigitta Show*: Tune in here! What you see is what you get!

Let's just say that Kwahnesum High School gave me an education.

On Natalie's laptop, Trent Yves playing Fox, second son of Presto the Magnificent, appeared floating in the air. Natalie paused the DVD. "See?" she said. "Note jaunty grin. Note tasty pecs. Note magic wand." She drummed her fingers on the laptop. "The imagination runs wild."

I pulled my hair into a ponytail. "Your point being?"

"That is so the guy at the arcade, Brigitta."

"His chin was different," I said. "Also, he had no wand." I attempted a laugh.

"Um," said Cheryl. "I'm sure he had a wand."

I blushed. Trust me to leave myself wide open, just like I had at school.

Mallory was a mighty senior when I came to KHS as a freshman: National Merit Scholar, head of the Random Acts of Kindness Club, founder of the Astronomy Society. Me? I spent three months drawing attention to myself and the other six trying to disappear.

I didn't know you weren't supposed to wear the patchwork coat your grandmother made you or drink nettle tea from a homemade thermos. You weren't supposed to like school food or English class or Democrats. You weren't supposed to audition for the musical unless you had been accepted by the "drama crowd." And playing the violin in the stairwell after you thought everyone had gone home? Uncool.

Natalie tried. But everything had changed between us. Suddenly, I was in her world and she didn't know what to do with me. We'd been almost like sisters all our lives—running through the woods singing and quoting Shakespeare. But at school I saw a new side to her—a side that wanted to make sure she was doing the right thing all the time—listening to the right music, watching the right shows. I swear I never saw her do the celebrity sighting thing until after I started at KHS. And then she'd be all, "I saw Whitley Sandstone at Disneyland," and I'd be like, "Whitley who?"

And she'd give me this look I'd never seen before.

After a while I stopped eating lunch with her and her friends. Sometimes she flashed me a smile, but she didn't seem to miss me.

Eventually it had been Devon who invited me to his table. He'd found fellow geeks right away. I was the only girl, and all we talked about was gaming and sci-fi. But the secret Brigitta was thankful that nothing had changed between me and Devon.

Now everything has.

I stretched out on the rug and stuck the cushion under my elbows. In this episode of *Presto!* Fox convinces Candace, played by Randi Marchietti, that he has real magical powers, passed from magician father to son.

"I heard he got Randi pregnant," said Natalie. "She had a secret abortion."

Sounded like Trent Yves.

Candace and Fox end up locked in the teachers' workroom. Predictably, they need a rope ladder. Predictably, Trent makes one out of his shirt, jeans, and jacket, leaving himself in nothing but boxers. The effect, I hate to admit, is breathtaking.

"Ahh," said Natalie. "You sure you don't want him?"

"That is so cheap," I said. "Can't you see how cheap that is?"

"Do I care how cheap that is?" said Natalie. "Look at him, Brigitta! You want a religious experience? There's your god."

I hated what the sight of Trent's biceps did to me. "Trent Yves has a different girlfriend every week."

"Brigitta!" Natalie poked me playfully. "I thought you didn't pay attention to Hollywood!"

"I don't." I am such a liar. "You told me that."

Cheryl popped out the DVD. "That's what the guy next door looks like?"

Natalie folded her laptop. "It's eerie."

"You know they don't have rottweilers, Brigitta." Cheryl had begun to succumb!

Natalie was bouncing up and down.

"I'm staying here." I moved to the window seat. "You can go without me." Maybe Devon would come for his coat after all. Maybe he'd bring chapters from the novel we'd been working on. Maybe he'd sit close to me on the window seat as we leaned over the pages, his arm bumping mine "accidentally."

I remembered the look on his face at the Burger Arcade. No. Probably not.

Natalie stopped bouncing. "But, Brigitta, it won't be any fun without you!"

Fun was not a word I had considered. *Mortification*, perhaps. *Ignominy.* "Angry Stud Muffin Reencounters Tabloid Girl."

Cheryl scrutinized me. "C'mon, Nat. Let's just stay. You didn't ask me to come here for Mr. Hollywood."

Then why had she asked her?

Natalie looked at her cell phone. "There's time! We could visit Trent and still do the rest."

"The rest of what?" I shifted on the window seat. The hinge was digging into my butt.

Cheryl cocked her head at Natalie and withdrew a velvet bag from her pocket. Natalie sighed and nodded, lowering herself back onto the rug.

Cheryl unveiled a pack of tarot cards. "Natalie says you need a reading."

"I do?"

Natalie patted my knee and looked at me earnestly. "I called Devon."

M y heart sank. "You called him?"

"Of course I did," said Natalie. "I told him he'd better get his sorry ass up here or you'd never speak to him again."

"Natalie, I already never speak to him again." I slid a window open. No sign of Devon on the trail. Cheryl's cards wouldn't tell me anything I didn't already know. And the thought of her using them to psychically vivisect me appealed to me not at all.

Natalie slid open another window and peered down sympathetically at the Devonless trail. "Do you have his coat?"

I pointed to the loft. Devon's coat had been there since March. I hoped it was full of spiders.

Cheryl began shuffling her cards.

"Hey," I said. "Let's just skip the reading."

Natalie's face softened. "It's Devon, isn't it, hon? Oh, God, I feel terrible." Sure she did.

Cheryl brandished her cards.

"It's a good idea, Brigitta," said Natalie. "You need the information." I sighed and gave in. If it would keep them from disturbing Angry Stud Muffin, it was worth being vivisected.

Cheryl laid the cards out in a pattern. I was more fascinated than I wanted to be. Devon would laugh.

"What does it say?" I leaned forward.

"Don't rush me. I'm concentrating." Cheryl examined the layout.

"Hmm," she murmured. She tapped the Emperor card and frowned. "Patriarchy." She sighed. "You're letting the male establishment control you, Brigitta."

Ha! The only "male establishment" around here was Dad, and he'd barely noticed me lately—unless he wanted work done.

She touched another card and closed her eyes. "The Knight of Swords sweeps in like a gale," she intoned. "He may charm you, vanish, and leave you devastated."

"That would be Devon!" Natalie clutched my shoulder.

A gale? It sure didn't sound like him. Devon was more of a mild draft. And why such enthusiasm over "devastation"?

Cheryl opened her eyes and drew one more card: The Lovers.

"Ooh!" squealed Natalie.

Cheryl sat back on her heels. "Whatever happens will unfold quickly." She surveyed her layout. "Your dreams are about to come true," she said. "But you're afraid of them."

With Hollywood timing, the floor began to shake. "It's him!" Natalie stage-whispered.

Devon's head and shoulders appeared. My treacherous heart tripped over itself.

"Hey," he said. "I heard there was pizza."

I fumbled for the last four slices, while Cheryl surveyed her layout again. "So"—she peered at Devon speculatively—"how's Jazmina_of_the_Night?"

"Oh, okay," said Devon. He shoved his hands in the pockets of his hoodie.

Okay! He didn't even have the decency to deny she existed.

Cheryl looked a bit deflated. Apparently her divination skills needed a brushup.

I had made Mallory invite Devon freshman year. She wanted her "club" to be about "women's empowerment," but I told her I wouldn't do it without Devon. I guess the joke was on me, because Cheryl had visited, decided Devon was an acceptable human being, and sent him a link to the Darkworlds forum where he became Master_of_Shadows and met Jazmina_of_the_Night (aka Erika from Vermont). Natalie said he'd met her in person at Norwescon. "You're so much better than her, Brigitta," Natalie had insisted. "Cheryl says she's really skinny—too skinny. Like emaciated, you know? He's going to lose interest. You'll see."

Devon's eyes flicked over to me and then down to the floor. He had a nervous little-boy look. Nothing like a gale.

I thought about how we'd done National Novel Writing Month the last three Novembers, racing to finish fifty-thousand-word novels in thirty days. Neither of us had ever gotten the full fifty thousand, but last November we'd almost done it. Near the midnight deadline, I was up to 49,901 and he was up to 49,892. We'd been sitting next to each other in the window seat, and he'd leaned over to check my screen. His hand was on the edge of the seat, not quite touching me. He smelled like soap and Altoids.

"We're close," I said.

"Yeah." He brushed a bug off my leg. "Almost there." He moved his arm to the cushion behind my back.

I started to sweat. "We've never made it this far," I said.

His eyes darted toward mine and then away. I could feel the heat of his skin. "I'm thinking of ending with a quote by Schopenhauer," he said. *"If we should bring clearly to a man's sight the terrible sufferings and miseries to which his life is constantly exposed, he would be seized with horror."*

"That'd work." I swallowed.

"It's twenty-seven words," he said. He turned, so that his face was inches from mine. "I like your book," he said.

"Thanks." My cheeks went hot. I could feel his breath. My lips parted slightly.

"How much more time do we have?" He swiveled his head back to the NaNoWriMo countdown clock on his computer: 0:00.

Devon's shoulders had slumped. "Oh well," he'd said. "Next year."

What about this year? NaNoWriMo was only four months away. Would we go back to where we'd left off? Maybe he realized now how shallow Jazmina was—that she only wanted him for his extensive knowledge of original *Star Trek*. "Brigitta!" he'd say. "It was only you, all the time."

I considered forgiving him.

"I should probably go," said Devon. "Brigitta, do you have my coat?"

I decided forgiveness was overrated.

None of us noticed my sister until she was actually in the room.

"Gita-girl!" Mallory flung her arms around me. She smelled like coconut shampoo.

"Hey," I said. "Welcome home."

She was tanner than when she came back for winter solstice, though Mallory doesn't tan exactly. We both have fair Irish skin like Mom's. Mallory's short, black hair fringed her face. Her UCal T-shirt clung to her flat stomach.

"Malloway!" Natalie hugged her.

"All my little chicks have grown up," said Mallory. She reached up and ruffled Devon's hair. "How's the rooster?" she said.

"Fine," said Devon.

"Still taking good care of my sister?"

Devon shrugged.

"Not exactly," said Natalie.

How could I be somewhere other than here?

"Not exactly what?" Mallory looked from Devon to me. "Is there a problem between the two of you? When I left in January, you were thick as peas."

Thieves, I thought. We were thick as thieves. Mallory always spoke in mangled metaphors.

Devon looked like he'd swallowed a coat hook.

Mallory got that rolling-up-her-sleeves look. "Sit down," she said. "We need to work this out."

We do not need to work this out, I thought, but Devon had already obeyed Mallory's order, and the others were settling in, waiting for the wisdom to drop from Mallory's lips.

She turned to me. "Brigitta, could you express to Devon how you're feeling? Try to use I statements."

Devon became interested in a knothole by his foot. I could not open my mouth.

Natalie touched my shoulder. "It'll help to talk about it, Brigitta. Men need to know how their insensitivity impacts other people."

Mallory turned to Devon. "Is there something you would like to say?" she asked, oh so gently.

"Um," said Devon. He rubbed at a cut on the back of his hand. "Well, I'm not trying to be insensitive." He was quiet for a moment. Maybe he was thinking of me, regretting all the grief he'd put me through. "But I really have to go home," he finished.

Maybe he'd never met anyone more boring than me.

Mallory stood up and blocked the door. "You can go home after we've had some honest dialogue."

Devon stood but didn't try to push past her. "I can't stay," he said.

"Devon," said Mallory. "I want you to look inside and ask yourself why you can't stay."

"I can't stay," Devon said quietly, "because I'm grounded. And if I don't get home before my parents, I will lose my car privileges for the rest of the year."

"Ohhhhhh," said Cheryl as if she'd suddenly figured something out.

"Why were you grounded?" said Natalie.

Devon picked at some dirt on his jacket. "Oh, you know," he said. "Chores. Stuff like that."

Cheryl folded her arms. "Chores? Really? Chores?"

Devon shifted. "I really have to go."

Cheryl stood up. "Or did your dad check your hard drive?"

Realization flashed.

"Eww!" said Natalie. "How can you look at that stuff?"

Devon ducked his head. He shrugged.

Cheryl looked ready to put an evil spell on him. "This is how patriarchy has held women down for generations!"

"I don't think it takes generations," said Natalie. "Only a few minutes."

I shut my eyes and wished for invisibility.

Mallory folded her arms. "Girls," she said, "we need to get a grip. This is all a normal part of psychosexual development in the adolescent male. Males use images from the Internet to—"

"Mallory, it's okay!" I said. "We get the idea."

To his credit, Devon did look like he wished he were somewhere else. Maybe in front of his computer looking at thought-provoking pictures, while dreaming of Jazmina_of_the_Night.

Mallory stepped aside so Devon could open the door. His narrow shoulders and brown curls disappeared down the ladder, leaving his coat behind.

I pulled my knees to my chest, feeling naked. And stupid. All that time I'd longed for him to kiss me when he had digitized perfection at his fingertips.

I thought of what was on my hard drive: Whitley, Daniel, even Trent. They weren't naked but...my porno? If anyone found that stuff, I would most surely die.

I thought again about the boy from the arcade, the only one who had seen my secret "starstruck" side. I prayed to God I'd never see him again.

chapter
four

At KHS I developed this fantasy about people reading my mind.
I *wanted* them to read my mind, because then they would say,
"Oh, Brigitta! Now we understand!"

Um…yeah. I got over it.

Dad used to kind of read my mind. When we made the long drive
to Seattle for violin competitions, he could sense what sections I was
nervous about without me even saying anything. If I was really freak-
ing out, he'd pull over and play them on his flute. Then he'd give my
shoulders a rub and say, "Relax, Gidget. You're my star whether you
win or not."

But all that changed when my grandparents died. After that, it was
like a door had shut between us.

My grandfather Opa died around the winter solstice during "that"
year—the year I went to KHS. And Nonni died near Valentine's Day.
It's a funny thing when people die. Okay, it's not *funny.* What I mean
is that before it happened, I wanted so badly to be known by people
at school, and after, I wanted to disappear. I couldn't risk bursting into
tears or something stupid. A few times I almost did, but I was able to
stop it. The trick is not to let yourself feel anything too strong. Just keep
everything sort of even. It's better not to play the violin, for example.

No sooner had I figured out how to disappear, than Mom and Dad's
chanting, drumming, eco-happy friends finished building The Center
out of old tires and dirt. The Center is an Earthship. Dad says it's "a

completely independent globally oriented dwelling unit made from materials indigenous to the planet." Translation: a half-buried building insulated with pop cans. Not that I'm allowed to drink pop.

The Center is Dad's dream come true. Mallory and I spent our formative years in a single-wide on our twenty acres so that The Center could finally rise out of the ground, gleaming with social consciousness. The whole thing is all adobe and solar panels and sloping greenhouse windows wedged into the hill like a glass stairway. The upstairs gazes from the hilltop like a tranced-out giant. The front door is his nose.

With its thick, rounded walls and trees growing inside, it looks like a combination of something out of *Star Wars* and an elf dwelling from *Lord of the Rings*. The *Seattle Times* featured it in their Living section, along with a complete rundown of what the Schopenhauers were up to: drumming in the sweat lodge (Dad), past-life regression workshops (Mom—who also talks to fairies, though, thank God, she didn't tell any reporters).

Needless to say, none of the other freshmen lived in Earthships (with or without fairies).

Dad got really busy after that. There was "no time" to drive me to Seattle for Youth Symphony, so I had to quit "for a while." (Right.) He lost his flute (he said), so we couldn't practice together. He started trying out this new "spirituality" thing, though he'd never even used the word *spiritual* before. (That was Mom's department.) Mostly that was a good thing, because he stopped exploding at us all the time. But it also made him a stranger.

And then nobody could read my mind.

What is it to be known, anyway? Maybe being known is overrated.

★ ★ ★

Something was wrong. I sat up in my sleeping bag blinking in the gray light of the loft. The air was cold, and my mattress had deflated, leaving me on the bare boards. Sleeping in the tree house had been more appealing than another therapy session with Mallory.

Wind in the limbs rocked the tree house gently. I'd named this tree Eve, and she was a good place to be when life went south. A cedar branch curved across the skylight like a protective arm. A few moths fluttered in the domed glass.

I quieted my breathing and listened to the outside: squirrels chattering near the window, the buzzing of a wasp. And down below…That was it! The kinglets and robins were sounding an alarm. Something was down there.

It was freezing outside my bag. I yanked on my jeans and pulled out my Nonni coat—the patchwork one she made me right before she died. No one knew I slept with it, but it made me feel better. I slipped it on and stuffed my feet into my sneakers.

Out on the porch I scanned the clearing. There! Twenty paces from Eve was…Oh, God, what was *he* doing here? Wasn't the Hansen acreage enough for him? If there was a God, why would he (or she) send me this?

He sat against the Douglas fir I'd named Adam, knees drawn up, arms wrapped around them. He couldn't see me on the tree house porch. I'd leave it that way. I could wait him out. I slowly sat myself down against the wall and put my hands flat on the damp boards. Pitch stuck to my fingers. Mosquitoes bit me. My hair probably looked like mice were living in it, and I hadn't brushed my teeth. He'd better go away soon.

At least ten minutes went by. Luke Geoffrey leaned back against Adam, ran his hands through the pine duff. He was beautiful. I hated myself for thinking that, but he was. He looked sad, and I had a ridiculous urge to go down there and hug him. Instead, I was spying on him. This thought came to me slowly. Most people who sit in the woods like that want privacy, and I was unabashedly scanning his face for clues about his sadness. His mother had died, I thought. No, he had befriended a homeless orphan child he'd found in a subway station in

Manhattan. She was six, and he'd convinced his parents they should adopt her. But she'd died, horribly of AIDS the following year, since her mother was a heroin addict. All Luke had left of her was a Raggedy Ann doll he had given her, and now he carried the doll in his pocket, crying into its stained apron when he was alone.

Luke got up from where he was sitting, and I was instantly, screamingly embarrassed about the orphan girl, as if he could read my mind from down there. This was the boy who had infrared humiliation-sensing capabilities. This was the boy didn't know anything good about me. He didn't know I was deep and philosophical or that I had won violin competitions. He only knew I read the *National Enquirer*.

He started walking toward Eve. *No!* I thought. *Go back!* Or at least don't look up. Every muscle in my body tightened. I would stay perfectly still and not breathe until he went away. He stopped and picked a few huckleberries, lifted his palm to examine them, and then dumped them on the ground and squished them with his foot. He crouched to tie his shoelace. I could see the back of his neck as he bent forward.

And then I saw her. She emerged from behind Adam, all in one motion: tawny gold fur, white muzzle outlined in black. "Cougar!" I heard myself scream.

She was probably seven feet long from nose to tail. I don't know why I decided she was female; I'd never seen a cougar outside of Northwest Trek Wildlife Park. Cougars don't let people see them unless they want to be seen. Dad says they can track a person for miles and he'll never know.

Luke fell backward, catching himself on his hands. The cougar's ears lowered as she locked eyes with him. She was terrifyingly beautiful: strong and sleek. Luke froze.

My knuckles were white on the railing. "Get big!" I yelled. "Stand up!"

He must have wondered where the disembodied voice was coming from, but he didn't dare look away from the cat. He got to his feet and began backing away from her. I could see that he'd soon be trapped against the bushes. I had to think like a cougar. Luke certainly wasn't going to.

I clambered down the ladder. The cougar didn't even look at me. I had nothing to fight her with. I tore off my Nonni coat, not sure how that was going to help. All I could hear in my ears was my own hollering. I had no time to consider whether I was crazy.

Luke was yelling "Get away!" At the cougar or at me, I couldn't tell, but I raced forward and began whacking at the cat with my coat. (Yes, I realize now, I was crazy.) The cougar shook her head, like the coat was an annoying insect. She laid her ears flat and opened her mouth. Four huge canines gleamed in the morning light. Her muscular shoulders rippled as she moved toward us, and a hiss like a rattlesnake came from her throat.

Luke was breathing hard. "Holy shit," he said. The cougar circled. She was fixed on Luke. I scooped up a handful of dirt, rocks, and fir cones and threw it at her face, but she didn't even flinch. I kept swinging my coat.

Luke grabbed a broken tree limb and thrust it at her. She snarled. My coat caught on a branch, and she swiped at it with a plate-sized paw. I felt naked without my coat. Undefended. I'd die here with Luke. Really die. Not like in the stories I made up. *Focus*, I told myself. *Breathe and focus.*

I read an article about a woman killed by a cougar in Colorado. The cat had sunk its teeth into her head and neck and peeled her scalp back. That's how they'd find us: scalped, covered in leaves with all our vital organs eaten out. I wished I knew less about animals.

Luke swung the tree limb in front of us. The cougar stayed in a crouch, her tail twitching, her eyes locked with his. I became a two-legged rock thrower. "Oh, God!" I kept screaming, "O-god-o-god-o-god-o-god-o-god!" I yelled myself hoarse and went on yelling. I was drenched in sweat. We backed, one step at a time, across the clearing, past Eve. The cat followed us step for step, tail low, icy golden eyes staring Luke down.

Then, as if she'd suddenly thought of something better to do, the cougar relaxed. Her canines disappeared, and her tongue came out to lick her nose. And then she turned and walked into the trees. Stopping for a brief moment, she looked back at us as if to say, "Not this time." As quickly as she had appeared, she disappeared.

I collapsed against Eve. I was shaking and couldn't stop. Luke's face was covered in dirt and maybe tears. I'd prayed never to see him again, but now it didn't matter.

He held his hand out to me. I took it. "Thanks," he croaked and pulled me to him. He wrapped his arms around me. He was shaking, too. We stood that way for a long time. I smelled the wet wool of his sweater. He put his chin on my hair as if we'd always known each other. I felt the fear drain out of both of us. Devon had never, ever held me like that. No one had.

Luke stepped back and looked at me, his hands still on my arms. Then he stepped into the clearing and picked up my Nonni coat from where the cougar had tossed it. Three huge rips ran down the back of it. I shivered and he put it around me. "Here's your hero cloak," he said.

His eyes were so blue I thought I'd fall into them and drown. I wanted to touch his jaw where it curved down to a strong chin streaked with dirt. His lips were wide and kissable. He smiled.

And then, in the middle of the most romantic moment of my life so far, I opened my mouth and said, "You do look like Trent Yves."

chapter five

O migod, omigod, omigod, Brigitta!" Natalie came tearing up the driveway of The Center and threw herself at me. "I'm so glad you're not dead and in little bloody pieces all underneath the tree house! Hi, Clare." Natalie threw herself at Mom, who hugged her distractedly. The air was chilly damp, and my Nonni coat now had cougar-installed vents. All morning Mom had been handing me mugs of motherwort tea ("great as a nerve tonic").

It had been four hours since the cougar. I was not ready for people, but Dad's friend Clyde Redd was here along with Buck Harper from up the road. Tarah from next door and her mom Rainbow arrived with lasagna. It had meat in it, so we wouldn't be able to eat it.

Luke had let me lead him out as far as the driveway and then had walked home by himself. He hadn't touched me again. I wished I hadn't wanted him to. All morning my body had been acting strangely—my skin buzzing like it was full of bees, my throat full as if something was pushing against it. I kept thinking about the eyes of the cougar—the raw power of her. And I kept thinking about how Luke's arms had felt around me—wanting him to come back and hold me again. A boy I hardly knew.

Several members of the Shivat Eiden group, all in skullcaps, were helping Mom harvest snap beans while watching the woods. Their row of bicycles was lined up along the porch rail. Even in my antisocial state of mind, I felt a pinprick of excitement at having them here.

This was the first real religion that had been at The Center in a while. For the last six months, it had been make-it-up-as-you-go groups like the Out-of-Body Travelers and the followers of Mamda, Channeled Ancient Warrior.

Tarah approached under Rainbow's careful gaze. She touched my hand. "Are you all in one piece?"

Natalie gripped my arm. "Brigitta fought that cougar off with her bare hands. She almost died!"

"It wasn't really like that, guys," I tried. "The cougar showed up. I chased her off. Everyone's making a big deal out of it."

"It is a big deal, sweetheart." Natalie hopped onto the hood of Mallory's car. "Cougars eat people."

"Not very often," I said. I didn't want to talk about it. My brain was still turning the whole thing over slowly—the cougar...and Luke.

I had expected the cougar to run off when I rushed her. But when she wouldn't take her eyes off Luke, I knew she was determined to kill him. And suddenly life had become my all-consuming goal—Luke's life or mine, it didn't matter. In that moment we both shared the same silver cord that held us to the earth.

But when Mallory had found me shaking in the entryway of The Center, the story had come out differently than it had happened: it had been *me* sitting on the ground in front of Adam when the cougar appeared, me she'd locked eyes with, me alone who had used a branch and rocks and my coat to fend her off. I'd meant to tell the real story, but it had been like telling a dream. When it came down to it, some parts wanted to be guarded, held only in my private thoughts.

In her usual running-the-universe way, Mallory had hustled me to Mom and called the Washington Department of Fish and Wildlife. Mom had cried and made me cocoa with real sugar from some secret stash I didn't even know she owned. Dad was busy with the retreatants and barely spoke to me. But that was normal.

Above us clouds moved away from the sun. Mallory was leaning against the adobe doorway chatting up Rainbow.

Dad stood on a large boulder staring into the trees and concentrating intently. He wore no shoes, and his blond hair, free of its usual ponytail, had blue feathers braided into it. He was bare-chested (cringe), and he wore a medicine pouch—a little bag of herbs—on a cord around his neck. Why, why, why did he have to do that today?

He started to drum, which made Rainbow look around nervously and Mallory wince. Mallory had persuaded her to let Tarah come to the Tree House Club back *before* Dad got weird and turned his "center for eco-sustainability" into a "center for spiritual education." He'd been an atheist until Nonni and Opa died.

"Mmm. It's finally getting warm." Tarah unzipped her hoodie.

I pulled the Nonni coat tighter around me. It didn't feel any warmer to me.

Mom and Dad never gave me and Mallory a religion. Being good flower children, they told us to choose our own paths. Mallory chose psychology at UC Berkeley. It's not a religion, but it allows her to know everything. It made her crazy that Dad stopped being an atheist after she left for college. It made her apoplectic that he was learning how to be a shaman from a mail-order course he found in the back of a magazine.

"So." Natalie lowered her voice conspiratorially. "Any sign of Trent? We should really go warn him there's a killer animal loose, don'tcha think?"

I felt a pang in the pit of my stomach. After I'd had a shower that morning and begun to come out of my daze, I'd wanted to call Luke. The thought had filled me with panic, but I knew he couldn't call me. He didn't even know my last name. And I needed to reassure myself he'd made it home okay. But there was no listing for any Geoffreys (or Jeffreys or Joffreys) in Kwahnesum. I tried Facebook but struck out there, too.

Now I gazed into the tangle of evergreens. Was the cougar still brooding there, waiting for her moment? As a kid I'd felt connected to every rabbit and squirrel. Dad had called me his Forest Girl. I'd *longed* to see a cougar, even making a little bed for them under a tree when I was six, with bunches of yellow flowers. (Turns out cougars aren't attracted by flowers.) Now the thought of leaving the safety of The Center parking area set me shaking. I'd been too afraid to go as far as the Hansen mansion, even via the driveway.

Behind me something moved. I jumped and shouted. But it was only a truck pulling up: blue, with a Washington Department of Fish and Wildlife insignia on the door.

"Easy, girl." Natalie put her arm around my shoulders. What was wrong with me?

A short, pocked man got out. He wore a tan shirt, like a Boy Scout, and a big hat. A rust-colored bloodhound hopped out after him. Dad came to greet him, drum in hand. "Paul Schopenhauer."

"Officer Mark Angeles." He shook Dad's hand, not even blinking at his Crazy Horse appearance. "And this is Mack." The dog sat obediently by his side. Mark and Mack. They were apparently a matched set.

"Good to see you, Mark." Buck Harper stepped forward and shook the officer's hand. "Don't know if you remember me, but I taught your daddy how to hunt when he was eight years old."

Buck was ten times that at least and had lived in Kwahnesum since it was accessible only by donkey cart. "That cougar's the one's been eating my sheep," said Buck. "There used to be a bounty on 'em. You could go out into the woods and shoot five, maybe six cougar and get fifty dollars a head."

Officer Mark nodded. "I've seen photos of that," he said.

"That is barbaric," said Clyde Redd.

Natalie nodded vigorously. "It's just so wrong to shoot an animal like that."

"You haven't seen a cougar-killed sheep, missy," said Buck. "And it could've been your friend, here. Cougars are a menace."

"Only because we're encroaching on their territory," snapped Clyde.

I almost thought they'd come to blows except that Clyde teaches nonviolent communication at The Center.

Dad gestured to me. "My daughter, Brigitta. She's the one who encountered the cat. It was my older daughter you spoke with on the phone."

Officer Mark turned to me. "Are you all right?"

I nodded. "She didn't touch me. Just"—I felt embarrassed to say it—"scared me."

"They're pretty awe-inspiring." He scanned a clipboard. "Especially if you're all by yourself."

I should correct him. I should tell him someone had been with me.

He eyed my coat. "Looks like she did more than scare you."

"Oh, this." I fingered the torn patchwork. "It wasn't on me. I was... hitting her with it."

Dad's eyes widened. Well, at least that got a rise out of him.

Officer Mark pulled out a pen. "So, where were you when this happened?"

Mom walked over, brushing dirt from her hands, and began to rub my shoulders. I licked my lips. "If you follow that path and cross a footbridge, it comes out in a clearing. Look up and you'll spot a tree house in one of the cedars. It's kind of hard to see."

Next to me Natalie and Tarah listened with rapt attention. Once I told about Luke, Natalie would pump me for every detail. And even if I didn't tell all, she'd still move in and try to manage everything, exactly the way she had with Devon. Not that Luke was my boyfriend. Not that he'd even promised to come back.

I took a breath. "Across from the tree house there's a Doug fir that's two hundred years old."

Dad had once let me count Adam's rings by using a hollow drill to take a sample of the tree's core. (That was before he decided such a violation would anger the tree's spirit.)

Tree house. Old growth Doug, Officer Mark wrote.

Of course, I couldn't leave Luke out. Officer Mark would need to know his part of the story. But the Luke aspect of the experience belonged to a tender place in me. Not the gossipy place Natalie kept all her mental boy files and her celebrity image gallery.

Dad fingered his drum, frowning. All his "journeys to the spirit world" and he'd never seen a cougar in these woods. Maybe it bugged him that I had.

As far as anyone knew, I had been by myself. It had just been Forest Girl sitting under a tree elder, communing with nature.

Mom rested her hands on my shoulders. Natalie, Tarah—every eye was on me. A breeze set one of Dad's feathers fluttering.

All Officer Mark needed were the facts about the cougar's behavior. Did it matter whether there had been one human or two?

"I was…sitting on the ground…"

"Was there anyone else in the vicinity?"

"No." I looked at Dad's bare feet. "No. I was alone."

chapter
six

When I'd finished, Officer Mark reached into his truck and retrieved a rifle-looking thing. Mom let out a long breath.

Where would they release the cougar once she'd been tranquilized? It would have to be remote—where she wouldn't encounter more humans. It seemed unfair. Weren't we in *her* forest?

"We contacted almost everyone on the surrounding properties," Officer Mark was saying to Dad.

Natalie leaned in on full alert. Most of our neighbors were already here: Tarah and Rainbow, Buck, Clyde. "How about the Hansen mansion, over that way?" She pointed.

"We've tried several times," said Officer Mark. "No one seems to be home."

Not home? Where was he?

Officer Mark whistled for Mack, and they disappeared into the woods. Mom went back to the Shivat Eiden group and her bean rows, which always calmed her nerves. Dad began drumming again. Rainbow smiled wanly and motioned Tarah back to the car.

"Trent's probably off on a press tour," sighed Natalie.

"That must be it," I said. "I'll keep my eyes peeled for swarming paparazzi." I browsed the huckleberry bushes as Rainbow and Tarah pulled out. That morning after I'd blurted out the Trent Yves line, Luke had let out a little groan. Maybe people had said that to him before. I wished *I* hadn't.

But then he'd winked and shot back, "And you look exactly like a dryad."

It occurred to me now that dryads are usually naked.

I imagined him really *being* Trent. Now that I'd saved his life, he'd invite me into his private plane and take me to Grauman's Chinese Theatre where I'd put my hand right into his handprint. We'd shoot a movie together—some epic adventure where we'd swing from a scaffolding onto the back of a galloping horse. I'd look into his blue, blue eyes and—

"Brigitta?"

I shook myself. I'd fallen headlong into Natalieland, like Alice down the rabbit hole.

Natalie scooped a few huckleberries out of my hand and popped them into her mouth. "Wake up, huh?"

A turquoise Toyota pulled up, and Felicity Bowen jumped out. Felicity was a friend of Mallory's who was doing a journalism internship at the *Kwahnesum Chronicle*. She had already transformed the paper from a haphazard ad flyer with a few articles into a weekly journal with interviews, a history of Kwahnesum column, and an event listing (mostly for events in Woodinville and Redmond—but Felicity tried). She made a beeline for me.

"Brigitta! What a story, hey?" Felicity's blond-red hair never needed combing because she kept it short as a boy's. She had a pencil stuck behind her ear—part of her reporter uniform. "You are something else, girl."

"Yeah," I said. "I guess." Felicity made me nervous.

"Well," she said. "I caught Mallory on her cell after she called the wildlife people. But I want you to tell me the story from the beginning, starting with when you saw the cougar."

I told the story as briefly as I could. Just the cougar and the branches and rocks. No blue-eyed Luke holding me. The more I told it this way, the more the real story became mine.

There was a shot. We all sucked in our breath. I hadn't expected a tranquilizer gun to sound like that. Felicity hurried out to the trail. Buck Harper was ahead of her, amazingly spry for an eighty-year-old. Dad set his drum down quietly but didn't start down the trail. We waited. Nobody talked. I'm not sure how much time went by, but finally Officer Mark appeared, lugging a black duffel bag on a rope. The dog Mack padded behind him.

"There she is!" chortled Buck. "Let's have a look!"

Before Mark could stop him, he had unbound the bag to reveal the face of the cougar. I faltered. Blood matted her neck and her eyes stared out, unseeing. Her fur was stiff and stood up strangely. She was dead.

Felicity began snapping pictures. Mom started to cry. Buck tried to comfort her by saying, "Now, Clare, that's one less man-eater we all have to worry about."

Dad stared soberly at me and didn't say anything.

I fingered the tears in my Nonni coat. I felt responsible.

Natalie's eyes widened. "You killed her!"

"And he's a good shot, too." Buck nodded at Officer Mark approvingly. "Just like your daddy."

Mark gave Mack a treat and didn't answer.

Natalie persisted. "But I thought…On Animal Planet there were these wolves. And they just took them somewhere with no people."

"They die," Officer Mark said finally. "When cougars are relocated, they usually die. A cougar needs a wide range—ninety to a hundred forty square miles can support maybe three of them. When we've relocated them in the past, we've radio-collared them. Invariably we find their carcasses within two years."

"Isn't that two more years she'd have gotten to live?" Clyde Redd jammed his fists into his coat pockets.

Officer Mark shook his head. "She threatened a human. We can't chance it."

"Why don't we lift her up?" said Buck. "I'll pose with her."

Clyde strode to his truck and slammed the door.

"Why is everyone so touchy?" said Buck. "I'll never understand you people. It was those damned sixties. All that marijuana ruined your minds." He shook his head. "Now is someone going to take a picture of me with this beast?"

Officer Mark pulled the bag back over the cougar's head. "With all due respect, Mr. Harper," he said grimly, "you didn't shoot her." He heaved the bag into the back of his truck.

"Let me know if you have any more problems," he said to Dad before he drove away.

Dad gave a brief nod and headed into the woods.

chapter
seven

I had some woods of my own once, but I lost them. The trees were
different from our Kwahnesum evergreens. Instead they were oaks and
dogwoods and sycamores. I had a house, but I lost that, too.

Nonni had named their place in Westfield, Indiana, Cherrywood—a
gingerbread kind of house with a big kitchen and screened-in porch. In
the back, the lawn rolled down to Nonni's garden, a rail fence, woods,
and a meadow where Opa rode his riding mower round and round
every evening. Opa was a builder and Cherrywood was his creation.
Nonni was its queen—a librarian in a floppy hat.

Every summer since I was nine, I'd been allowed to fly out to
Cherrywood by myself to visit Nonni and Opa. Mallory wanted to stay
in Kwahnesum most of her summers. But Cherrywood seemed more
like home to me than our cramped single-wide, even though it was
probably an eco-monstrosity.

And since I've been gone from it, I've felt lost.

* * *

The evening sun was hitting the bedroom windows. I cranked the
skylight open and sat at my computer. The Shivat Eiden group was
moving around in the downstairs kitchen. Downstairs is where retreats
happen. (Our apartment is upstairs and takes up as little room in The
Center as possible.)

The Mallory Invasion was well underway. My Hindu statues were
gone from the bookshelf, replaced by a copy of the *Diagnostic and*

Statistical Manual of Mental Disorders. Clothes covered the second bed. Mallory had disappeared shortly after the cougar party ended with its guest of honor's execution.

I couldn't blog about the cougar; the thought of her was jagged and cold in my gut.

Absently, I typed NationalEnquirer.com into my browser. "Whitley's Prayer with Dying Child" was the top article and, I had to admit, it was for this I'd disgraced myself in the Burger Arcade. Whitley and his prayer beads were at the bedside of a cancer-stricken nine-year-old from Fresno. I considered blogging about it but couldn't admit to my source material.

I scrolled down the page and noticed another headline: "Trent's Mom Hurls Chair at Daytime Emmys." (Had the Emmys been injured?) Trent grinned cockily at the camera, apparently unconcerned about his chair-wielding mother. Did he look like Luke? Not exactly. Did I expect him to?

Mallory chose this moment to barge into "our" room. I switched to Word fast and grabbed yesterday's poetry book purchase.

"It's freezing." She cranked the skylight closed. "You know, Mom could use some help downstairs." As if *Mallory* had been helping run The Center all year. Evidently I'd made a full recovery from this morning's near-death experience.

"Where's Dad?"

Mallory gazed at the ceiling. "He's still in the woods banging on his drum. Clearly in full-blown midlife crisis." Three quarters of psych and Mallory's diagnostic skills were at the level of fine art. "Whatever happened to him walking around the woods with his flute?"

I sidestepped the question. When I'd asked Dad about replacing his lost flute, he'd said it would be a waste of money because he was no longer interested in playing "Eurocentric music." "Dad's been drumming for years," I reminded her. Mallory knew this. Dad's master's thesis was on northwest native drum art.

"Not so he can talk to spirit guides." Mallory stashed her suitcase, knocking a chunk of adobe off a corner of the closet. Dad had never completed the finish work on the upstairs, and you could still see the even rows of tires that made up the walls. Mom said they looked like modern art. But really they looked like tires. And the adobe, made from straw, clay, and dirt we'd mixed in our driveway, had a habit of falling off if you hit it wrong.

"The least our father can do is to pay attention to his primary relationships," Mallory said. "Mom's down there by herself taking care of a dozen people. This is really dysfunctional, Brigitta." She threw the chunk into the trash. *She* could mix more adobe.

"Mom and Dad are fine." My head hurt.

She pulled off her T-shirt and chucked it into the hamper. Light filtered through the glass bottles embedded in the wall, turning her skin pink and green. She wore a shiny silver bra over her perfect size B breasts. (I'm a double D, and all my underwear is boring.) She peered at my screen. "What are you doing, anyway?"

"Paper for Mom."

"A paper? It's summer, little sister. What are you doing a paper on?"

"Donne."

"Well, I'm glad it's done." She leaned into the mirror and examined something on her chin. "Good God, Gita, relax a little."

"Not 'done,' Donne. The poet. Sixteenth century." I couldn't help feeling a little smug.

"Oh. Him. Troubled, troubled man. Probably bipolar." She yanked a blue silk tank top over her head. An answer for everything. It must be comforting.

* * *

Dad finally appeared at dinner, tired and mossy. The feathers in his hair had wilted.

Mallory pressed her lips together when she saw him. She yanked the vegetables and goat cheese out of the oven while I cut greens from the indoor garden. (We grow most of our food. It's an Earthship thing.)

Mom ran her hands up Dad's arms, and he half smiled, hugging her close. Mom likes this new spiritual version of Dad better than the skeptical one we grew up with.

"You smell like cedar," she said.

Mallory cleared her throat. "If we're done sniffing each other, we can eat."

Dad tied his hair back and washed his hands. He hung his drum in the window distractedly before sitting down.

Mom stroked his arm. "How was it?"

"Disturbed." He salted his potatoes. "Bear spoke to me yesterday, but now…a lot of confusion. Killing cougar like that…" Dad shook his head. "The energy field is contaminated." He didn't look at me. Did he think this "contamination" was *my* fault?

Mallory got one of her "indulgent" looks. She used to save them for me, but now Dad was fair game.

Mom divided a piece of bread. "Could you do a mourning ritual?"

Dad gazed out at the bench by Mom's garden. "I could." He nodded slowly. "Near the western edge…"

Mom dipped her bread in olive oil. "What's there?"

"I don't know. Something forceful. Strong, strong magic." Dad swirled the wine in his glass as if he was reading tea leaves.

My mouth went dry. A pair of golden eyes flashed into my thoughts. An open maw. Teeth like knives. The cougar's ghost? Was she angry?

Mallory propped her elbows on the table. "I find this fascinating," she said.

Mom sighed. "I'll bet you do."

Mallory straightened. "Well, no offense, Dad, but animal spirits? This isn't reality."

Dad used to talk a lot about "reality." Especially to explain how far out of it Nonni and Opa were—they'd gone to one of those churches where people spoke in tongues and fell on the floor. I used to go with them, and it wasn't so bad. No stranger than the people who channeled Mamda, Warrior Spirit.

Dad sipped his wine and didn't reply, but Mallory was just warming up.

"This is what we call magical thinking," she pronounced.

Mom pressed her lips together. "Your father, also, has taken Psychology 101."

"Actually," said Mallory, "we discussed this in abnormal psych. I wrote an entire paper on why primitive thought appeals to certain personalities. It's a kind of escape, a stress reducer. The problem is it can be debilitating." She looked at Dad significantly.

Primitive thought. Certain personalities. Exactly what Dad used to say. It was as if he'd come back to haunt himself.

My shoulders and head hurt. Couldn't Mallory leave it alone? Couldn't she see how much better Dad was doing now that he had his shaman thing? He was calmer, more relaxed.

After Nonni died, he'd been dangerously quiet. He'd paced a lot. When he did speak, his words were short and sharp. I'd learned to stay out of his way. Shamanism had centered him, connected him with the land—"bound him to it," he said.

And yet part of me wanted to bite back the way Mallory did. The cougar had come to me—or at least to Luke. If she had a message for anybody, it wasn't Dad. And now Dad was all grief stricken about an animal that had nearly killed me? Why did I feel as if I was disappearing? Probably because that's the way it's been since Dad started wearing feathers in the first place.

Dad put his hand on Mallory's cheek. "My love, there are worse things than primitive thought."

She glared at him and stabbed her lettuce. "By the way, Mom, I don't think Brigitta should be expected to write papers this late in the summer. It's July first, for God's sake."

July first. The date surged through me like an electric charge. "It's Nonni's birthday," I blurted without thinking. "She'd be seventy-five."

Dad looked away from me. He took another swallow of wine and resalted his potatoes. Even Mallory had nothing to say. It was as if I'd dropped a dead cat on the table.

Mom put her hand on mine. "That's right, she would, Gita."

Nobody said anything for the rest of dinner.

* * *

Mom left me with the upstairs dishes and took Mallory downstairs to do dinner cleanup. Dad went out to his office.

I sat on the indoor garden wall, wiggling my toes in the dirt. Faint wisps of Jewish music drifted up from the meditation room. Nonni might have liked that. She'd always said Judaism was the "roots" of Christianity. She'd have loved for me to become a Christian, but I couldn't do it, not even for her. I guess I do need to "choose my own path."

Someone downstairs had a violin. It made me want to get out mine, but what would I do with it? Walk into their service like a strolling minstrel?

Mom and Dad wanted us to give the retreatants space when they were doing their rituals. We weren't supposed to go barging in.

I brushed off my feet and put the kitchen shears away. Maybe I could just stand outside the door.

Our meditation room faces east, and the back wall is completely glass. Outside, the trees were silhouettes in the darkness. A woman in a prayer shawl was up front. Two candles illuminated her face. A bearded biker-looking guy in a leather skullcap played the violin.

I've only been to a synagogue once: Natalie's bat mitzvah. She read the Torah in this gorgeous river of Hebrew, and it made me cry (surreptitiously).

The singing was sad and slow. *Baruch Atah, Adonai, Eloheynu Vaylohey avoteynu v'emoteynu.* One of the men brought me a booklet. He motioned me to join them, but I shook my head.

I squinted to read the translation: *Blessed are You, Eternal One, our god and God of our Fathers and Mothers. God of Abraham, God of Isaac, and God of Jacob. God of Sarah, God of Rebecca, God of Leah, and God of Rachel.*

God of Brigitta? Who could say?

In front of me, the group joined hands, their prayer shawls draping together like a wall of wings. The melody spiraled out like smoke: *Eileh chamda libi: chusa na v'al na titalem.*

This is my heart's desire: have pity; do not hide yourself.

My throat tightened. "You're hungry, Brigitta," Nonni used to say. "You're hungry for God."

I slid into the hallway and set the booklet on the floor. Why did I want to hurl it at something? Mom and Mallory were laughing in the kitchen. At least my room would be mine for a while.

Upstairs I wrapped myself in my Nonni coat. Nonni had called it my "coat of many colors," like Joseph's in the Bible story, she said. I stroked a frayed corduroy patch. Being mad was ridiculous, but I was— furious: at Dad for talking to spirits when he'd always said religion was unreasonable, at Mallory for making everything mysterious into a psychological problem, and at Mom and Dad for making us choose.

Why couldn't we be Baptist like Tarah's family? Or Jewish like Natalie's? We'd be together in a religion, not at this potluck Mom and Dad called "spirituality," where everyone floated around in an individual bubble.

At Cherrywood Nonni and Opa would pull me into a group hug and pray with their heads bowed and touching. I'd felt linked to them. Now I couldn't mention their names *or* their prayers in front of Dad. He had his own, far superior world.

Eileh chamda libi. What was my heart's desire? And why did God love to hide?

eight

After four days, I was beginning to wonder if I'd dreamed Luke Geoffrey and the cougar. But Thursday the *Kwahnesum Chronicle* came out with Felicity's front-page photo: the cat limp and heavy in the bag.

Luke had not reappeared, except in my imagination. Had he really looked at me that way? Had I really been in his arms? The Hansen place seemed deserted, and I couldn't bring myself to knock on the door.

I pinned the clipping on the tree house wall. The cougar's eyes were huge, blank marbles. I sat on an orange crate and stared back. Where had she gone?

Mom talks about past lives and karma. When Dad was an atheist, he talked about how the body's decay feeds the planet. Now he talks about the spirit world. I don't like to think about any of that. Even if you go somewhere, everything familiar ends: no more birthday parties, no more brushing your hair. I shivered. The cougar's vacant face gazed from the photo. She'd been so alive. And in that moment of her aliveness, I'd been about to die. How could death and life be sisters like that?

* * *

When Opa died we stayed at Cherrywood for a week. We'd planned to come for Nonni and Opa's fiftieth anniversary. Dad and I had adapted portions of Josquin's Mass *Pange Lingua* for flute and violin. We'd practiced together for months. "We'll tour it, Gidget," Dad had joked, "and we'll make a mint. I'll pay my parents back for all those flute lessons they forced on me."

But no one was joking now. Dad and Mom hid in Dad's old room. Mallory rummaged through the attic. And Nonni sang. Nonni had always sung. Every night she tucked me into bed with the Shepherd's Psalm. Even when I was fourteen I didn't mind.

But this was different. Nonni sang hymns as she dusted, hymns as she salted the snow on the front steps. Opa was dead. And all she could do was smile and sing.

Dad avoided her. "Give your mother time," I heard Mom say. "She's in shock. We all are."

On the third day I stepped out to fill the bird feeder while Nonni sorted fabric scraps at the kitchen table, singing "Crown Him with Many Crowns." Stop! I wanted to say. Instead I flung the scoop hard into the wooden seed bucket. It rattled over, the closest I'd come to defying her.

Nonni looked at my face and was back for a moment. "Oh, Brigitta-Lamb," she said. "Don't you see? He made it! Opa made it! He's dancing on the walls of heaven! How can I not be happy for him?"

Two months later, she had her first stroke.

*   *   *

Mom taught us early to listen to animal language. Dad taught us to track, but Mom taught us to listen. We'd sit for ten minutes, completely still. Eventually I worked up to an hour. A few times birds landed on my head. Once, a hummingbird had perched on the back of my hand, like a small jade fairy. Some days I'd track deer, holding my head alert like they did, sniffing the air, leaping. When you assume the deer's rhythms, they accept you. You're one of them. But somewhere along the line I'd stopped listening. Sometimes animals still came to me, like the cougar maybe had. But I'd closed the door. Now I wasn't sure I could open it.

I lit a candle in front of the clipping. The cougar needed a name.

I stroked the picture. "Onawa." It's a native name from one of Dad's drum books—not sure which tribe. It means "wide awake." "Onawa." I circled Eve's trunk, trailing my hand over her bark. Could Onawa hear me? Somehow she didn't seem angry anymore. I said it again. "Onawa."

A thrush and two flickers flew past suddenly, letting me know someone was here. I peered down. Yesterday the Shivat Eiden group had left and was replaced with nine Buddhist poets who were regulars at The Center. Peter, my favorite of the Buddhists, strolled the path, bowing. He'd go all the way down, his head drooping almost to his feet. Peter always reminded me of an elf—with a baseball cap and a trimmed gray beard.

Buddhists don't kill things. Did he know about Onawa? That she'd been killed on my behalf? That was a load of karma. Maybe I'd reincarnate as a mosquito. I knew I should slip away while he was bowing. Ritual's a private thing.

Peter tipped his head back and smiled up at me, completely unsurprised. He bowed to me. All the way down, then up.

"Hi." I descended awkwardly. "Good weather for bowing?" Gaa! Why do I say things like that?

"It's always good weather for bowing." A red-tailed hawk landed on a northern pine. "Would you like to try?"

"Okay." I felt shy.

He brought his hands together. I did too. It felt complete, like I was connected to myself.

"What do you see?" he asked. "One small thing."

"That frond of bracken fern?"

"Ah," said Peter. He bowed, his head almost touching the dirt. I decided not to feel silly. I bowed, too.

"Am I bowing to the fern?"

Peter straightened. "To the fern, or to the ant, or to the ground that supports you. To your loved ones, to your enemies."

To Onawa?

"When you bow," he said, "you give your whole self away. You breathe out. You die."

"I'm tired of death." I blushed.

Peter nodded. "Death is the great teacher, Brigitta."

After he left, I practiced bowing. I bowed to a beetle, a slug, a clod of dirt. I wanted to bow but not do the dying part.

A ways from the path I noticed something: scratch marks—cougar marks—on the trunk of a maple. The grooves were smooth under my fingers—the power of those claws: a message from Onawa? I bowed low.

A sudden crashing-through-the-brush sound and Natalie emerged, breathless, from the foliage, twigs tangled in her hair. She stopped abruptly. "What are you doing, Brigitta?"

Swiftly, I became vertical. "Hard to explain."

She wasn't interested in an answer. "Hey, I'm back from boring Aunt Jo Ann's." Natalie's boring aunt was legendary. She lived in New York and, according to Natalie, spent all her time discussing bargains she'd gotten at Macy's and decorating her bathrooms.

"At least it was only three days. I called a bunch of times, Brigitta."

I had meant to answer. But every time her number came up, I'd let it ring through. She could always call Cheryl, couldn't she? "I'm sorry."

Natalie hugged me. "No worries. It wasn't all bad. I saw Kirsten Dunst at MoMA."

"Oh?"

"Really, Brigitta. She got into a cab, and I went charging out there—four photographers on the sidewalk! Aunt Jo Ann was all, 'Natty, Natty! Come back!'"

"So how'd she seem? Kirsten, I mean." A mosquito landed on my arm.

"Truthfully? Tired. Like she wished everyone would go away." She leaned against Eve. "Guess what I TiVoed for you?"

"No telling." I tried blowing on the mosquito.

"Trent! On *Letterman*! Oh my God, Brigitta, you have to see it! That boy is so ripped."

"One of the many things he offers the world." I sent the mosquito onto its next life and felt immediately guilty.

"Come on, Brigitta. How can he not make your mouth water?"

The thought of Trent made my head hurt. "Not hungry, I guess."

She pushed off from the tree and made her mission clear. "I've driven past the Hansen place like ten times. But you know I wouldn't go visit Trent without you."

"Luke Geoffrey is not Trent Yves." It came out meaner than I meant it to, but Natalie only smiled and wiggled her eyebrows. "Ah," she said, "you remember his fake name." She took off, squishing the bracken fern.

My mind formed a horrible image of her on Luke's porch whipping out her cell phone camera. He'd see me cringing by the fountain. It wasn't funny. "Natty! Natty, come back!" I tried my best Aunt Jo Ann voice.

Natalie laughed. "Come on, girlfriend." She took off running.

When Natalie and I were younger, we used to roam these woods, becoming different things: flower fairies, elves, girl pirates, and finally sixteenth-century mercenaries. Maybe Natalie can still play because she has her little sister Bekah to entertain. Me, I don't frolic in the woods anymore.

But I did follow her, arriving where the trees thinned to a row of maples and we were looking out at Luke's house. During our pirate stage, Natalie and I had spied on Hansen Manor fund-raisers for things like the vanishing western mole rat. We'd watch people promenading the terrace in black tails sipping vintage Ste. Michelle.

Now the place had an empty feel. An overturned lawn chair lay in the scraggly grass. "Well," said Natalie. "Let's knock."

In a way I wanted to knock, though my courage had failed me every day before this. Maybe Luke would be there. He'd smile at me the way he had in the woods—his Trent Yves smile.

Natalie started across the lawn. "What are you waiting for, Brigitta?"

I shook my head. "I'm going." I turned back toward the tree house. Let her knock. At least she'd be making a fool of herself instead of me. I twisted off a thimbleberry vine. *Smack!* I hit a hemlock. *Smack!* An alder.

Six alders and two spruces in, Natalie caught up with me. "Brigitta, what's going on?"

"Let's just not bother him."

"Oh, come on," Natalie teased. "Someone's got to welcome him to town."

"I already have."

Her smile faded. I couldn't believe I was playing the I-saw-him-first game with Natalie, who knew all my crushes from age ten on. Natalie, who smuggled me Cheetos.

"It was just for fun, Brigitta. Don't you remember fun?" Her usual kidding was gone. "Geez," she said. "Don't you remember when we used to serenade all the neighbor houses every May Day? At six o'clock in the morning? Don't you remember when we did plays out here? Don't you remember convincing everybody at Camp Eagle's Nest we were sisters? From a remote island off New Zealand?"

"We were twelve!"

"So? Who said you couldn't act goofy anymore? Who said you had to go all grim reaper? Who said you had to spend all your time up in a tree house studying the mystical whatever-it-is you're after? We're sixteen, Brigitta. We don't have to be dead."

"I'm not dead."

"Yeah, well"—Natalie made a zombie face—"you're doing a pretty good imitation." She pushed through some branches and headed for the road. Burrs stuck to her shirt. She was so clueless if she thought strolling up to Luke's front door was like May Day serenading.

A woodpecker drummed an oak snag. I dropped the thimbleberry vine and followed a deer path back to the property line. Inside Luke's house a thin-faced woman moved a lamp. Her hair was long and wavy. Brown, like Luke's. She turned toward the window. I pulled back behind the maple. When I peeked out again, the drapes were closed.

Seeing Starzz

Celebrities Find Their Deep Space
Hollywood's Hidden Spiritual Quest

Who Knew?

Starlet's hoping Trent Yves will show up on her doorstep with a dozen roses and serenade her.

Meanwhile, I have an admission to make. I have seen *Rocket*. All of it. And I may have misjudged Trent, just a little. It's surprising what he can do with a decent script. (Yes, I'll even admit the script was good.) I think that—at least this time—he can act.

Aquarius0210 responds:

Mystic, you've finally seen the light! The fight scene at the end? It was done in one take. I saw him on *Good Morning America*, *Leno,* and *Ellen*. Every time someone asks him about that scene he just says, "It was pretty intense," and changes the subject.

Cindylou responds:

Denzel was amazing as Theo. So sad when he got shot.

Trentsbabe responds:

i hav seen it 9x. i cry and cry at the end. best trent movie EVAR!!!!!!!!

Pandapriestess responds:

denzel's a classy ex-hit man. & trent...wow! i was surprised b/c the

only other good thing he's done was imlandria. the scene betw. rocket
& his evil father @ the end blew me away.

Cindylou responds:

The dad isn't evil.

Pandapriestess responds:

let's see…he's cold, heartless, beats his son, forcing him to run
away…no, he's really a nice guy.

Cindylou responds:

His wife died. And he lost his multimillionaire job. He went a little crazy.

DapperDan responds:

Excellent casting choices. I, too, was surprised by Trent Yves' emotional range. A demanding role for one so young. I think we'll see more
of him in serious roles. BTW, Mystic, I've been perusing your blog and
have added it to my links. You might want to have a gander at mine,
www.filmbuff.bloggapalooza.net. I am a film student at VFS. You're
asking important questions.

DragnMonkee responds:

this movie was stupid. it wuz supozd 2b an action movie, but it wuz
realy just "o i hate my daddy" & then he was all crying & crap at the
end. y wud anyone see it 9 x? imlandrea was stupid to. my sister made
me sit thru it. thot id puke.

Aquarius0210 responds:

Mystic, what did you think of the church scene?

Mystic responds:

Where Rocket is praying when Theo gets sick? Or his mother's funeral?

DapperDan responds:

The church scene (first one) was intriguing for the camera work. Why do you think the director showed first the gargoyles, then the saints? The long down-the-aisle shot with Rocket the sole person in the building was provocative. In an action movie, one would expect fast cuts at this point. I don't think this director was aiming for *Die Hard,* even with the gritty motif of the film.

DragnMonkee responds:

yah hes all "o my poor boyfreind theo. pleez god dont let him die."

Trentsbabe responds:

i hav seen imlandria 29x. btw theo wasnt rockets bf. theo just took care of him on the street. y do u think they were bfs?

DragnMonkee responds:

"i hav seen imlandria 29x." u must be realy stupid. only gud thing abt imlandria was gwen meliers ass.

Aquarius0210 responds:

DragnMonkee, why don't you go play with yourself?

Mystic responds:

Good to meet you, DapperDan. Aquarius, I'll respond about the church scene later. DragnMonkee, you are history.

nine

I blocked DragnMonkee from my blog and signed off. It was quiet without Mallory home. Mom and Dad were with the Buddhists, who were mostly silent. I flipped my bedroom light off (using it when there was still daylight was cheating) and went to start dinner.

The movie trip had taken most of the afternoon. Monroe is forty-five minutes by bike, which is my only transportation. (Mallory thinks I need to grow up and get a driver's license, but cars kill people. Besides, bikes save the earth.)

I lopped off some radish tops and dropped them into the compost jar. I felt guilty for seeing *Rocket* without Natalie, but if I was going to break down and see it, I had to do it alone. Now my insides felt upside down. The movie had done a number on me, and I couldn't get it out of my mind.

Trent as Rocket was more dangerous than I'd ever seen him. He was deadly angry. After surviving a brutal beating by his father (Christopher Walken), he takes a gun and is going to shoot him in his sleep, but freaks out and runs away instead.

I culled some cucumbers from the vine. The leaves had little white-flies again. Maybe the ladybugs would eat them.

Trent's long *Imlandria* hair was short and dyed black. Rocket wore bondage pants and a black shirt that had a bloody knife on it. He had piercings in his ears, eyebrow, and chin, and two leather wristbands—one with skulls and one that said "follow your dreams."

His eyes were gray, almost black. What color were they in *Imlandria*? in *Presto!*? in *Sparrowtree*? Because every time I looked at him I kept seeing them blue.

The last scene had stunned me—the one Aquarius said he wouldn't talk about. After living on the streets for several months with Theo and refusing to go home, Rocket finally does go back on the night a hired killer is stalking his father. The killer tries to shoot Rocket, but Theo takes the bullet for him and dies.

I grabbed a can of tahini from the pantry along with a jar of Mom's chickpeas. Why had the story taken hold of me this way? That scene was stuck in my head—Rocket's dad coming in as Theo falls; Rocket exploding, beating on his dad, punching his face, kicking, knocking him down. And his dad lets Rocket whale on him. He doesn't defend himself, until finally Rocket breaks down sobbing.

It would have been completely cheesy if Trent hadn't acted it so well, but I believed every second of his rage, and the tears were just…I don't know. I felt like I'd witnessed something private. Like Trent wasn't acting.

The falafel balls sizzled in olive oil. I transferred them to a bowl and set the table. What would it be like to have Luke over for dinner? Was he there at his house? Was he staying away on purpose? Would he ever come back? Was I only dreaming about him because I wanted him to be Trent?

ten

Onawa's face haunted my sleep: the ruff of fur around the ears, the staring eyes. I heard the shot over and over. On day six I stopped again at the tree with the scratches. Touching them, I almost felt I could hear her speak. But what was she saying?

I was almost afraid of Luke coming back. What if he looked exactly like Rocket: the strong cheekbones, eyes that shot fire but had sorrow locked behind them? Yes, it was stupid. Okay, it was extremely stupid. But every time I thought of Luke now, he morphed into Trent.

What if he really hadn't made it home? What if Onawa had killed him behind his mansion? What if he really was Trent and a strange, hippie princess had allowed him to be eaten? Would weeping Trent fans come to The Center with lit candles? Would photographers in helicopters hover overhead? Would *Entertainment Tonight* call me the most hated girl in America?

I crossed the bridge. Was that him, leaning against Eve?

My heart bounced a couple of times.

Luke's hands were in his pockets. An easy smile spread across his face. Rocket's smile? Of course not. The corners of his mouth were wrong. But then, Rocket had hardly smiled.

He was wearing jeans and a black shirt with snap buttons. The breast pockets had metal side zippers, and the shirt was open at the collar. I had to refrain from launching myself into his arms.

"So," I said nonchalantly, "you're alive." (And not under a pile of leaves with all your organs missing.)

"Yeah," he said. "Mum and I had to get away for a few days."

"Oh," I said. "To escape your adoring fans?" I attempted a laugh.

"Uh-huh," he said. "That's it exactly."

"I mean," I rambled on, "it was kind of a media circus here. Well, maybe not a circus, but there was one reporter and people came with lasagna."

I should have told him Felicity had no idea he'd been here—that his secret was safe with me. I smacked myself mentally. Why had I gone to that movie?

Luke shrugged. "I was on vacation." He ran a hand through his hair: brown hair, with threads of blond. I tried picturing it black.

"Yeah? So where did you go?" I hadn't meant it to come out so pissy.

"Aruba."

"Aruba? You mean like snorkeling? Tropical fish? That Aruba?" He did look tanned. And his hair had gone lighter.

Was it a movie shoot? I asked myself. *Stop it!* myself answered back.

"Mum wanted to go. We only got a few days. But it was nice."

Nice. A little jaunt to Aruba? Life's tough for some people.

Luke stared at a chipmunk darting into the brush. I picked at an oak leaf. I wanted to talk to him. I wanted to tell him how it had been since Sunday. I wanted to tell him I'd had dreams about him holding me. But I wasn't crazy.

"Did you read the *Chronicle*?" I said finally. "There was a big photo of the cougar after she was shot."

He looked up, surprised. "They shot her?"

"Well, of course they did." I felt irritable again. "She almost killed you, remember? What planet are you from?"

He laughed, and I instantly regretted how I was acting. "Illinois," he said. "I'm from Planet Illinois where cougars, also known as pumas, also known as mountain lions also known as species *puma concolor* are not an everyday thing."

I smiled. "You've been doing your homework."

"Wikipedia. The homeschooler's friend."

"You homeschool, too?"

"Yeah. You?"

I nodded. "Hey!" I remembered. "I've got that clipping up top. Do you want to see it?"

"Up top?"

"The tree house. Above your head."

He looked up and realization dawned. "That's where you came from! I thought you were, like, Jane of the Jungle swinging from the trees."

"You didn't know there was a tree house?"

"Well," he reminded me, "I was a little preoccupied."

I went up first, showing Luke where the ladder boards were hidden. He pulled himself through the trapdoor after me and stepped through the main door, running his hand along the walls. When we got to the clipping, I suddenly felt exposed. He touched the dripping candle and read the word I'd pinned under the picture. "What's 'Onawa'?"

"It's a Native American word. From a book." I wanted to escape. Even if it meant leaving Luke here.

He studied the picture. "It's her name," he said quietly. "You named her."

For a minute I thought I'd cry. I bit the inside of my cheek. "It means 'wide awake,'" I told him.

"Yeah," he chuckled. "She was."

We stayed an hour. I told him about The Center, and he didn't think it was weird at all. He told me about some of the places he'd been: Ireland, the French Pyrenees. He told me about his dad's property in Illinois—woods, but different from here, with a pond. He had two horses there.

He was easy to talk to now that he was warmed up, much easier than

Devon had ever been. I thought if he'd showed up when I was bowing to grass blades, he'd have understood. But I was glad he hadn't.

It struck me that he'd hiked all the way back through the woods today not knowing the cougar was gone. And that now he was sad she was. Maybe he was the kind of person who would get why I wanted a religion. Natalie thought it was weird. Mallory didn't believe in anything except psychology and "the indomitable human spirit."

Would Luke understand all this stuff? I wanted to believe he would. But I also wanted to pretend he was Trent Yves.

I am pretty sick.

"So," I said. "What else do you know about cougars?"

He stretched his legs out on the floor in front of him. "They have very big teeth. How about you? You must know a lot about them."

I didn't want to admit that even after living in cougar country my whole life, Onawa was my first cougar.

"I can show you where she's been."

Luke stood. "Lead on!"

He was amazed by the cougar scratches. "And look here." I pointed to a slight dip under a cedar tree, where the earth was matted down. "That's where she was sleeping."

Would Onawa mind my sharing her secrets with Luke? She seemed to have chosen him. I might have seen the cougar marks before if I'd paid better attention. But I'd been preoccupied with Devon. While I hunted for more cougar signs, Luke stepped off the trail. "Don't get lost," I called.

A minute later, I heard him shout.

I followed his voice to an old cedar snag that stood like a chimney a foot or so taller than me. Mallory and I had played in it until she'd outgrown that sort of thing. Luke poked his head inside the opening at the bottom.

"What is it?"

He reached in and lifted something out. It was a kitten, the size of a small house cat. Round, curious nose, spotted fur.

"That's a cougar kitten!"

He handed it to me. The kitten fit into my arms like a baby doll. It had a wild smell—strong and pungent. It laid its head listlessly against my hand. Vibrant blue eyes looked up at me.

"There's another one." Luke lifted out the sibling.

They had huge paws, but their limbs were so floppy. Mine began to purr. Luke's gave a pathetic mew.

"Onawa's babies," I said.

Luke nodded. "Orphans."

My kitten opened its white-mustached mouth, but no sound came out. It was spotted, almost like a leopard. They must outgrow their spots, the way fawns do.

Overhead, a woodpecker drummed. A gnat buzzed in my ear. I rolled the kitten on its back. "Mine's a boy," I said. "I think."

Luke checked his cat. "Another boy?"

I peered at his cub. My cat Ophelia had borne two litters before she'd been spayed. "I don't think so. Male cats have hidden genitals. See the round spot on mine? That's the p—" I felt myself redden. "Anyway. I'm guessing yours is a girl."

Luke sat cross-legged and tucked the kitten into his lap. She batted at him weakly.

My kitten began to purr again and to knead my chest with his paws. "Ouch!" I unhooked his claws from my shirt. He looked at me languidly. I ran my finger across the fuzz of his chest and could feel his ribs underneath loose skin. How long since they had eaten? Onawa had been dead five days. It had rained once since then, so maybe they'd had water. Maybe.

Luke rubbed the girl cat's ears. "What are you going to do with them?"

Me? What was *I* going to do with them? I shook my head.

Luke knocked a bug off his forearm. "Aren't there people who deal with things like this? Some department somewhere?"

"Are you kidding? That would be Fish and Wildlife."

"So call them." He put his nose against the girl kitten's nose and scratched behind her ears.

"Fish and Wildlife?" Was he really that stupid? Only a few minutes ago he'd been calling the kittens orphans. He'd understood why I had to give their mother a name. At least, I thought he had.

"What?" Luke looked up at me with those blue, blue eyes of his. They were almost the same color as my kitten's eyes. He smiled, rather adorably, and I decided to forgive him his stupidity.

"Fish and Wildlife sent Officer Mark." I tried to speak patiently. "The guy who shot Onawa?"

"They wouldn't shoot kittens."

"Luke! Kittens grow into cats. Big cats."

"Yeah." He stood, cradling the girl cat. "They'll die if they don't eat," he said. "You have to do something."

Me again. *I* had to do something. "Don't you care what happens to them?" I glared at him.

"Of course I do," he said, surprised. "They have no mother. They should be in a zoo."

"They live here," I said. "It's not their fault we shot their mother."

"We?"

"Yes, 'we.' Consumerism. Greed. America shot their mother."

Luke raised his eyebrows. "Not bad," he said.

A ridiculous sense of pride overcame my irritation momentarily. My kitten nipped feebly at my finger. Onawa's child. I had a sacred obligation to her. We had to keep the kittens secret. If I called Fish and Wildlife, they would send Officer Mark. He'd shoot them with a sad, sad look on his face, but he'd shoot them. Or Buck Harper would do it and want to get paid. A cougar's a cougar. Even a kitten would be a threat to people like Buck. "You haven't lived here long," I told Luke. "I'm not turning these little ones over to be killed."

Luke sighed. "Isn't there a zoo in Seattle?"

"A zoo? Yes, there is a zoo, where these creatures, who are indigenous to this very woods and who have lived here for thousands of years could be put on display like circus freaks for the entertainment of spoiled twelve-year-olds whose daddies work at Microsoft and who would rather be playing Xbox. Is that the life you'd pick for the animal the Snoqualmie Tribe called Protector?"

"Wow," said Luke.

I blushed.

"Brigitta." Luke stroked his kitten. It was the first time he'd said my name. "How are they going to survive?"

I had now officially painted myself into a corner. I pictured Buck Harper coming onto the property with a hunting rifle and a bunch of cronies, including Officer Mark's father, who he'd taught to hunt. They'd be accompanied by wildlife agents and zookeepers with huge cages on poles like the one in *Horton Hatches the Egg*. Felicity Bowen would be snapping pictures. I would face them all down. I'd block the cedar snag with my body. I'd call on the spirit of Onawa. "No closer!" I'd command, and I'd be so fierce that they would shrink back, convicted of their evil intentions. Luke watched me questioningly.

"I'll be their mother." I decided it right then. "And if you're interested, you can be their dad."

I couldn't believe I'd blurted out such a bold suggestion. I couldn't imagine saying something so pushy to Devon.

Luke gazed at his kitten thoughtfully. Then he smiled. "Okay," he said. "See if you can find some water."

I had three jugs of it in the tree house. I fetched one. It took a lot of tries to get the kittens to drink. When we poured the water into a bowl, the kittens wouldn't lap it.

Luke put some water on his finger and dribbled it into his kitten's mouth. He had a scratch on his arm and was watching the kitten intently through his dark lashes. In my mind, Luke kept shape-shifting into Trent and I wondered what he was doing here. I was no better than Natalie. The kitten licked at the water. Luke dribbled more in. I remembered Natalie's 4H project where she weaned a calf. I dribbled water into my kitten's mouth and lured her to the bowl with my wet fingers. Finally, finally, the pink tongue darted in. Victory. When Luke's kitten figured out the water trick, I thought he was going to do a jig. "Sweet!" he whispered.

"So the cougars are gone from Illinois?" I stroked my kitten's ears.

"Some people say they're not." He sheltered his kitten in his lap. "But I've never seen one."

"Same in Indiana," I said. "I used to spend my summers there."

"Really? Where?"

"Cherrywood." I felt exposed again for having said it. Cherrywood wasn't a town. It was like sharing the name of my teddy bear. "I mean, Indiana. My grandparents' place. They had a house, some acreage." My throat tightened. I peeked through the white fluffs of fur in my kitten's ears and examined them for mites. His ear canals were pearly and clean. Onawa had seen to that.

Luke watched me and didn't ask more questions. "I'm hardly there in the summer," he said. "Usually we go to Switzerland or something."

Switzerland. "What does your dad *do* anyway?"

Luke frowned. I'd offended him. I wanted to crawl into the snag and pull the cubs in over the top of me. "I'm an idiot." I examined a troop of ants near my foot.

"No, you're not." Luke brushed my hair back from my face. His touch jolted me.

"My dad's in telecommunications," he said. "He's part-owner in one of the larger cell phone companies in the Midwest. He just got in at the right time, when I was really little."

"So you haven't always vacationed in Aruba?"

"No." Luke stretched his legs out. "So," he said, "what are you naming our kids?"

"What? Oh! The kittens!"

Luke let out a laugh. "Brigitta." He said it as if he'd known me forever, as if he knew my quirks and liked them. He was so easy with his words, so not like Devon, who clammed up whenever he might be called upon to register an opinion of me, good or bad.

"Let's name the boy Felix," I said impulsively, "and the girl Kalimar— you know, from *Imlandria*."

"You sure?" Luke tickled his cougar's chin. "Kalimar croaked at the end."

"Aha! You do too follow movies!" Felix licked the back of my hand with a sandpaper tongue.

"What?" Luke draped Kalimar carefully over his thigh.

"You told Natalie you didn't follow movies. At the arcade? When I… oh, forget what I did."

He paused. "Oh, yeah," he said. "That *was* you, wasn't it?"

My cheeks went hot. "I didn't mean to throw myself at you."

"Don't worry about it." His eyes were laughing at me. "Girls do that all the time."

"Oh, really?" I shot back.

"Yeah." Luke grinned. "They think I'm Trent Yves."

Seeing Starzz

Celebrities Find Their Deep Space
Hollywood's Hidden Spiritual Quest

July 6

What Is Death?

An exploration of this topic yields interesting answers from various religions:

Ancient Egyptians believed the dead were ferried across Lily Lake by "He-Who-Looks-Backward," who took them to the Fields of Rejoicing. But only the rich got to go.

Hindus believe the dead are reincarnated but make a stop in one of many realms between lives. Swami Sivananda says that some souls "become gods and enjoy the happiness of heaven for a long period."

Christians believe the dead stand before the throne of God where they are judged. The righteous spend eternity with God, dancing on the walls of heaven.

Buddhists believe that after many incarnations, they hope to reach Nirvana, "the out breath," which is the state of oneness with God.

Tomorrow I will talk about Native American, Islamic, and Jewish views on death.

Aquarius0210 responds:

Wazzup with this topic? What happened to "Mystic-at-the-movies"?

Trentsbabe responds:

no offense mystic but this is realy deppresing. what abt that guy u saw? who looks like trent? did u see him again? maybe starlet is right. if he likes her she is lucky.

Xombiemistress responds:

Actually, Buddhists don't believe in "God" in the same way Christians do. But you're mostly right.

Mystic responds:

Xombiemistress, I just used the word "God" because it's the easiest way to explain it.

Cindylou responds:

speaking of death, mystic, it's all over rocket. i mean, that's the theme of the movie, isn't it? his mom is dead, he wants his dad dead, his father-figure gets shot. so much of it is like trent's real life.

Trentsbabe responds:

what??? trents mom died? when??? mystic is that guy still there? i wish i lived where u live. i wuld tear all his cloths off.

Aquarius0210 responds:

No Trentsbabe, Trent's mom is not dead (though she may be crazy). And he has a terrible relationship with his father. After his French movie, *Le Petit Chose* flopped (it's supposed to be like the French *David Copperfield*), his dad left him and moved back to France. Pix of him seeing his dad off at the airport are <u>here</u>. He looks ready to kill the photographers. That is not a happy face.

Mystic responds:

Xombiemistress, are you Buddhist? Does the good karma of nursing a sick animal back to life erase the bad karma of killing an animal?

Trentsbabe responds:

i m just trying to find out, mystic—dose trent live in ur town?????!!!!!

chapter
twelve

At 3:30 in the morning, blogging was getting me nowhere but halfway to sleep—where I couldn't go because I had cubs to tend.

I had come home before noon, hoping to go directly to Google—and cougar care instructions—but Dad had waylaid me at the top of the stairs.

"There you are! I need all hands on deck, Brigitta. I can't have you running off. I've got fourteen people coming for the sweat lodge tonight, and we have no power."

"No power?"

"Something's wrong with the turbine. Clyde's coming in an hour."

Because Earthships are designed to be "off the grid," we don't use city power. Dad installed a hydroelectric turbine in the stream that runs through our property. Usually it works fine.

"No power means no Internet?"

Wrong question. Dad hates the Internet. He calls it "a purveyor of intolerance and corporate-culture bullshit." He refuses to use a computer unless he absolutely has to. He shot a do-not-mess-with-me look. "Help your mother fold laundry, and then you and Mallory clean the kitchen and sweep the dorms. I won't have time. I should have started the fire already."

Mallory came up the stairs and handed Dad a cluster of sage. "Is this what you were looking for?"

"No, no," he said impatiently. "I have sage. I need tobacco. For the prayer ties."

"What on earth are those?" said Mallory.

"Prayer ties," said Dad evenly, "are small bundles of tobacco. We use them to summon help from the spirit world."

"Of course," said Mallory. "I should have guessed."

"I'll get it." I left and went downstairs. Why Mallory was so intent on baiting Dad I didn't know, but I wasn't sticking around for it.

I knew Dad was especially tense because Wise Crow was coming to the sweat lodge for the first time. Even though he wasn't Dad's teacher, Wise Crow had been a shaman for years. I knew Dad wanted to impress him. For someone whose spirituality was mostly a solo act, Dad sure got nervous around people who knew more than he did. When Dad was planning The Center, Michael Reynolds, the guy who invented Earthships, came from Taos, New Mexico, to teach a workshop on our property. Dad had yelled at us for a week before he arrived.

The rest of the day I ran stairs, scrubbed, and toted. Every hour or so, I stole out to Felix and Kalimar. It scared me to death that I didn't know what to do with them. Should I call someone? A zoo or a wildlife refuge? But if I called the wrong someone, it could be all over for them. So I filled water bowls and rubbed their furry bodies and checked for their warm breath. They drank and purred. For the first time in a while, I prayed. Not like when I hadn't ever wanted to see Luke again—that was more a wish than a real prayer. This was an "Oh, God" prayer, out loud, like Nonni's. "Oh, God, I'm clueless. Help me keep them alive." Just to be sure, I prayed the same thing to the four directions like Dad does and called on the spirit of Onawa to help me tend her babies.

Luke had left after that first feeding, saying that he "had to go." I squelched my disappointment. Every so often I'd start off in the direction of his house and then think better of it.

One of those times I returned by way of the stream. Dad and Clyde were packing up their tools, having set the turbine in motion again.

I detoured around a fallen fir I'd always called the Grandfather Tree, whose roots made an earthen wall higher than my head. I had no intention of tangling with Dad again.

"Got to say this shamanism of yours has been a stretch for me, Paul," Clyde was saying, "but it was worth it seeing the look on that Morgan woman's face here the other day."

I peered through a net of moss.

Dad stuck the dead motor into a cardboard box. "You mean Rainbow?"

"God, yes. She's one of those Bible ladies who keep showing up at board meetings." Clyde was a teacher at the high school. I think he'd taught practically every subject.

"I can imagine," said Dad.

Clyde rinsed a screwdriver with creek water and dried it. "It's always something: they want abstinence education, or prayer at the football games, or a ban on Halloween. Jesus."

Dad chuckled. "I'm sure I alarmed her. *The devil prowls like a ravening lion.*' I grew up with that crap." He settled a wrench into his tool kit.

I winced. Why did he always make it sound like Nonni and Opa were stupid? They didn't go around preaching about the devil. Nonni hadn't been harassing the school board.

Clyde said something I didn't hear and Dad laughed.

I crept away quietly and went to check on the kittens.

★　★　★

Even after the turbine was running, we had no Internet until midnight, when Mom gave in to my begging and fixed it.

I cruised for two hours, Googling "cougars," "cougar kittens," "starving cougar kittens," and "care and feeding of wild animals." I hit cougars' size, weight, range, hunting habits, but not "What to Do If You Find a Cougar."

I crept out to them at 12:30 and again at 2:30. The air smelled of Dad's wood smoke. My stomach hurt. I was afraid to give the cubs meat or milk, but how long could they live on plain water? Would they die because of me?

Mallory was out again. Our room seemed especially empty. Strangely, I wanted her here. I wanted to tell her about the kittens. And then I didn't want to tell her. She was the one who'd called in the Death Squad.

At 3:00 a.m. I put my head on my desk. What was the magic Google Cougar-Rescue Code? I tried once more with "cougar cubs eat" and got a big, fat nothing.

The screen blurred. I let myself think about Luke. Why had he said that about girls throwing themselves at him? Was he toying with me? What if he really was Trent? Would he fly me to Paris, where we would watch the sun set over the Seine while sipping expensive wine and evading journalists? Next week would the tabloids say, "Who Is Brigitta Schopenhauer?" Would I be discovered by Trent's agent and star with him in his next blockbuster, where we would have to do a nude scene? Aak! Cancel that thought! I was turning into Natalie.

I typed "Trent Yves" into the search engine.

There were eight million results. EIGHT MILLION. I should have kept searching on cougars, but I was so brain-dead. Trent Yves stared out at me with long hair, with short hair, blond, brown, in a Mohawk. Trent with a shirt, Trent without a shirt, Trent without much on at all. Sad Trent, happy Trent, sexy Trent. Trent looking dodgy in *Rocket*, heroic in *Imlandria*, smart-alecky in *Presto!*, resilient in *Sparrowtree*, even small, cute, and triumphing-over-evil in *Laser Boy*.

And the more I studied him, the more he wasn't Luke. Trent had perfect teeth, perfect pecs, perfect everything; he was made of plastic. Luke had zits (quite a few), a crooked smile, and he was shorter than Trent. It was neurotic to compare them, but at 3:00 in the morning lots of things seem logical.

What was illogical was that I was falling for him. After only two days with him. Without even knowing him. This was nothing like crushing on Devon. This was new and wild, and even though it was insane, I didn't want it to stop.

★ ★ ★

Mallory slipped into the room at 4:00 a.m.

"Gita! What are you doing up at this hour?"

I looked at her. What was *she* doing up?

She turned away and stripped off her denim jacket.

"Where were you?"

"Out."

"By yourself?"

She toed off her shoes. "Gita, I'm nineteen. And you're not my mother, dear." She disappeared into the bathroom.

When Mallory got that "decisive" tone to her voice, you didn't argue.

We were both in our beds with the lights off when Mallory sighed and rolled over. "Gita?"

"What."

"I'm not trying to be a bitch."

I was quiet, processing this. Mallory wasn't the apologizing type. But she was different tonight. Subdued.

She propped herself up on her elbow. "Everything's changed. You go away to college and your family mutates." Her voice got softer. "I'm not used to it."

In the darkness, I could make out my guitar and Mallory's old telescope. When she started the Tree House Club (for me, she always points out), we'd go out on clear nights and find Jupiter. Mallory would be there, adjusting the focus. We don't do that anymore. But I don't play guitar anymore, either. Some things you outgrow.

"You are so rude to Dad." My voice was unintentionally shrill. Why was it Dad I was upset about? But I couldn't talk about the cougars or Luke. Not now.

"Brigitta, honestly." Now she was her old self. "Bear has been talking to him?"

"Well, maybe he has."

"Good grief, Gita. Has he been tutoring *you* in this dysfunctional grandiosity?"

No. Dad hadn't been tutoring me in anything. He was too busy running The Center to even teach me Pacific Northwest history like he'd promised. I wasn't sure why I was defending him. "Mom believes in fairies. You don't seem worried about her."

"Dad and I have always worried about Mom." Mallory pulled up her sheet. "Don't you see? Dad was the balancing force in this family. He needs to return to the real world."

I picked at some fuzz on my blanket. "And that would be?"

"Well, Webster says, 'Those who make you believe absurdities can make you commit atrocities.'"

"Atrocities? You think Dad's committing atrocities?"

"I didn't say that, Gita. Just that absurd beliefs can lead to dangerous things."

Mallory came right out and said things. I'd never have said Dad's shaman thing was absurd. Just different. Before, Dad had considered himself a "freethinker"—which never included thinking freely about religion. He'd warned me against "abandoning my intellect" (particularly when I'd just returned from Cherrywood). He'd said you didn't need God to have beauty. The earth itself and all its functions were beautiful—in part because life was fleeting.

But now he went out every day and waited for an unseen world to come to him.

I don't know what Nonni and Opa would have said about his shamanism. It didn't have Jesus in it, and they were all about Jesus. So he was still making sure he wasn't like them. And I was still caught between his world and theirs—only now neither would let me in.

I gazed at Mallory blearily across the room. She thought all religions were absurd.

"You found that quote in *Webster's*?" I yawned. "I thought I was the only one who read dictionaries."

She shifted. "Webster. Dr. Lampson. A friend of mine."

"A 'friend.'"

"Yes," said Mallory. She rolled over. "A friend."

chapter thirteen

Kalimar was glad to see me. She put her nose into my hand and chewed my finger. I'd slept until ten and missed their seven o'clock watering. I'd barely escaped making herbed zucchini hash with Mom, who was getting ready for the Parents of Indigo Children. Mallory had rushed to assist her. It made me wonder.

Felix lapped from the bowl, and I lifted Kalimar to my shoulder. Sun filtered through the maples warming the forest floor. Kalimar dug her claws into my arm. I'd have to search my closet for combat wear. She purred, a sound I was beginning to relish. It was more rumbly than the purr of a house cat. Her ears twitched as I rubbed my fingers over the silky spot between them. Her eyes were shinier. Yesterday they'd been sunken. She blinked at me. Had she been able to do that yesterday? I swayed and sang to her—my own version of a sea chantey Opa used to sing us:

> *What do ya do with a spotted kitty*
> *What do ya do with a spotted kitty*
> *What do ya do with a spotted kitty*
> *Earl-eye in the mornin'?*

"You're a good mama."

Luke. I was embarrassed to my toes.

He wore a black T-shirt that said "Murphy's Pub." He unhooked a blackberry cane from the hem of his jeans. "But it's not so earl-eye in the mornin'."

"Yeah?" I found my voice. "So where have you been?"

He scooped up Felix. "Patience, my dear, patience." He smiled that slow smile, and I wanted to throw something at him. Or kiss him.

I got busy with Kalimar's water bowl. Why did just standing near Luke turn me into a blithering idiot? "I've been giving them water all night." It sounded as if I was asking for congratulations.

His smile faded to surprise. "All night? You must be exhausted, Brigitta."

I nodded. "And I'm not any nearer to figuring out what to feed them." I hadn't wanted to admit this.

The smile came back. "Pedialyte," he said. "That clear stuff you feed babies when they're dehydrated? It restores their electrolytes. You can get it at the grocery."

"You know this how? I've been Googling for hours."

He looked smug. "You have to know what to search on. For sick animals, you give them Pedialyte."

So he did care. How many hours had he Googled? If I'd Googled more on cougars and less on Trent Yves, would I have figured it out for myself?

Luke sat down on a log and cradled Felix. "How's it going, cat?"

What would he look like with long, blond hair? I'll admit to loving *Imlandria* from the start: Felix, the peasant boy, who is secretly a prince; the quest through the magical forest; the horses. Even with Trent Yves in it, I was a sucker for a good fantasy. And since I'd seen *Rocket*, Trent hadn't seemed so bad.

Luke caught me watching him. "What?"

"Oh. Nothing." I am definitely a sucker for a good fantasy. When would my Hollywood-clouded brain return to the real world? I checked Kalimar's neck for fleas and tried to regain my composure. "Why don't we go to town for the Pedialyte?" Unbidden, images of strolling down

Main with the beautiful Luke Geoffrey paraded through my senses. If people thought he was Trent, I wouldn't disabuse them. Trent Yves, Tinseltown playboy, found me irresistible. He couldn't even go to the grocery store without me. We'd pass Devon on the street, and he would regret ever passing on me. And right in the middle of Main and Cherry, with 18-wheelers stopped at the crosswalk, Trent would sweep me up in his arms, his lips would find mine. Who cared if anybody saw? Goodbye, Gwendolyn Melier, bon voyage, Randi Marchietti—Brigitta Schopenhauer is on scene and ready for action.

"Actually." Luke stood and settled Felix back in his den. "I've got to shove off. Promised Mum I'd do some stuff." He reached into his pocket and extracted his wallet. "Here." He held out a twenty. "Buy as much as you can." He put the money in my hand and sauntered away without another word.

I watched him disappear down the path, arms swinging, moving branches out of his way. I almost went after him, but Kalimar was still nestled against my neck. I deposited her in the tree with her brother and slid the twenty into my pocket, feeling slimy.

fourteen

Family Grocer had only five liters of Pedialyte. I was about to throw them all into my cart when Natalie appeared at the end of the aisle. She slowed when she saw me. I smiled and began perusing the shelves for a more explainable purchase.

"Hey, Brigitta." Her upside-down smile was halfhearted.

Other than Pedialyte, this aisle had diapers, bottles, "feminine hygiene," and condoms. I snagged a box of eco-friendly panty liners. "Hey, Natalie."

"Any sign of Trent?"

"He's not Trent, and he's not home." It came out sharp. "I'm sorry, Natalie. I haven't had much sleep."

She held up a bag of Cheetos. "Want to come over? Cheryl and I are going to watch *Sparrowtree*."

"Can't." I couldn't leave the kittens for a whole evening. "Dad has this sweat lodge thing." It was only a small lie. So what if the sweat lodge had already happened?

"Oh," she said. "Okay." She glanced at the shelves: the pull-up pants, the bottles, the condoms. "Did you ever give Devon back his coat?"

"Devon? No, I…haven't had time." Devon's coat was stuffed into the window seat. I'd gotten tired of tripping over it. How long could the kittens wait for their Pedialyte? How long would it take me to bike home with all that stuff in my pack?

"So you really hate him now?"

"What? Oh, no. I don't hate him."

"That's good," said Natalie.

I'd need to get bottles, too. Bottle-feeding would be easier.

"Brigitta." Natalie shifted the Cheetos to her other hand. "What is going on? Is there something you're not telling me?"

"I…No, Natalie. Why would you think that?"

She looked hurt, but she smiled encouragingly. "Because Cheryl says she saw Devon's car on the way to your place last night. And he's being really secretive. Are you back together with him?"

"Devon?"

"No, Trent Yves. Of course Devon. Unless…*Is* Trent back?" Her eyes shone with renewed possibility.

I imagined what would happen if Natalie found out about Luke. She'd want a script of every conversation. She had with Devon. And then she'd want to be the director. I saw her gathering my life into her lap like a long scarf. I needed to pull it back into my own lap before it was too late. "Devon and I have known each other a long time," I ventured. "There are things between us that nobody else knows."

This was mean, even though it was true. I had shared secrets with Devon that I hadn't with Natalie. For a moment I felt the pain of losing him. He had been a good friend, a really good friend. Now that I had met Luke, I could see that what I'd had in Devon was a buddy, not a boyfriend. But I missed that buddy.

"So he was there last night?"

"He might have been…nearby," I said vaguely.

"Oh, come on, Brigitta." Natalie stopped smiling.

"Okay, yeah." I felt sick with the lie. I didn't carry lies well. I couldn't deal them out smoothly like some people could.

"So you've forgiven him for Erika…and the porn?" She looked hopeful.

"He's…turned over a new leaf." I hugged her. "I'll call you."

I bought the panty liners, even though I didn't need them, wheeled my bike around the side of the building, and waited until she drove away. Then I went back in and bought what I'd really come for.

* * *

Luke squatted by the snag, scratching Felix between the ears. He flashed me a smile, and I forgave him for his hasty departure.

"Your mom happy now?" I snapped the top off one of the Pedialytes.

"Yeah. She needed some pictures hung. She's not tall enough to do it without a ladder."

"Nice guy."

"I aim to please."

At first the kittens choked on the bottles, but soon they had the hang of it and were slurping happily in our laps. They seemed to like it better than water.

We decided on an every-three-hour feeding schedule, based on Luke's info. I would do nights, of course, and he could cover mornings. It exhilarated me that I'd be seeing him every day, even if he never stayed long. My chest went all fluttery just thinking about it.

On the way back to the house, I stopped at the spot where I'd first spied Luke from the tree house. I laid my hand on Adam's bark. He'd done his treeish part in protecting us, I was sure. But then, why us and not Onawa?

I sat down and leaned against his rough trunk, where Luke had been—a dip between two roots that had always made a kind of chair. Only today something was poking me. Another root? No. Something gray jutted out of the dirt. It took my hands and then a stick to loosen it enough to pull it out—a long, metal box.

I set it across my lap, feeling the weight of something inside. Had Natalie and I buried it when we were kids? We'd done stuff like that— particularly during our pirate phase. But the box didn't look that old. It wasn't even rusty—just dirty.

I pried the lid off. Under it was a blue plastic wrapping. I peeled it back: a case—black, with silver buckles. I sucked in my breath. Dad's flute!

I snapped the buckles open. The flute sections were nested in their red velvet compartments: mouthpiece, body, foot. I brushed my fingertips over the keys and listened to their soft clicks. Had Dad done this? Had he buried his flute? When? I felt a wave of sadness. Why?

"Brigitta!"

Dad! Coming across the footbridge! Hurriedly, I closed the case, shoved both case and box into the plastic bag, and dropped the entire thing back in the hole.

"Brigitta!"

I raked leaves and dirt over the top, just as Dad appeared under Eve. "I need some help with the hermitage. I had a call from a Sufi sheikh who would like to stay there in August."

The hermitage was to be a small cottage a distance from the house where people could take private retreats. Of course, it wouldn't do to have it built like an ordinary cottage. No, we had to haul out the tires again.

Something crinkled. A bit of blue plastic was showing between my feet. I scooted some leaves over it, trying to keep my eyes off the ground. "Do you need me right this minute?"

Dad tugged at the sleeve of his blue work shirt. "Right this minute would be preferable, but I could wait half an hour."

"Half an hour, then." I nodded earnestly.

Dad cocked his head and winked, surprising me. "Thanks, kiddo," he said, almost like the old Dad. Did I dare ask about the flute?

The moment passed.

After he left, I pulled the bag out of the ground and filled the hole. Up in the tree house, I assembled the flute and brought it to my lips. I couldn't play, really, but Dad had taught me a few basics. I blew a gentle stream down and across the mouthpiece, and the tone emerged, low and silky. The opening notes of the *Pleni* from the Josquin mass went through my head. I hadn't played it since Opa died. And this was the first time I'd seen Dad's flute since then.

I took the instrument apart and set it back in its case, then settled the case back inside the metal box. I looked around for a place to hide it, and my eyes fell on a silk scarf of Mom's. Its purples and greens and blues looked like a stained glass window. She'd given it to me to protect my violin, but it was too pretty to keep locked up, so I'd hung it from the window.

I set the box on the shelf under Onawa's picture—my altar, I suppose. I draped the scarf over it and set the candle on top. It seemed to belong there. At least for now.

At the hermitage, Dad was surveying the past month's work. So far it was roofless. The back and sidewalls had been bermed with sloping hills of earth, so that it reminded me crazily of the baby Jesus' stable—except lined with tires. A middle partition wall, built entirely of tires, was taking shape and was now up to my knees. Next to it was a wheelbarrow full of earth. One of Dad's drums hung on a tree spur nearby—evidently at the ready if he suddenly needed to go into a trance.

Dad moved to one side of the wall and I to the other. He hoisted a tire onto the stack, and we moved it into position. "That looks good," he said.

We scooped the soil in with our hands and pressed it into the casing. Much as I'd hated building The Center, I had developed a kind of rhythm with tire filling, and it really wasn't unpleasant. I liked how the earth felt in my hands—as if I was making myself a part of it.

The first few measures of the *Pleni* drifted through me again. "Full are heaven and earth of Thy glory" was what the Latin words said. Mom told me the Josquin had been performed at Nonni and Opa's church when Dad was a teenager. How had she known that? Had he told her?

When we'd done as much hand filling as possible, Dad grabbed his sledgehammer and I grabbed a shovel. I scooped dirt out of the wheelbarrow and emptied it into the tire. Dad climbed onto the wall. Tentatively, I hummed the opening notes of the *Pleni*.

Dad lifted the sledgehammer and began to pound the dirt into the casing. The next few notes were too high to hum, so I sang the Latin, "*Pleni, pleni.*" Each word stretched out for measures and measures.

Dad pounded harder.

I dumped in another scoop of dirt and sang a little louder, "*sunt coeli.*" Dad pounded louder still.

My cheeks began to burn. I switched to his part instead of mine, "*et terra.*"

He didn't look at me; he focused entirely on the tire. He began to pound in a contrary rhythm. I dumped in another shovelful and began to sing the next section—a difficult passage we'd had to play over and over before we got it right—"*gloria, gloria, gloria a tua.*"

Dad stopped pounding and climbed down onto his side of the wall. "Let's take a break, Brigitta." He brushed his hands on his jeans. "There's some iced tea in the house." He reached for his drum and made for the sweat lodge.

I put my hand on the stack of tires. Dad and I hadn't created much of anything together since he'd abandoned the mass. And now we were making a wall. I almost laughed.

* * *

My alarm clock and I settled into the tree house about 10:00. I'd told Mom I was at Natalie's. It felt strange. Another lie. And to Mom, who I'd never lied to.

When I woke up, it wasn't to the alarm. I squinted. 2:00 a.m.

"Don't worry. I got the one o'clock feeding." It was Luke. I nearly jumped out of my skin.

He sat with his back to the wall, barely visible in the clock glow. "Thought I'd let you sleep," he said.

"Before giving me a heart attack?" Did my breath stink? I was acutely aware that all I had on inside the sleeping bag was my T-shirt and a pair of white cotton panties. "How long have you been here?"

"Long enough. Wasn't tired anymore. Lying in bed running movies in my head."

"Movies?" I didn't say, "Like *Imlandria*?" but Luke could hear it in my voice.

He chuckled. "There you go again, Brigitta. But seriously, don't you do that? When you can't sleep? Make things up and watch them roll?"

I clicked on the mag light and sat up carefully, with the bag gathered around me. "I guess so. What were your movies?" My brain was moving slow. This was so surreal.

The shadows made odd angles on his face. He wore a hoodie, and his hair was sticking up. He rested his arms on his knees. "Well, in one I got in my car and just drove."

"Where'd you end up?"

"I don't know. I didn't get that far. It was just me and the car and the road."

"That doesn't sound like much of a plot."

He smiled. "No, probably not."

"So, where are you going? What are you looking for?"

I could never have asked that question of Devon.

Luke was thoughtful. "Eden," he said.

I was surprised. "As in, 'The Garden of'? You even know that story?"

"Why wouldn't I?"

"I just didn't think you were into spirituality. You seem so..."

"So what?"

"So...into other things," I finished lamely. "I mean, do you believe in God?"

He shrugged. "I don't know. Maybe you wouldn't need God if you had Eden."

I turned this over in my mind. "I'm not sure that makes sense. In the story, God made Eden and walked around in it with Adam and Eve."

"That's one way to look at it. Or maybe Eden is God."

"I don't know any religion that teaches that."

"Does there need to be one?" Luke picked up the mag light and cast beams on the wall with it.

I yawned and lay down again in my sleeping bag. "Now you sound like my mom."

Luke frowned. "Better than sounding like my mom."

I hesitated. "What does your mom sound like?"

Luke stretched out on the floor. He propped himself up on one elbow. "How about you, Brigitta? Do you pray?"

I thought about my cougar prayer—my first conscious prayer in a long time. For some reason prayer wasn't a regular thing with me anymore. "I used to." I couldn't say that it was with Nonni I used to pray. Some afternoons we chatted with God on the screened-in porch while we turned Nonni's sewing scraps into doll dresses for the homeless shelter. It was as if Jesus was sitting there between us, making his scraps into loaves and fishes.

A breeze blew through the cracks in the tree house wall. "Do you need a sleeping bag? There's another one inside that bench. Just lift the seat up."

Luke took the mag light and pulled out a board game, Devon's coat, a tube of hand lotion, and finally retrieved the bag and a pillow. He moved close enough that I could feel his breath. A crane fly looped over our heads. I wanted to swat it but felt sleepy, so sleepy.

"I used to pray, too," said Luke.

I thought, as I drifted off, that I felt him touch my hair.

chapter fifteen

Luke's sleeping bag was beside me, rumpled, in the morning. I hadn't dreamed him. My back hurt from sleeping on boards again. I sat up and secured brushes from the cupboard—tooth and hair. 8:30! How long since the kittens had eaten?

Devon's coat and the hand lotion were strewn across the floor, along with the board game, a belt, and a pair of Luke's socks. Had he gone home barefoot?

The tree house began to shake. He hadn't gone home! I brushed my hair furiously and checked my face in the mirror. Plain, pale. For once I wished I wore makeup.

Footsteps on the porch. I dabbed toothpaste on my tongue. The door opened.

Natalie.

Her eyes took in the room: me, the two sleeping bags, my jeans, the belt and socks, Devon's coat.

"Whoa," she said. "Brigitta. Wow. Should I go?"

I opened my mouth and then closed it. What if Luke came back while she was here?

She looked up toward the loft and pointed. "Devon?" she mouthed.

This was what I got for making stuff up.

"No!" I pulled some hair out of my brush. "It's not what you're thinking, Nat." It was one thing for her to think Devon and I were back together; it was another to give her the impression that we were—

"He's not here?"

"No. Just me."

Natalie eyed the belt. "Well, you'll be happy to know I covered for you. Your mom thinks you're with me. I came so I wouldn't be lying." She squinted at the game. "Risk? I know that's his favorite game, but…" She picked up the socks and twirled them.

"Natalie, it's really, really not what you're thinking."

"Yeah, hon, I know." She winked.

I forced myself not to look out the window. Was Luke still out there?

Natalie moved to the window seat and sat. She took a breath. "We need to start talking again, Brigitta. You're different."

I didn't answer.

Natalie wrapped one curl around her finger. "Is it because…is it because you've done things I haven't done?" She looked down.

"Natalie, I haven't done anything."

"Okay." She brushed some dirt off her sleeve. "I get it. You're into him, and I guess it makes you pull away from everyone else."

She stood, as if she was going to leave, then plopped back down. "But, Brigitta, I always thought you'd tell me…your first time…was it, you know? Was it what you'd dreamed of?"

"Natalie, I did not have a first time!"

She stood all the way up this time. "I believe you, Brigitta." She dropped my jeans in my lap. "And I won't tell your mom. Why don't you come by sometime?" She opened the door and didn't bother to close it before climbing down the ladder.

I stayed where I was, planted, feeling small and mean. I waited until she had disappeared down the path.

★ ★ ★

Luke was at the cougar den, dangling some beaded leather strings from a thick stick. Felix leaped for them. Luke grinned when he saw me. He looked haggard. "You sleep a lot," he said.

I colored. "Did you do the entire night shift?"

"Yup. Look at them."

Luke wiggled the stick. Felix pounced, missed the strings, and captured Luke's hand. "Ow!" Luke flipped Felix on his back and detached the teeth and claws. He had some impressive welts. He ruffled Felix's stomach.

"Have you done a miracle or created a monster?" I plunked my butt onto the pine needles.

Luke chuckled. "I'm sooooo tired. I am never having children, ever, ever, ever." He balanced the wood on his knee. It was about eight inches long, the width of my wrist, and the bark had been peeled off.

I picked it up. Three leather laces were tied around one end. Carved into either side was a cat face. "Did you do this?"

Luke nodded. "It's part of the branch I used to—well, to fend off their mother. Thought it should become something."

I twirled it, and the beads clicked softly—three blue ceramic balls with dots of green. The carvings were rough, but they were unmistakably cougar faces. "These are good. Where did you learn to do this?"

"Scout camp." He grinned. "It would be better if I could sand it. But it's for them. See? This one's Kalimar." He traced her round chin and extra-long whiskers on the wood. "And this one's Felix." He flipped the stick over and showed me where Felix's left ear was bigger than his right. "I found the strings in my pocket. Part of a shirt I used to have." He hadn't shaved. It made me want to touch his face.

"Did you stay here all night?"

"Mmm." His head drooped. He had a cut between his forefinger and thumb.

"Isn't your mom going to wonder?" Kalimar crawled out of the snag and batted at the wood curls by my foot.

Luke shrugged. "Mum sleeps like the dead."

Kalimar swiped at the beads, whipping one around the stick.

"Unfortunately, Mallory never sleeps. That's why I had to stay in the tree house. And she's taken down all my Pablo Neruda poems and replaced them with Maslow's Hierarchy of Needs."

Luke rested his head against the tree trunk, his eyes half closed. "I have no idea what you are talking about," he mumbled. His eyes closed completely.

I had a sudden impulse to pull his head into my lap, but (fortunately) lacked the nerve to carry it out. What was coming over me?

Felix wandered out and sniffed at some deer scat. "Not so far, buddy." I hauled him back. What would we do if the kittens began to roam? He wove between me and Luke and started climbing Luke's shirt.

Luke woke with a start. His head flew up.

I couldn't help laughing.

Luke leaned back again, while Felix sniffed at his neck. "Looked like you had a visitor."

"You saw her. Natalie. She thought I spent the night with Devon."

"Devon?" He frowned.

"Devon, he's—an old friend."

Luke nodded slowly. "Is he an old friend you often spent the night with?"

"No! I mean, sure, when we were little, but not…it's not what you're thinking." How many times would I say that today?

Luke watched my face. I was the first to look away.

"Hey." Luke pulled something out of his jeans pocket. "Look what else I found." He opened his hand. It was a red feather.

"Cardinal!" I said.

"That's what I thought. You have them here? They're all over the place in the Midwest."

Unexpectedly, my eyes teared up. "No," I said quietly. "No cardinals here." I blinked, hoping he didn't notice. "Where did you find it?"

"It was at the base of that tree, the one where we met Onawa."

I loved him for calling her by her name—for remembering it.

I thought of what else had been at the base of Adam. Had Dad planned to unbury his flute? He'd packaged it carefully against damage. But maybe that was like those steel-lined coffins they'd tried to sell us for Opa: they know you can't really preserve what's inside.

In Luke's other pocket a cell phone began to ring. He silenced it without pulling it out. "Here." He put the feather in my hand and heaved himself up. "Why don't you keep it? Maybe a cardinal made its way here, just for Brigitta." He raised his hand and walked off through the woods. I didn't follow. He needed to sleep.

chapter sixteen

I stroked the feather across my palm and tucked it carefully into my pocket. It had drawn back a curtain on my heart; I'd better close it fast while I still could.

A squirrel high on a cedar began a *pchieooo* that jerked his whole body with every cry. A drumbeat caught my ears: hard-soft, hard-soft—the rhythm of a heartbeat. I skirted a mossy stump and stopped just before the tree house. Dad stood in the clearing in full shaman mode.

His bare chest and face were painted with black-and-white stripes. More stripes went up his temples, cougarlike. This wasn't the first of Dad's rituals I had seen, but this new person who had stepped out of Dad's body still caught me off guard. After years of studying indigenous cultures as if they were in a petri dish, now he'd climbed into the dish himself.

Dad walked in a circle, around the base of Adam's trunk, beating the drum with every step—PUM-pah, PUM-pah, TOE-heel, TOE-heel.

I wanted to go, but if I moved I'd call attention to myself.

He crouched and put his hands on his thighs. He began breathing, breathing. He stretched, clawed the air with his hands, twitched his butt like it had a tail attached; his spine undulated.

I knew what he was doing: he was calling on Onawa, just like I had.

I almost envied him. It had been a long time since I'd followed the animals' movements. I could be uninhibited when I was little, but it's different now. People see you; they make judgments. And pretty soon you find out you're alone. Maybe that's why I hadn't sensed the cougar when she was alive. Yet when I'd finally called her, Onawa had led me to her babies. Or rather, she had led Luke to her babies.

Luke! Turning my head, I saw him just out of Dad's view. He would be stuck just as I was, reluctant to draw attention. How did Dad's antics look to him? I felt suddenly alien, part of an alien clan. At Kwahnesum High School, people had called The Center "that bizarro place in the woods." Those people hadn't mattered to me. Luke did.

Dad began to yowl. He crouched and sprang on what could only be described now as his hind legs. His eyes moved and his head followed in a smooth motion. He looked fully cat now in his every gesture. Except that he wasn't a cat. For the first time I saw him as Mallory did—disconnected from reality, possibly mentally ill. Was that what Luke saw?

Finally, finally, Dad drummed his way backward across the bridge and toward The Center. Luke stood and drifted to the base of Adam's trunk where Dad had been having his fits. He would understand—he had to understand—that The Center was a place for spiritual things. I stood behind Eve for a moment and realized I was hiding. Luke turned around, and I let myself be seen. He took a step or two toward me, an odd expression on his face. His cell began ringing again. Once more, he silenced it in his pocket, then he waved, turned, and was gone.

I wanted to run after him, but I refuse to chase people. He had talked about prayer and the Garden of Eden. But that look, just before he walked away—it made me uneasy.

I fingered the cardinal feather. Mallory was right. Dad had changed a lot, and quickly. But even if shamanism was a form of mental illness, at least he was more honest. About most things. Certain territory was off-limits.

The feather lay on my palm like a small flame.

* * *

At Cherrywood cardinals were everywhere, along with rabbits, foxes, and bobcats. Nonni gave them all names from Beatrix Potter stories or from the Bible.

A few nights after Opa's funeral, we were all on the screened-in porch. Mallory was reading something she'd found in the attic. I tried (unsuccessfully) to nap on the chaise lounge. Mom shook Nonni's rugs out the porch door and went to start tea. Dad stared into the woods, one hand on the screen. Nonni balanced a small tower of fabric scraps as she patched together what would be my Nonni coat. She was smiling distantly and singing, "*When peace like a river attended my way—*"

Dad strode to the opposite screen and stared toward the road.

Nonni went on, "*When sorrows like deep billows rolled—*"

Dad sighed and drummed his fingers on the wood frame.

"*Whatever my lot, Thou has caused me to say—*"

Dad stopped drumming.

"*'It is well; it is well with my soul.'*"

Dad pivoted.

"*It is well—*"

"Mom, enough."

Nonni looked up. "Enough what?"

Dad leaned against the love seat, his hand gripping the wicker under the vinyl cushions. "You know what I mean."

"No, Paul, I don't. You'll have to explain." She fixed him with a steely expression I didn't know she had. I was wide-awake now.

Dad straightened and ran his hands through his hair. "You always do this, Mom."

She looked at him questioningly. Challenging him. I'd never seen her like this.

"You never miss an opportunity to preach at me."

Nonni kept her mouth shut. She folded her hands in her lap, and the scrap tower scattered on the brick floor.

"There is nothing out there, Mom. You know it. I know it. There are no fluttering angels bringing us manna, no Lazarus coming out of the grave. Nobody's walking on water. It's all very beautiful, but it's just not true."

Nonni didn't answer, so Dad kept going. He was on a roll now, pacing across the bricks. "I am so sick of you acting like I am damned to hell because I won't buy into your fantasy. I've got a goddamned master's degree. I've studied more tribal mythologies than you can shake a stick at. They're all trying to do the same thing: defeat death. And it can't be done. We live; we die. Full stop. End of sentence."

Nonni's hands tightened around her remaining fabric scraps. She pressed her lips together.

Dad swept his arms out. "This is what we have. This! Jesus isn't coming down to catch Dad up in his fiery chariot. He is gone. And I'm tired as hell of your religious manipulation."

"No one is manipulating you, Paul," Nonni said quietly.

"Like hell you aren't." Dad threw open the porch door and slammed it shut behind him, heading for the woods.

Nonni put her head in her hands and began to cry. It was like nothing I'd ever heard before—high and fierce, like a wild bird. Once, I'd read the word *keening* to describe crying like that. It was the first time I'd heard Nonni cry.

Mom came through the French doors carrying a tray of tea mugs. She set them on the table and went to Nonni. She put her arms around her from behind and leaned her head against Nonni's. I huddled on the bricks at Nonni's feet and took her hand. She ran her fingers through my hair and went on wailing and wailing. Mallory stayed on the love seat, with tears running down her face. I must have been crying, too. We were like wolves making that noise they make at the moon. We were trying to find something we didn't know we'd lost. We were trying to find each other and Opa and Dad in the great, dark night.

seventeen

You're quiet, Gita." Mom and I squeegeed the windows in the meditation room. Rain dripped down the outside, which, to me, made window washing pointless.

Luke hadn't come back. Last night, sleeping in the tree house yet again, I had awakened every hour and scanned the dark for him. And this morning I'd played with Felix and Kalimar extra long, hoping to hear his ambling steps in the leaves. But apparently I was kidding myself. His desertion gnawed at me, but even worse was the realization that the kittens' lives were now entirely in my hands.

I found a *Caring for Kittens* book Nonni had given me for Ophelia when I was ten. Yesterday I had sneaked all the goat's milk and most of our eggs to the downstairs kitchen and made "emergency formula." Felix had been so delighted he'd bitten the nipple off the bottle.

"Gita?" Mom stepped around the bucket. "Are you in there?"

I sat back on my heels. "I'm fine, Mom." I forced a smile. It was 3:00. The formula was almost gone. What could they eat next?

Mom gave the window another rub while the rain jostled the sweet peas outside. "Is it Devon?"

Devon again. It was rotten that I kept using him as a cover. It would come back to bite me. I nodded.

"Oh, honey. Boys can be confusing, can't they?"

What would she think of Luke if I introduced them? Why hadn't I? I was keeping a lot of secrets these days.

I'd told her I was spending another night with Natalie, banking on Natalie's loyalty to cover for me one more time. It was getting easier to lie. It was like delivering a line for a play. I was a character in this play and maybe Luke was, too. But if that look on his face yesterday had been any indication, he may not be back for the curtain call: the Schopenhauers had outweirded him. Otherwise, why had he gone off like that without a word?

I dropped my squeegee into the water. "Why did Dad have to get so strange?"

Mom wiped her forehead with the back of her hand. "Is that what's bothering you?"

I shrugged.

"Gita, I know he's chosen a path that seems odd to some of the neighbors. Are they gossiping again?"

"No. It just *is* weird. He's jumping around like a cougar and yowling and—it's like six steps beyond you and your friends howling at the moon last summer. At least you didn't wear face paint."

Mom caught my eye. She remembered me leaping around the woods like a deer. I got busy with the squeegee.

Mom smiled a secret smile. "Well." She folded her hands in her lap. "It's more interesting than the way the Christians pray."

I remembered Nonni and Opa's church and the people falling down on the floor. "Not much," I said. But I'd liked it at Nonni's church. And I liked Jesus, all full of light and magic. I even talked to him sometimes, though I could never tell Dad that.

Mom had always kept quiet about her beliefs. I think she'd had to with Dad the Doubter. Once or twice I'd found a bowl of milk out in the grass after a full-moon night—something you gave the fairies for their revels.

"I'm sorry, sweetheart. I shouldn't say negative things about Christians. I know you loved your grandparents."

I shrugged again. Even though it felt like a truck ran me over every time I thought about Nonni and Opa.

And Dad. When I thought about Dad right now my head hurt. Dad with his drum and his face paint and his dancing. Dad and his sweat lodge and his animal spirits. He would have laughed at all that before. "There's nothing there," he would have said. And now he was a spirit world unto himself—he'd found his own Eden, after dispensing with mine—if I had even known where mine was.

The sound of a car in the driveway ended Mom's questioning session. "That must be Alana from Parents of Indigo Children. She wanted to see the dorms before Thursday."

A red Porsche was parked outside. Out of it climbed a tall, thin man with a brown beard. He wore a Greek fisherman's cap and a tidy raincoat. Mom extended her hand. "I'm Clare," she said. "I was expecting Alana. Are you here to see the dorms?"

The guy took her hand. "No, actually, I don't know an Alana. I'm Webster Lampson. I'm here to collect Mallory." He winced as a raindrop hit his face.

Mom's smile wavered. "Ah!" she said. "Mallory is not here. She's running some errands for me. Won't you come in?"

Webster Lampson studied us, the driveway, the entrance of The Center. He was getting wet. "Yes," he said, "I think I will."

I'm not good at guessing ages, but this guy was old. Almost as old as my parents. He must have been like forty or something.

Dad was in his office tapping numbers into a ten key when we came into the foyer. "Paul." Mom stuck her head in. "We have a visitor."

Dad came out wearing his wolf sweatshirt. His ponytail was held with this bone and feather thing that dangled from the nape of his neck. "Paul Schopenhauer." He shook Webster Lampson's hand.

"Schopenhauer." Webster Lampson grinned. "Mallory tells me that great German mind was a relative of yours."

"Distant cousin," said Dad. "You aren't here about the Indigo Children?"

Webster chuckled. "I should say not," he said, "though I have heard of their movement. An article on pseudoscience in one of the journals."

I disliked him more moment by moment.

"I see," said Dad. "Can I get you anything? We have fresh goat milk from the neighbors. And there's tea."

No goat milk, I thought. *Don't let them check the goat milk and find out it's all gone.*

"We just got some very potent oolong tea," said Mom. "It's great as a colon cleanser."

"I'll pass," said Webster. "I had an espresso on the way here. Any idea when Mallory will be back?"

"Mallory is here!" My sister shouldered her way in the door, dropping her packages on the floor, and flung herself at Webster Lampson.

She wound her arms around his neck, and he hugged her to him. "Here's my best student," he said. "Is she not beautiful?"

"Yes," said Dad grimly. "We think so."

"Well, my love," said Webster Lampson. "Are you ready to go?"

"Go?" said Mom.

"Yes," said Webster. "You didn't mention this to them, Mally?" He nodded to Dad. "We're taking a few days at the coast."

Mallory at least had the decency to blush. "I, um, haven't finished packing yet, Webster." She tried to look at Dad, but only succeeded in looking past him at Mom's knuckles. "Dr. Lampson is researching coastal environments and their impact on brain chemistry. I said I'd help him with some fieldwork this week. You know—two heads are better than none."

"Paul," said Mom. "Why don't you give Dr. Lampson a tour of The Center? Dr. Lampson, I'm sure you'll find the Earthship concept fascinating. It may even take your research in a new direction." She began picking up Mallory's dropped packages. "Mallaboo, please help me put these away, dear. We've so much to do in three days."

Webster looked as if he was about to protest, but when Mallory went meekly with Mom, he followed Dad downstairs.

I took the chance to slip out. Kalimar and Felix were snuggled in a furry heap out of the rain, like two spotted plush toys. Still no Luke. I pulled up the hood of my raincoat and gave them the last two bottles of formula. Felix ate sloppily, goat milk dribbling onto his chest. Kalimar was more fastidious. They drank it all.

Now what? Should I just start them on cat food?

If Luke had a car, he could drive us to town. I'd never thought to ask him. Maybe he was sick. Maybe he was wasting away from some rare illness that came from handling cats. It had come on suddenly in the night, and now he was weak, covered in spots, longing for me to bring him some cool water. Maybe his mother kept asking him to get out of bed and hang pictures, and he was trying to do her bidding because he was such a dutiful son and hoping against hope that I would come and rescue him. I would help him through the woods on my shoulder and tend him in my own bed. Mom's tea would heal him. No! Cancel the tea.

I gave Kalimar a final pat and hiked in the direction of the Geoffrey place. I could just check.

At the property line I peered out at Luke's rainy driveway. How hard could it be to knock on the door? A light was on in one of the upstairs windows. Was Luke inside?

But if he was inside, why hadn't he come back? He'd promised to help me with the kittens, and he hadn't even given me his phone number or email.

I put my hand on a maple trunk and let the rain drip off my hood. What if I had lost him before anything had even started? I'd be languishing in my tree house when I was seventy in a faded tank top. The rats would be scuttling over my granola bars. Every day Natalie would send me a bag of Cheetos in the pulley bucket. And there I would finish my days, desolate, with only the depressing poems of John Donne to comfort me.

I turned around and trudged back to The Center. I had kittens to care for.

* * *

Mom and Dad were distracted enough with Mallory's "friend" that I was able to get back online and track down an exotic pets website. It said that once they were weaned, big cats could be fed cat food two to three times a day. How was I to know whether they were weaned? I didn't even know how old they were. But with no goat milk and no Pedialyte, I was going to have to try.

Looking at the exotic pets site made me think I could make this work. Most people had enclosures for their exotic animals, but Felix and Kalimar weren't "pets." They deserved to roam free in the woods where they'd been born. It was the least I could do for them. If I could learn how to care for them properly, they could live out their lives with us in peaceful coexistence. That was how Dad said we were supposed to live with the animals—to share the forest with them and respect their wisdom.

I bought thirty-five cans of cat food at Family Grocer—all I could fit in my backpack and still make it up the hill on my bike.

* * *

I didn't dare spend another night in the tree house. Besides, it would be cold with the rain. I had to hope Mallory would sleep soundly enough for me to sneak out.

Mallory was quiet all through dinner. Webster wasn't there, but he came back about 8:00, and Dad gave him a dorm room downstairs. No one told me what had happened while I was gone. Mallory seemed cowed at first, but as the evening went on, she began to shoot little dagger looks at Dad. She was unpacking her suitcase when I came out from brushing my teeth.

"Are you staying home?"

"Not that this is home," she snapped.

"Did you think they wouldn't freak out? I thought they did pretty well. They're letting him stay here, aren't they? How old is he, anyway?"

"Brigitta, that is irrelevant. Besides, I am more than usually mature for my age. You know that."

"Does he give you As?" It was nasty of me.

Mallory slammed her duffel bag onto the shelf. "I am not even going to answer that!"

I put my cell phone underneath my pillow, with the alarm set for midnight, hoping only I would hear it. I needn't have worried. When it woke me, Mallory's bed was empty.

My neck hurt. Something was poking my back. There was a sound—purring. And in my lap—kittens. I had come at midnight just to check. I had only meant to stay a little while.

Felix put his wet nose against my arm, and Kalimar stretched and dug her dagger claws into my leg. "Ow!" I lifted her off. Note to self: buy leather jeans. Pale light filtered in from the triangular "doorway" and the chimneylike opening above. My butt hurt from sitting all night.

Felix and Kalimar hovered as I opened cans. The website said two to three feedings a day, but it made me nervous. They were used to eating every three hours.

Inside the tree I felt the spirit of Onawa so strongly. She had been there in the night with me, too, a silent guardian over her children. I needed to begin thinking ahead. If they'd been with her, they'd have her milk and her warm body to sleep against. I was a poor substitute. Onawa would have been teaching them to hunt soon. How would I do that? Maybe I'd cover myself in animal skins and let the cubs follow me, skulking through the undergrowth. I'd follow the deer trails, and when a deer appeared, we would watch and wait. Then I'd suddenly leap into the clearing and—

And what? And Luke would be standing there and I'd be wearing nothing but animal skins. And while he would be intrigued by this, it would not be enough to keep him from concluding I wasn't suffering from the same insanity as my father.

How much cat food would it take to feed two full-grown cougars? How much money was in my college savings? How long was it possible to have secret cougars?

I decided thinking ahead was wrecking my morning.

Kalimar looked up at me and licked her whiskers. She slowed down her attack on her breakfast. Felix was still snarfing his. I found Luke's toy and dangled the strings over Kalimar's head. She swung her paws at the beads, then tried to bite them. Wood shavings from Luke's carving peeked out amid dead needles on the den floor. He had sat up all night carving and then he had abandoned ship.

*   *   *

I was checking the exotic pets website when Natalie popped up on IM.

guess what?!

What? I thought back guiltily to the last time I'd seen her. I hadn't even tried to call her since then.

TY was in seattle sunday!!

I groaned. Trent Yves was the last thing I wanted to think about. I clicked to the "Big Cats" section of the website.

Natalie started typing again. *4 real! cheryl saw it on the news! he was feeding lunches 2 homeless ppl dwntwn.*

It made sense. *Rocket* had been filmed in Seattle, so it was probably a publicity stop. Of course Trent *would* show up fifty miles from us just when Natalie might have let the whole thing go. *Nice of him,* I typed.

not so hard 2 run 2 seattle when your mansion is local ;-), Natalie persisted.

I sighed. I didn't want to be mean, but I had enough on my mind without Natalie's obsessive speculations about Luke. *The Trent thing is getting old.*

you'll see. this time i'm right. i asked ruby chavez @ the po. so-called "luke geoffrey" lives there w/only his mom. just the 2 of them in that huge

house. *ruby wd know, she's the postmistress. AND trent is an only child.
AND his dad left them and went to france.*

I stretched. *Why Kwahnesum? Not exactly an entertainment hub.* I
needed to wash my hair and get back to the kittens.

*that's the point!! we're small. out of the way. media's horrible 2 him.
wouldn't u want 2 escape?*

Not to here. I took off my shoes and wiggled my toes.

*it's perfect. woods, mountains. he cd use it as the location 4 his nxt film.
we cd b in it!*

Right. My cat Ophelia jumped onto my bed and began licking her
calico paws.

*y not? gwendolyn melier was an unknown til imlandria. & omg, that
kiss at the end? how many x do u think they practiced that? lol. & now he's
going out w/ her.*

Why did this make my head hurt? Even if Luke was Trent, which
was ridiculous, he wasn't going out with Gwendolyn Melier. He'd
only been seen with her at a party, which didn't mean anything at
all. The kiss, though, had been spectacular. Surprising the camera
hadn't melted.

cmon, B, uv got 2 have seen him. he lives nxt door 2u.

Ophelia curled up on my pillow. My own eyes were at half-mast. *I'm
tired, Nat. Need 2 take a nap. ttyl*

I signed off.

* * *

Kalimar was lapping water from a puddle when I got back to the
den. She had eaten about half her breakfast. Felix still had a little
clinging to the bowl, too. He was feisty, batting at my hair. Kalimar's
tail twitched as she practiced pouncing. I let Felix curl up in my lap.
Was it just a coincidence that both Luke and Trent were onlies living
with their moms? Luke had never mentioned brothers or sisters, but
that didn't mean he didn't have any. When I thought about it, I didn't

know that much about him. I'd never met his mom or been inside his house. I thought of all the Trent Yves pictures I'd looked at on the web. Luke kept transfiguring into Trent in my imagination. What if Trent really had chosen Kwahnesum for a hideaway? What if Natalie's fantasy was true?

Seeing Starzz ⭐ **Celebrities Find Their Deep Space**
Hollywood's Hidden Spiritual Quest

July 10

Breathlessly Awaiting Trent

Starlet is so certain Trent Yves lives here that she's practicing for her screen test at the grange hall. My, oh my, who'd have thought our little hamlet would be visited by such greatness? As for me, I haven't had a tender moment with Trent since at least Sunday.

Aquarius0210 responds:

Your "Starlet's" a hoot. I check every day for the next installment. Who do ya think'll show up next?

Trentsbabe responds:

mystic, i am so confuzed. r u realy having sex with trent?

Mystic responds:

Trentsbabe, if you look up, you'll see the word "gullible" written on the ceiling.

Seeing Starzz ★ **Celebrities Find Their Deep Space**
Hollywood's Hidden Spiritual Quest

July 10

Hideaway
Fan Fic by Mystic

Chapter One

The pressures of Hollywood had exacted an awful price from Trent by the time he found the town of Idyll Grove. Despite his passion for his art, the shallow attacks of the paparazzi had left him helpless and hopeless, needing respite, needing a place to disappear. And who would recognize him in this small valley where the main entertainment was fly-fishing—or rodeos two towns away?

It was in this state—flattened, beaten, exhausted—that Trent stumbled into the woods near his new mansion. He never suspected how fateful that morning walk would prove to be.

He followed a creek. There was something magical about it, something that drove him forward—a musical sound on the breeze. Was it only a meadowlark?

Trent stepped off the trail and began fighting his way through brush with his bare hands. He felt like Felix of Imlandria, searching for the scrolls. But there were no cameras here, no costumes, no props, just Trent Yves, blessedly alone and following a sound that stirred his heart.

The sound grew louder, more mesmerizing. He emerged into a circle of tall cedars, and it was there that he saw her.

Her golden hair cascaded like a waterfall to her slim waist. She wore a gown the color of sapphires. Her eyes were closed, and she was playing an instrument. It had strings the girl was stroking with a bow, but also little holes the breeze blew through, with an effect that was purely numinous.

When she stopped playing, he was filled with sadness. "Go on," he said. "Please?"

The girl opened her violet eyes. "I knew you'd come," she said. "I've been waiting for you."

Trent tried to step back but found he couldn't. Had the girl bewitched him, or was it only that he didn't want to leave? "Who are you?" he asked.

"I am Eoindyllandra," she said. "And you are Michael."

How did she know? Michael. His real name, not the one chosen for him so many years ago when his soul had been stolen by a glittering dragon with a relentless appetite.

She knew too much. Wasn't this the very thing he'd been escaping? To be watched, his secrets exposed? "What do you want of me?" he demanded.

Eoindyllandra held out her hand. "Don't be afraid," she said. "I know what you seek."

How could she? *He* didn't even know. He was only aware of an aching emptiness that filled him with despair.

"It won't be easy," she said.

And now he was intrigued.

"We must journey together, you and I, to a land you've never heard of. You will face many things. Even death. But if you survive, you will gain your heart's desire. If you wish to turn back, the time is now."

He was torn. To go would be to leave everything familiar. His family, his fans. He was known in the world he lived in. Known and loved. Adored, even.

The girl smiled, and he felt the warmth of it like a sunrise. He had thought she was a siren or even a goddess. But now he saw something else: power, yes, but also pain and a hint of sorrow.

"Michael," she said.

He took her hand.

The ground dropped away, and a rushing filled his ears.

chapter nineteen

Inside Cougar Bungalow, total sleep was impossible. As soon as I dozed off, Felix would put his whiskers on my face or Kalimar would walk over my legs. And their purring was like the engine of the *Titanic*.

I could have stayed in my room. Mom and Dad still hadn't clued in that Mallory was sleeping downstairs with Webster. The crap Darling Mallory got by with. If I said half the things she said to Dad, he wouldn't just pat me and smile. And he certainly would not invite my boyfriend to vacation at The Center where I could creep into his bed at night. If Mom and Dad thought I was creeping into anybody's bed, they'd have simultaneous heart attacks. Possibly because they thought I was about twelve.

My body fit inside the curve of the cedar trunk. It was buggy, and the kittens smelled strong and earthy, especially at close quarters. Natalie would gag, but I didn't mind it. I was becoming a woodland creature again.

Once or twice in the night I made my pathetic way to the tree house, just in case. So lame. Luke clearly didn't want to come back. Why did I even like him so much—a guy who would be weirded out over a little shamanism? Even if Dad was a freak, at least Luke could have said good-bye or "Your dad's a freak" or something. Did I only like him because he looked like Trent? How shallow was that?

Drifting in and out of sleep, my mind played with the idea of Luke being Trent-incognito. Maybe he'd left to make another movie. His next movie, *The Lamplighter*, was about cliff diving. Was he standing at the edge of a cliff right now, wishing I were there? If I were, would I hold his hand and jump?

Kalimar's claw caught on my Nonni coat. "Kalimar, no!" A patch tore away, leaving a bare spot. I shoved her off me. The scrap was from a Cherrywood sundress—gold with a green vine twining across. I rubbed it between my fingers, remembering against my will.

When Nonni had her stroke, Aunt Julia hadn't seen any reason for us to come. She had it "all under control," which meant she had already stuck Nonni in a nursing home. Dad and I went anyway.

Without Nonni, Cherrywood had been stopped in time: a rack of cold gingersnaps lay on the tile counter, a book of Anne Morrow Lindbergh's poetry facedown on the chaise lounge. And on her recliner, a stack of sewing scraps with a spool of thread on top.

I'd gathered them into my lap—bits of red and blue from my first recital dress, a green print from my "princess" skirt, denim from a bag she'd made me. Most had made their way into my Nonni coat.

I'd found scissors and a needle. If Aunt Julia, who lived ten minutes from Nonni, couldn't grasp that she needed her sewing, I'd have to bring it to her myself.

In the morning the kittens were snoozing hard. Figured. Felix tickled my cheek with his whiskers. I pressed the gold scrap into my pocket and stumbled back to the house to shower before I could be missed.

★　★　★

It took two hours to get out of the house after everyone was up. Mallory rose early and made us breakfast, even though she was not a morning person. Webster was in a good mood (naturally) and asked Dad non-sarcastic questions about Native American drum art. I didn't like him any better than I had the first day. Mom was baffled by the lack of goat milk but didn't say anything. She probably figured Webster had drunk it all and didn't want to embarrass him. Why, I am not sure. A little humiliation would have done him good.

Webster drove away after breakfast, and Mom and Dad left an hour later. Aunt Julia had given them an "overnight getaway" at a time-share in the San Juans. It had to be used on a July weeknight between Monday and Thursday, and they were required to be there at noon to hear a sales presentation. They'd put it off so long they had to go today or lose it.

Mom threw suitcases into the car with a determined smile on her face.

"Enjoy!" called Mallory from the doorway. "Don't forget to stop and smell the posies."

It had stopped raining, and I lugged my violin outside. I was ready to play again, Dad or no Dad. Since I'd quit competing, my practicing had gone from four hours a day to two hours, and finally to about once a week. But I needed to play now. It had always sorted me out when I was tangled.

Tomorrow night the hills would be alive with Indigo Children—a "new," highly evolved breed of human, bearing a cosmic message of peace and harmony. For once I wanted a week with the woods to myself—no chanting, no spirit quests, no kids with psychic powers.

I gave the cubs breakfast, but neither of them ate much. Felix licked my hand with his sandpaper tongue and curled back into a ball.

Out in the clearing under Eve I nestled the violin under my chin and let the bow take over. I played Vivaldi's Concerto in A Minor, then went on to the Toreador song from *Carmen*, which was fast and full of fury. My feet pressed into the mud, and the notes came up from the ground. A cold breeze blew at my cheeks. Six measures in, I had the feeling of being watched. I lowered my instrument. Luke stood, scowling, one foot propped behind him against Adam. "I must be a season ticket holder," he said. "I'm catching every performance."

Onawa, Dad, and now me. Performers. My fantasies of leaping through the air with him abruptly hit the ground.

"Thanks." I put my violin in its case. Maybe the edge in my voice could cover my exhilaration. "What are you doing here?" I began letting down my bow.

"Brigitta…hey." He laid a hand on my shoulder. "That was—it sounded great. I'm just in a bad mood."

I closed my case, with my back to him. "I wasn't playing for your benefit."

"Hey." He turned me to face him. "Don't be this way. Please?"

I liked his hands on me. They cupped my shoulders, warm and steady. His face lost its hard edges. I looked away. "Why did you leave like that?"

"Leave like what?"

"It's Thursday. Where have you been since Sunday?"

"Somewhere else."

"Where?"

He let go of me. "Do you require an itinerary?"

"Well, it would have been nice. I've been feeding kittens all by myself."

"Yeah, well, I'm sorry. I had to be somewhere."

"Uh-huh. I know. Anywhere but here. Anywhere but out in the woods with some strange girl, watching 'performances' by her freakish family!"

Luke's hands fell to his sides. "Is that what you think? That I left because of your dad?"

I picked up my violin and started across the bridge. "Just forget about it," I said.

"Brigitta, wait."

I stopped.

"Come with me," he said to my back.

I turned around. "Come where?" My stomach did a flip. Was he inviting me to his house finally? What was wrong with me? He could waltz off after promising to be here and then I was ready to chase after him as soon as he resurfaced?

"Aren't you even slightly interested in seeing Felix and Kalimar?"

His face fell. "Yes. Yes, of course I am. Are they all right?"

"No thanks to you." I was relentless. Was it just my exhaustion?

"I am sorry," he said. "Truly."

"I'm sure you are." Now I was being awful. He was tugging at my heart, so I was being awful.

When he saw the cubs, he got down on his hands and knees in the wet ferns. "Ohh!" His face relaxed.

Felix had finished his breakfast and was cleaning his enormous paws. Kalimar had her nose in her bowl, her ears peeking out over the rim.

Luke peered into the den and saw my pillow. "You slept with them?"

"Two nights. They don't sleep much, though."

"And they're eating solid food now?"

"Twice a day." I leaned my violin against the cougar tree.

"They look bigger."

"Do they?"

Kalimar grabbed Luke's sleeve with her teeth. I picked up the cougar toy and teased her away from him. Felix had already curled up to sleep. I set Kalimar next to him. They liked to sleep after eating.

Luke knelt in the leaves. He had dark circles under his eyes.

"I was rotten," I said.

"I deserved it." He stood and offered me a hand up. "There's nothing freakish about you, Brigitta. You're—I've never met anyone like you." He kept hold of my hand.

Heat spread across my cheeks.

He looked into my eyes with his blue, blue ones. "I missed you when I was gone," he said. "I wish—" He stopped. He let my hand go gently. "I will be back," he said. "I will." He patted the cougar tree and walked away—again.

My heart turned over as I watched him duck around a fallen birch. It was a couple of minutes before I snapped to attention. He had said, "Come with me." And then he'd just gone! And here I was standing, like a stick in the ground. Well, it was time for me to get unstuck!

I hefted my violin and took a deer path to the property line, arriving as he emerged from the row of maples. A look of sudden joy crossed his face. He stepped into the driveway, and the skies opened up. "Quick," he called as his shirt darkened with raindrops. He sprinted to a black Jeep Rubicon and opened the passenger door. "Come on!" He was getting drenched.

The car? He was taking me somewhere in his car? I hesitated only a few seconds and then ran for it. I stuffed my violin in the backseat and climbed in with my heart racing.

Luke started the engine and leaned back against his seat. His hair curled at the ends with dripping water. His damp T-shirt outlined his muscles. My shirt was just as damp, and I wished I had a jacket to wrap across my chest. He looked at me and grinned. "You're soaked, beautiful. I think there's a blanket in the back."

I reached behind me and felt for the blanket. I couldn't answer. He'd called me beautiful! Me, beautiful!

He took a breath as if he was about to say something else but didn't. He pulled out the driveway and accelerated on Mountain View.

I found my voice. "Where are we going?"

"For a drive?" He looked at me questioningly.

This was crazy. I should insist on knowing where he was taking me. But he looked like a little boy about to hand me a wonderful birthday present, and I didn't want to break the spell. The cougars wouldn't want another meal until nightfall. There was no reason I couldn't go for a little drive.

He wound down Eagle Lake Road and on into town. Past the Dusty Cover New and Used, past the Burger Arcade, past the post office, and onto the highway.

opened my eyes. I was in Luke's Jeep. How could I have fallen asleep? We were at a gas station, and Luke was filling up. He wore a blue Mariners cap and sunglasses against the glare. Nothing looked the least bit familiar. "Where are we?" I asked when he climbed back in.

"Olympia," he said. "See? There's the capital building." He made a left turn, and the dome came into view.

"Olympia!" I sat up straight. "Luke, that's, like, eighty miles from home! What time is it?" I looked at the dashboard. We'd been driving an hour and a half. "The kittens!"

For the first time, he looked concerned. "Aren't they on twice a day feedings?"

I let out my breath. "You're right. But I've never left them alone for more than a couple of hours."

"Do you want to go back?" His shoulders sagged.

It was only noon.

"There's a place I wanted to show you," he said.

"In Olympia?"

"No, not exactly."

"Are you going to tell me?"

"Do I have to?" He winked.

We were already so far away, and Mom would freak if I wasn't home by 6:00. No! Mom and Dad were gone! They wouldn't be back until tomorrow, just before the Indigo Children arrived at 7:00.

Luke watched me as he waited at a stoplight, his face shifting from disappointed to sexy to unreadable.

This was crazy. I'd known him less than two weeks. He disappeared regularly. If Natalie's daydream were true it would make him a liar: even his name would be a lie because Trent Yves' real name was Michael Boeglin. But Natalie was not exactly Sherlock Holmes.

I thought about how Luke had stayed up all night with the kittens, how he'd taken my turn at feeding them to let me sleep. I thought about his longing for Eden and how he had touched my hair. And I thought about how he'd held me right after we met Onawa—the stark honesty of his face that day. There was something irresistible about being in a car with him going who-knows-where. Natalie was right about one thing—I'd forgotten how to have fun.

My clothes were almost dry, and it was getting too warm. I peeled the blanket off. "Okay," I said. "I'll trust you."

Relief hit his face like a sunbeam. "Best news I've heard all day." He turned onto Highway 101 and stepped on the accelerator.

He flipped on the radio and surprised me again. Classic King FM. A symphony of violins and horns boomed out. He listened for a moment. "Music for Royal Fireworks," he said. "Handel."

"You're right," I said. "What was I playing when you showed up this morning?"

"Bizet," he said. "Something from *Carmen*. And before that it was either Vivaldi or Corelli." He looked pleased with himself.

"Vivaldi," I said. "A Minor Concerto. How do you know this stuff?"

"Oh, I used to sing," he said. "And my grandmother had a doctorate in music. I've been dragged to symphonies all my life."

The music changed movements, and Luke, with a silly grin, began singing the French horn part, *"Da-tada-tada-tada-tada-tada-tada-tada."*

I picked up the trumpets' answering phrase, *"Bada-bum-bum-bum-bum-bada-ba."*

We sang the whole movement, lobbing clarinets and percussion and horns back and forth. He let me carry the meandering violin themes. I reveled in the feeling of being on fire with music. I hadn't realized how much I missed being part of an orchestra. Outside the clouds moved away, revealing a cobalt sky. I felt like I was flying in it with Luke, swooping over the landscape like a couple of swallows. He reached across the seat and took my hand. I laced my fingers through his, as if it was the most natural thing in the world.

"You sing pretty well, too," he said when the movement ended.

"I played that a couple of years ago when I was still in Youth Symphony."

"Why aren't you in Youth Symphony anymore?"

"Oh, Dad got busy building his dream retreat center," I said offhandedly.

"But you're good. You should be in Youth Symphony."

I shrugged. If Dad's buried flute was any indication, it would be a long time before he lent his energies to my "Eurocentric music."

Luke squeezed my hand. He didn't let go.

We ate teriyaki in a town called Elma. I had only three dollars and forty-five cents, but Luke wouldn't let me pay. "I kidnapped you," he laughed. "The trip's on me."

"Kidnap me anytime," I shot back.

His smile was like the Fourth of July.

We were headed west most of the time. I could tell from the trip navigator on the dashboard—and the location of the sun. "Are you even going to give me a hint where we're going?" I teased.

"Learn to cultivate mystery, Brigitta." He touched my cheek.

"Such as the mystery of where you've been since Sunday?"

He gave me a sideways glance. "California. Mum was in one of her rare good moods, said she needed some sun."

California?! The word zipped around my head, crashing into my fantasies. "Not enough sun in Aruba?"

"You don't know my mother."

"No," I said. "I don't."

Luke rubbed his neck as if it was sore and didn't elaborate.

"So," I went on, "where in California?"

"LA. We went to a horse show."

"LA?! Are you serious?"

"As a heart attack."

I couldn't think what to say next, so I said, "Did girls throw themselves at you?"

"Not this time." He winked. Was he toying with me?

"Do you go there a lot?" A truck rolled by us with a sign that said HAZARDOUS. FLAMMABLE.

"Some." He sped up to get ahead of the "hazardous" truck.

"Do people mistake you for Trent?"

He didn't answer at first. Was I irritating him with my Trent talk?

He started to chuckle. "Once," he said, "I was in a mall in Encino with my dad and an entire Girl Scout troop mobbed me. They were all shoving pens at me and squealing."

"What did you do?"

"Well, Papa said go ahead and sign. So I did. Made their day. See? My looks perform a useful service."

He wasn't irritated. I relaxed. "That must be really strange."

"It was at first. It's only happened for a couple of years. Apparently Trent wasn't such a big deal before that."

"Well, there was *Sparrowtree* when he was nine. And he's been acting since he was five."

"I know."

"You do? You, who 'doesn't follow movies'?"

"Hey, I had to say something. Your friend looked like she wanted to swallow me whole."

"Natalie does that. But she's really very sweet."

"You're cuter." Luke grinned.

His hand found mine again.

"So, what do you think of his acting?" I forged ahead, not sure why it seemed reasonable that Luke knew anything about acting.

"Whose?"

"Come on."

"He's okay. What do you think of him?"

I hesitated and then yanked myself back to reality. Luke and Trent were not the same person, for heaven's sake. I could say what I thought.

"He's a jerk. But I'm beginning to think he can act."

Luke laughed. "What makes you think he's a jerk?"

"Oh, you know—I-am-so-sexy-let-me-show-you-my-pecs-again. And I heard he got Randi Marchietti pregnant."

"Where was that? The *Enquirer*?"

Flames shot up my neck.

Luke squeezed my hand. "I'm just giving you a hard time, Brigitta."

I forced a laugh. "Anyway," I fumbled, "his acting in *Rocket* showed surprising emotional range." I quoted DapperDan from my blog. "I think we'll be seeing more of him in serious roles."

Luke looked impressed. "Could be. He was weak in *Imlandria*. And *Le Petit Chose* was a disaster."

"I think it's pronounced 'shoze.' I took French for a year at the School from Hell. Why do you think it was a disaster?"

Luke slowed down as we entered Aberdeen. "What's the School from Hell?"

"Kwahnesum High School."

He laughed. "I'm glad I homeschool. So what was it like?"

"Awful. It was like being a zoo creature. 'This is a rare Brigitta Schopenhauer, of the family Schopenhauerensis. Members of this family live in unusual structures in the woods and like to decorate themselves with feathers. Schopenhauerensis should be approached with caution, as they engage in evil ceremonies. The Brigitta Schopenhauer is particularly dangerous. One should avoid eating lunch with the Brigitta, but it is permitted to gossip about her loudly from the next table.'" I stopped. I was making myself sound pathetic.

Luke laughed again. Then he paused for a train crossing and turned toward me. "You are rare, Brigitta."

A silly smile blossomed on my face. I couldn't suppress it.

He crossed the tracks and made a left turn. "You can't be raw in front of people like that," he said. "They do that because they don't get it. You can't let them under your skin."

"Easy for you to say, Mr. Homeschooler. You live in the protective bubble."

"Maybe so," he said pensively. "But those people don't deserve your pain, Brigitta."

It was a surprising thought. I felt…known when he said it. Like he saw the me I don't show to anybody.

The highway ended in Westport. Luke kept going, down a narrow road and then up a sandy rise. The Pacific Ocean opened out in front of us, glorious with whitecaps—the first time I'd ever seen it. "Oh!" I exclaimed.

Luke drove all the way onto the beach. He jumped out of the driver's seat, ran around the Jeep, and threw my door open. "We're here!" He seized my hands and pulled me to my feet. I tumbled after him, pelting across the sand. He ran directly into the waves without stopping to brace himself. "Woohoo!" he whooped.

I followed him in. The water was heart-stoppingly cold, but all around us little kids and dogs were playing in it. My jeans stuck to my legs, and I went splendidly numb.

An older couple with a kite smiled at us.

A wave knocked me off my feet, and Luke grabbed my waist to steady me.

We rode the waves in and chased them back out, holding hands and jumping. I felt wild and bold and dangerous. And Luke was sweeping me out to sea.

chapter
twenty-one

Being in love must be something like being drunk. But I couldn't know because I'd never been either. All I knew was that I was giddy with Luke, wheeling around in my squishy sneakers like a five-year-old. "Your lips are blue!" he called over the wind. He tugged me back to the Jeep and wrapped the blanket around me. He was shivering himself, water dripping off his lashes. He opened the back of the Jeep and found a big duffel bag. "Here!" He pulled out a pair of green sweats and a blue shirt with a parrot that said "Jolly Roger." He handed them to me along with a pair of socks and a green hoodie. I tried to give back the blanket, but he waved it off, pointed at the restrooms, and said, "Meet back here, okay?"

The bathroom was cold and had a loud auto-flush toilet. I rolled up my wet jeans and shirt along with my socks. My bra and panties were uncomfortable, but I couldn't take them off. What would I do with them? Stick them in the pocket of Luke's hoodie? It was strange to wear Luke's clothes. They smelled good—like clean laundry and spices. The sleeves on the shirt and coat were too long for me. What on earth was I doing here? Would Mallory notice I was gone? My belly was filled with a strange excitement. Suddenly the world had no boundaries.

Luke was at the Jeep wearing jeans and a thick denim jacket. The sun glinted off his sunglasses. He stashed my wet stuff and opened the door for me like a footman. He bounced into the driver's seat, crowing as sand sprayed out from our tires.

"Can we do this?"

"It's a Jeep. It can do anything!"

"I mean, is it legal?"

"It's a state highway," he said as a cop in a 4x4 pulled onto the sand behind us.

Luke frowned and slowed down to twenty-five. The cop left us alone. Luke pointed to the right. "There," he said. "Isn't it great?" Ahead of us was a lighthouse—white, with a red top, poised like a rocket ready to be launched. "It's the tallest one in the state."

We left the Jeep and walked. The sound of waves dropped suddenly as we descended the other side. The wind blew off Luke's Mariners cap, and he ran after it.

At the base of the lighthouse, five kids in "Camp Octopus" T-shirts waited with a couple of counselors. A wiry man with a weathered face stepped out. "Are you the last bunch?" he asked. The girl counselor nodded.

It felt a little like going into an Egyptian pyramid. But then I've never been in an Egyptian pyramid. A stubby kid stepped on a little red-haired girl's heels. "Ow!" she yelled. The sound bounced off the walls.

"Vincent!" The girl counselor, a bleached blond with a whistle, steered Vincent around the desk at the base of the stairs. Luke exchanged a glance with me.

"The Grays Harbor Light Station was commissioned in 1898," began the guide. "It stands one hundred and seven feet tall, and we are about to climb one hundred and thirty-five steps. Are you ready?"

"Yes!" shouted Vincent.

The guide eyed him. "Let's start with safety rules. Hang onto the stair rails and no pictures. We don't want cameras dropped off these stairs. A dropped object could attain the velocity of a bullet."

"Cool!" said Vincent.

"It is not 'cool.'" The guide stared at him levelly.

Steel stairs spiraled up the walls. The knobs on the stair rail had various shapes pressed into them—a kind of braille for lighthouse keepers carrying whale oil up to the lantern.

The girl counselor stayed close behind Vincent. Once or twice she seemed to study Luke, who had taken off his sunglasses.

The antique lens filled the lantern room—a huge transparent flower. We all circled around it. Two long old-fashioned bulbs sat inside. Outside the window a thumb-sized electronic lamp warned ships away from the rocks.

Behind us a drapery cut off the sun's glare, but it was hot. Luke pulled off his jacket and tied it around his waist.

Feet scuffled on the other side of the lamp. A small "wheee!" and a sharp pop echoed up the column.

"Vincent!" the guy counselor barked. I peeked around the edge of the lantern. Vincent leaned over the stair rail.

"It was just a penny," he said.

"All right," said the guide. "Tour's over."

"I'm so sorry," the girl counselor began.

"Time to go," he cut her off.

One by one everyone descended the stairs. Luke cast a glance behind us. We were the last to reach the bottom. A neat hole shot through the desk.

"Whoa!" said Vincent, clearly impressed with himself.

"Let's see! Let's see!" The other children pushed in for a look.

"You are in such big trouble, Vincent," said the little red-haired girl.

The tour guide strode to the door and opened it. The boy counselor took Vincent outside, and pretty soon a man with a Camp Octopus hat hurried over. The girl counselor herded out the rest of the children. I was about to follow them, but Luke put a hand on my arm. He edged toward the desk and lingered over the lighthouse books. Outside, the tour guide walked toward the Camp Octopus bus with a phone to his ear. Luke put a finger to his lips and guided me back. "What are we doing?" I mouthed.

"Living dangerously," he whispered in my ear. He crouched behind the desk and pulled me down with him. I put one hand on the stone floor to steady myself. Luke's arm rubbed against mine.

Between the desk legs I saw the tour guide's feet returning. My pulse pounded in my ears. There was a click and the lights went off. The slam of a door. A key in the lock. "Luke!" I hissed.

"Don't worry," he whispered. "It unlocks from the inside. I checked."

Under the desk a penny-sized spot was the only light. Luke kept a hand on my back. He breathed. We waited until we there were no more footsteps. My hands were clammy. Sweat trickled down my sides. When all was silent, Luke helped me to my feet. High above us was a circle of light like the mouth of a well. The stairs wound out from it in a faint line, a giant apostrophe. Luke led my hand to the stair rail. "We can't do this!" I panicked.

"He's gone," said Luke. "Trust me."

"What if he comes back?"

"I've scoped out hiding places on the upper levels."

Part of me wanted to bolt—to run out that door and back down to the beach. But another, shivery part of me knew that if I didn't climb those dark stairs with Luke, I would regret it for the rest of my life. He put a steadying hand on my waist. "Go slow," he whispered. "And feel for the knobs."

The column opened out below us like the inside of a conch shell. It lightened as we climbed. We reached the "foyer" level, right below the lamp, and we didn't have to feel our way anymore. We took the last set of steps and emerged into the lantern room.

Below us a forest of trees stretched out toward the water. The Camp Octopus bus was pulling away. The tour guide climbed into his car. I let out my breath. Maybe we wouldn't go directly to jail with Vincent.

"I came here with my dad when I was nine," said Luke. "Only I didn't drop pennies off the stairs."

"Were you a good little boy?"

Luke smirked. "Oh, yeah. All the time."

He touched my hair lightly as we looked out toward the beach. We could see a sailboat and a little farther out a fishing boat.

"Did you go fishing?" I asked him.

"My dad took me out in a crab boat."

"Did you like it?"

He laughed. "I was terrified of the crabs." The sun shone through the prisms of the lens and cast rainbows on his face.

"I didn't think you were afraid of anything."

Luke looked away from me and out to sea. "Oh, yeah," he said. "I am."

I moved the drapery behind us, so that we were between it and the outside glass encasing the lantern room. "What?" I asked him. "What are you afraid of?"

I thought he wasn't going to answer. Maybe I'd pushed him too far.

"Myself," he said.

I searched his face. "You're not frightening," I said.

He turned toward me and lifted a hand to my cheek. His lips were warm when he kissed me. The joy of it ran all the way down my spine. He put his fingers in my hair, and we kissed some more. I wrapped my arms around his waist, and we swayed there like dancers. I thought that living in the lighthouse and kissing Luke for the next three months could happily replace eating and sleeping. I was glad Devon had never kissed me. It couldn't have been anything like this.

"I like you," he said. "A lot, Brigitta. You've figured that out, haven't you?"

"Well, I hope so." I felt rather breathless. "You're not in a regular habit of doing this, are you?"

He laughed and tucked my head against his chest. "Hardly at all," he said.

twenty-two

In a sheltered V of driftwood logs, we ate fish and chips (mozzarella sticks and chips for me). The wind blew sand into my chips. I blew back, but only succeeded in shooting sand into Luke's eyes. "Hey!" he said. "You're gonna make me cry."

"Want me to kiss you and make it better?" I teased, astonished with myself. Brigitta in Kwahnesum was responsible and steady. This Brigitta who had shown up in my body was just short of outrageous. I flopped back onto the sand and let him kiss me. His lips were cold this time. His blue, blue eyes stared down at me.

"I don't want to go home." I sighed.

Luke sat back against the logs. "Neither do I," he said. His gaze shifted to the beach grass. He plucked a bit of it by his foot.

"Are you in there?" I moved to the log beside him.

He shifted his eyes toward me. "Yeah, I'm here." He put an arm around my shoulders.

I snuggled against him. "You're awfully quiet all of a sudden."

He rubbed my shoulder. "Just running movies in my head again."

I looked at him sideways. "Movies."

"Yeah." He didn't smile.

"Okay, so what's in these movies?"

He ran a hand along my arm. "The plot's a little thin."

"How about the characters?"

He scooped a handful of sand and let it trickle out his fist. "Well, there's this kid and there's this woman." He shook his head. "Oh, forget it."

"No!" I turned to him. "There's a kid and there's a woman. Tell me about them."

He laughed dully. "It's a stupid movie, Brigitta."

I put my head on his chest, amazed at my audacity. He needed me to not look at him.

He kissed my hair and rested his cheek on the top of my head.

"The kid in this movie thinks he's smart." His voice rumbled through his rib cage. "So see, this movie's a comedy. Because when the woman's had enough Scotch she's got lots of entertaining things to say to her kid. Plus, she's able to hit a French door with a Chinese vase from fifteen feet. And the kid figures out he's not as smart as he thought."

I sat up. "Luke, is that what's happening at your house?"

His eyes clouded, and he didn't answer. I had broken the spell.

"Hey." He gave my back a quick rub. "We've got to get back. Kittens, right?"

The kittens! I pulled my cell phone out of my pocket. "It's 8:30!"

Luke scrambled up.

At the Jeep Luke peeled off his sandy jacket. His shirt rose up, flashing a hard, muscular belly. It gave me a strange quivery feeling. I glanced away quickly, hoping he hadn't noticed. He tossed the jacket in the trunk with the blanket and unzipped his duffel. Inside I could see two pairs of jeans, several pairs of socks, a clear carry case with toothbrush, razor, comb. He extracted a pair of black sneakers.

"How long were you planning to stay here?" I asked him.

"A while." He dumped the sand out of his shoes.

He had packed the car before he heard me playing Bizet. He had planned to go alone, to escape. Only I had changed his plans.

Luke put on the black sneakers and stuck his blue ones next to the sandy clothes.

"What are you going back to?"

"A pair of adorable cougar cubs and a girl who lives in a tree."

"Is your mom violent? Does she hurt you?"

He closed the hatch. "She's fine, Brigitta. I can handle myself."

I'd gone too far.

He jingled his keys. "Ready to hit the road?"

I retrieved my half-finished Coke from the running board of the Jeep and dumped it out. "I'll be right back." I nodded toward a trash can at the far end of the parking lot.

If he was going home, it was only because of me. And if I didn't get to those kittens soon, I'd be putting them in danger. But was Luke in danger? Was his mom on some kind of drinking rampage?

I threw the cup away. I could see him leaning against the hood of the Jeep, watching the waves. He had the drawn look he'd had when I first saw him from the tree house. How could I buy him a little time?

Mallory answered on the third ring. "Hey," she said dreamily. "What's up, Gita?"

"Can you do me a favor?"

"Where are you, Gita? I only stopped home to get clothes. I'm not planning to stay."

Webster's voice probed in the background.

"Will you not tell him if I tell you?"

"I suppose. What's this about, Brigitta? Webster, give me a minute? Little sister has a crisis." A car door closed.

I was tempted to hang up, but Felix and Kalimar were waiting. I talked her down the path and out to the cougar tree.

She exclaimed when she saw them. "They're so sweet! They're licking me! Pew, they stink, though. Brigitta, why didn't you tell me?"

"Can you feed them? And make sure there's water?"

I could hear her cranking open a can.

"Are they okay?"

"They look great. Their eyes are so blue. They're gobbling this food."

"Mallory," I started tentatively. "If I was gone overnight, could you check on them?"

"Brigitta, you still haven't told me where you are."

"You never tell me."

"Are you with Devon?"

I didn't answer.

"How far away are you?"

"I'm at the coast." At least I'd give her that.

She laughed. "Now that's a switch! You've taken my trip! Oh, the big one's cleaning himself. Is it a he or a she?"

"The big one's Felix. You won't tell Mom and Dad?"

"Mom and Dad don't have to know everything, my little saint. God, Brigitta, you never do anything, do you?"

"Can you look after the kittens?"

"No worries. They're so cute! I'll just tell Webster we're sleeping here." She paused. "Brigitta, are you prepared? Do you have condoms?"

"Mallory!" Alarm bells went off in my head. No, I wouldn't need condoms. Luke and I had slept in the tree house, and the subject of condoms had never come up. But my chest tightened as I looked across the driftwood at him, still staring at the water.

"Just be smart, Brigitta. Do you have any questions you'd like to ask me?"

"No!" I collected myself. "Mallory, thanks for watching the kittens."

"No problem, little sister."

Luke smiled when he saw me. "Ready?"

I was afraid to touch him after Mallory's condom talk. And after glimpsing his stomach. I put my hands in my pockets (which were actually Luke's pockets, since I was still wearing his clothes). "The kittens are fine. Mallory fed them." I hesitated. "She said she'd watch them… all night." I focused on my shoes.

Luke looked at me sharply. "Really?"

"My parents don't come home until tomorrow night."

Luke put his hand on my arm. "You don't have to do this."

"You need time away from that woman in the movie."

This time, he met my eyes.

twenty-three

Luke stepped up to the desk of the Sea Star Motel as if he knew what he was doing. Now that we were here I was beginning to panic. Was I really going to spend the entire night with him? The lobby was small: '70s wood paneling, a spindle of paperbacks. The girl behind the counter looked up from filing. Her name tag said "Liza." She was a perfect tiny-waisted blonde with impeccable makeup.

"Two rooms?" said Luke.

I let out the breath I didn't know I was holding. Two rooms would be okay. We could talk and then go our separate ways to sleep.

Liza scrutinized him and then glanced at me. "It's the Street Rods show tomorrow," she said. "All the old cars? Every room in town is booked."

A mixture of relief and disappointment swept over me.

A white-haired man poked his head in from a back room. "207's open," he said. "I just had a cancellation."

My pulse quickened again. We were back to one room. What on earth was I doing here? The silk potted palms stared at me, as if they were wondering, too.

"Okay." Liza looked on the computer. "That's one of our Jacuzzi fireplace suites. Real nice. View of the water. Queen bed."

Bed? Singular? My heart dropped to my toes.

"Fine," said Luke. He pulled a card out of his wallet, studiously keeping his eyes off me.

Could he hear my heart slamming against my rib cage?

Liza ran the card through her machine and handed him a keypad for his PIN. "Hey," she said, giving him a closer look, "you're not—"

"No," said Luke. "I'm not him." He pocketed his wallet and took the key.

Liza watched us go out the door. She was whispering something to the white-haired man.

"What did I tell you?" he said, when we were back outside. "That's always happening."

My mind was still stuck on bed, singular, so that I almost didn't know what he was talking about. He grabbed the duffel from the Jeep, and we climbed the stairs. I couldn't avoid staring at his broad back. I took long, slow breaths as we stepped onto the second floor walkway.

"Is this it?" My voice had gone all squeaky.

Luke put the key in the lock.

The door opened and my eyes took in the room: a kitchenette, a fireplace, a Jacuzzi with huge mirrors mounted on the walls behind it. And the bed. A four-poster. Only one. Luke closed the door behind us and went silent.

I was afraid to touch anything. Luke put his duffel on the luggage rack and emptied his pockets onto the bedside table while I perched on the edge of an armchair. He hung his denim jacket in the closet. "There's, um, probably tea in the kitchen," he said.

"I don't want anything." I kept my hands in the hoodie pocket, over my belly.

Luke went into the bathroom, and I got up, tentatively, to explore the room. There was a switch for the fireplace. I turned it on, then off. The Jacuzzi was deep—big enough for two people. A rubber duck peered at me from a stack of towels. In the mirrors my face stared back at me. My hair was tangled, and my cheeks were pinker than usual. A sprinkling of sand ran across my jawline. I brushed it away. In Luke's clothes I looked like a different girl. I pulled the hoodie off and draped it over a chair.

On the bedside table were Luke's car keys, a handful of agates we'd found on the beach, his wallet. I willed my mind to stop whirling. Downstairs, Liza was probably calling the press. Silly. Just like Natalie.

Still, the parallels between Luke Geoffrey and Trent Yves were hard to ignore: the unexplained absences, the crazy mom—and especially his looks. Even he knew he looked like Trent. I sat down on the bed and fingered Luke's wallet. If I opened it and pulled the card out, would it say Luke Geoffrey? Or would it say Michael Boeglin? The wallet was worn and brown in my palm. How could Luke afford to pay for a room like this? He didn't have a summer job that I could see. Did his wealthy parents just drop money into his bank account?

In the bathroom, the shower was running. I tried not to think about Luke in there naked. I flipped the wallet open. Inside was a picture of a man and woman, who had to be Luke's parents. They had their arms around each other and were laughing. A few cards peeked over the tops of the wallet pockets: a blue one, a red one, a Bank of America card. I could see the top of Luke's head in the picture. I hesitated. If I were Natalie, I'd want him to be Trent. But that was fake, a fantasy. Luke was a real boy with real pain. I wanted to be with him, not Trent. I ran my finger over the cards. How could I snoop like this? I'd told Luke I trusted him. If he wasn't who he said he was, wouldn't he have been honest with me by now?

I dropped the wallet back on the nightstand. The sun was setting. I went to the sliding door and pulled the curtains back. The sky was orange-rose over the water. The clouds shifted colors. Luke came up behind me and put his hands on my waist. His hair was wet, and he had on a different pair of jeans and a red T-shirt. My heart began to pound again. I wanted to bolt and I wanted to stay. I leaned against him, and he laced his hands across my belly. "You're beautiful," he whispered and an electric jolt ran through me. I turned into his arms, and his mouth came down hard on mine. His hands moved across my back; he pressed me to him. This was different from on the beach. My insides sped up, my blood racing through my veins in a rapid circuit. I felt his hard muscles as my hands, with a mind of their own, slid up his arms and shoulders. He kissed my eyes, my cheeks, my neck, and then came back to my lips. Nervously, I opened my mouth like I'd seen in the movies, and his tongue came in and tickled mine. Before I knew it, we were on the bed, his fingers tracing my jaw, my throat. He trailed his hand down, and his fingers slipped under the blue shirt and made circles on my belly. I was entirely electric.

"You're so amazing," he said.

I wanted him to stop; I wanted him to keep going. His hand moved up until it cupped my breast. *Is this a good idea?* my brain asked. *Yes!* my body answered.

Luke's fingers ran along the edge of my bra, touching my skin. It felt both delicious and terrifying; I was shooting the rapids—about to go over the falls. He slid his fingertips under the cloth.

"Wait!" I pushed away from him.

He sat up. His face was flushed and his hair was tousled. Both of us were breathing hard. He looked at and then away from me. "I'm sorry, Brigitta. I—I'm an idiot."

"No, *I'm* sorry. It's just—you're going too fast. I'm not ready."

He swung his legs over the bed and bowed his head, his back to me. "I'm not either," he said in a low voice. "I mean, I'm not unready..." He ran the curtain through his fingers. "I don't want you to think I brought you here for that. I mean..." He let out his breath. "God, I am such an idiot!"

My mouth was dry. I looked at my still-damp sneakers. I was the idiot. I hadn't told him I wasn't ready for sex before I let him rent us a room. Maybe I wondered if I was. My ankles chafed with sand inside the cuffs of the green sweats.

Luke put his hands on his knees. "Do you want to leave?"

I walked around the bed and slid the door open. Outside the waves rolled and splashed. The sun was gone. I stepped onto the balcony, and the air cooled my face. I turned back to him. He looked so miserable.

"Do you have any other sweats in that bag of yours? I don't think I'd fit in your jeans." I blushed.

Luke rolled across the bed and lobbed a pair of black sweats and a white T-shirt at me.

Even after I'd locked the bathroom door, showering felt awkward knowing he was out there. I looked down at my bare body, and it felt new—worthy even. I touched my breast where his hand had been. Had I stopped him too soon? Or not soon enough?

I brushed my teeth with my finger and some of Luke's toothpaste. Using his toothpaste seemed even more intimate than wearing his clothes. I slid on the clean sweats and shirt and found a comb in a plastic wrapper, which I ran through my hair. I could hear Luke pacing. Would Trent Yves be this nervous about a girl—about me? That seemed unlikely. I was glad for not having pulled out his debit card. What if he'd walked in when it was in my hand?

He was back out on the balcony when I emerged. I sat down in one of the fireplace armchairs and gave it a twirl. It spun slowly so that I was facing the sliding door when Luke stepped into the room. His cheeks were flushed and his hair was still messy. He looked less and less like Trent and more and more like Luke. He sat in the other armchair. "Are you okay?" he said. "Do you want to go?"

"I'm okay," I said. He was so not Trent. If Trent had a girl in a motel room, he would definitely not be offering to drive her home before he got what he wanted.

He stood up and went into the kitchen where he opened the fridge and then closed it. He came out empty-handed and peered into the Jacuzzi. Then he went to the sliding door and shut it, straightened one of the wall pictures, and walked to the fireplace where he flipped the switch on and off.

"Luke," I said. "It's all right to sit down."

He left the fireplace on and sat, shifting in his chair several times.

"Could you possibly be more nervous than I am?" I surprised myself by saying this aloud.

He gave a short laugh. "Yes." He surveyed the carpet. "I really blew it, didn't I?"

All the anxiety drained out of me. "I like you so much," I said.

He rewarded my brazenness with a broad grin. "Same back," he said.

twenty-four

Outside the waves tumbled over themselves. Luke gazed into the fire, now the only light in the room. "Remember when I said I was looking for Eden?"

"Yeah."

"This feels like Eden."

I looked around. "The Jacuzzi fireplace suite?"

He chuckled. "No, not that. I mean here with you."

A wisecrack about forbidden fruit leaped to mind. I squished it. But a wave of joy washed over me.

Luke put his feet up on the leather ottoman. "What's your Eden, Brigitta?"

For some reason I began telling him about Cherrywood, about Nonni and Opa and the birds and the raspberries and the hot cicada-filled summers. I told him about their "spirit-filled" church services and about Nonni singing me to sleep.

"What happened to them?"

My throat tightened. "Strokes. Both of them. Opa went first."

"That's rough," he said. "My grandmother, too. She had a bunch of strokes before she died. It was hard to see her like that."

"Yeah." I stared at my lap. Aunt Julia had said Nonni wouldn't recognize me or Dad, that it was silly for us to go see her, that the nursing home was providing everything she needed. The memory pushed at me. I pushed back.

"Hey," said Luke. "I shouldn't have brought it up."

"No, it's okay. It's been over a year."

I'd never told this story before. It was like a bruise—as long as I didn't bump it, I was fine.

Luke tipped his head. The firelight made shadows on his face. "You sure?"

I focused on the armchair upholstery buttons. It would be lame to talk about it—like I was looking for attention. But my mind's eye could see the lockdown wing at the nursing home, the color-coordinated hallways, the doors that clicked shut behind us. And Nonni. A different Nonni. Her eyes were all wrong. One side of her face was frozen. She'd shuffled forward with the nurse holding her arm. "Six-one-six-one-six-one," she mumbled. An address? A phone number?

Luke put his feet on the floor and leaned toward me, forearms on his knees. "Are you okay?"

I shook my head. "She was just so lost," I whispered.

"Yeah," he said quietly. "I know."

Did he? I longed to tell it all the way through: Nonni—who I loved like my own hands—her eyes darting around the room. Crying out, scared when Dad touched her. He'd left me then. Gone to see the nurses and left me alone with her.

"The room had this maroon wallpaper with flocked roses on it," I began tentatively. "*I* felt marooned."

Luke nodded.

"But I knew she was in there. I knew Aunt Julia was wrong about Nonni being 'too far gone to care.'"

Luke moved his chair closer. The memory was too fierce to stop. I told him: how I'd put the sewing scraps in Nonni's lap, how she'd pushed them away, crying "Ba-ba-ba-ba!" How the nurse had come then and tried to take her back to her room.

"No! Don't take her yet!" I'd said. I hadn't meant to raise my voice.

Nonni had slouched in her chair. "Six-one-six-one," she had mumbled.

The nurse had nodded. "Okay. She seems less agitated." She'd touched my arm. "It's hard the first time you see them. I know."

Luke listened. His eyes never left my face. It felt good to let the memory out—like lancing a wound.

"I didn't reach for Nonni after that. I couldn't bear to see her scared." Luke nodded.

"Instead I...I sang to her. The song she used to sing me."

Nonni had turned her face to me as I sang, *"The Lord is my Shepherd, I shall not want."* I'd gone on singing: the green pastures, the still waters. Her eyes glistened. I didn't want to sing the next part, but she was with me now, drinking it in.

"Yea, though I walk through the valley of the shadow of death
I shall fear no evil..."

I had to stop and take a breath. Luke reached for my hand the way I had reached for Nonni's. I'd wound her cold fingers through mine, and she hadn't pulled away. Her eyes had carried me to the last line: *"I will dwell in the house of the Lord forever."*

"Forever," mouthed Nonni. And then, clear as a bell, she'd said, "Forever, Brigitta-Lamb. Don't you forget."

* * *

That was as much of the story as I could tell. I rolled the upholstery button back and forth in my fingers. Luke knelt in front of me, his eyes red. He had brought me to the door of the memory and then gone through it with me. How had he done that? Why had I let him?

He brushed away my tears with his thumbs and led me to the balcony. The moon was a bright, fat almond. In the cold air Luke wrapped his arms around me. I leaned back against him, and he put his chin on my shoulder. We looked out at the water. I felt safe with him. We stood without talking for a long time.

When I began to nod, he scooped me up. I rested my head on

his shoulder, and he carried me inside and set me on the bed. "Don't worry," he whispered. "I'm tucking you in." I was too sleepy to protest. He pulled the bedspread back, and I slid between the sheets. He went to the fireplace and turned off the switch. Then he climbed onto the other side of the bed but stayed on top of the bedspread. He reached over and took my hand.

I didn't think I'd sleep, but I did. And then around one o'clock I woke up thinking of the kittens. I had banished them from my mind most of the day, but now they were back, demanding attention. How could I have left them with Mallory? Would she really know how to take care of them?

I could feel the warmth of Luke beside me curled deep asleep with his back to me. Was he cold? I slipped out of bed and retrieved a blanket from a drawer. I brushed back his hair, and he didn't wake up. I memorized him with my eyes: his long, dark lashes, his strong jawline. Behind his ear was a small white scar shaped like a bird's beak. Asleep, his face looked like a little boy's.

I thought of his lips on me, his hands under my shirt. My insides felt strange. Mallory wouldn't have thought twice about going further. Had I stopped him because I was too immature? Mom had always said I should wait until I was eighteen, but I don't know if she'd have been that shocked—just freaked out that I didn't have condoms like Mallory insisted.

I'd have been freaked out, too. Getting pregnant would be a definite glitch in my plans. But it wasn't just that. In that back of my mind, I could hear Nonni's voice. "Treasure your virginity, Brigitta. It's a gift you can only give once."

Natalie would have thought it was corny. I didn't know anyone but Tarah who thought like Nonni did about sex. But even so, there was a part of me that didn't want to disappoint her.

★ ★ ★

I woke to the sound of the room phone and Luke's voice, thick with sleep. The clock said it was nearly noon. "Hullo?" His voice slumped. "Yeah, it's me." I watched him through half-closed eyes. He rolled to a sitting position. "Yeah. Yeah. Are you sober?" He traced a bird on the bedspread with his finger. "How did you find me here? Oh. They can do that? Who else knows? Yeah, well, I'm sorry. Okay." He stared at the ceiling. "Okay. Yes, I'll come home. Just don't send anyone. Yes, I'll turn my cell back on." He stuck one leg out of bed. "Well, it hasn't been easy for me, either. Look, we'll talk about this later." He hung up and saw that I was awake. "Debit card," he said. "I just failed lesson 101 in the Art of Disappearing. Don't use a debit card."

"Your mom called the bank?"

He nodded. "At least she thinks I'm alone," he said.

chapter twenty-five

Luke didn't hold my hand in the car. His face was taut as we pulled out of Westport. We stopped for a light in front of a surf shop. Outside was a chainsaw carving of a surfer girl, her wooden hair flying—topless, with huge nipples. Luke hit the highway and I watched the speedometer climb. I punched my redial for the fifth time and heard, "This is Mallory Schopenhauer. Your call is extremely important to me…." I shut the phone. Where was she? Would she remember to give the kittens water? What if they were afraid of her? Would they go looking for me? My stomach acid kicked into overdrive. Maybe I had ulcers.

Luke passed a green SUV, an old Dakota pickup, and a Lexus. "Is your mom mad?" I tried.

"No more than usual." He passed an RV.

"How mad is she usually?"

He snorted and didn't answer.

I felt the sudden loss of him. Once more he'd gone somewhere and left me behind. Only this time he was right next to me.

I tried Mallory and got the voice mail again. How could I have left the kittens? I'd lost my head. If they died it would be my fault.

Luke swerved to avoid a bale of hay in the road.

"Whoa!" I said. "Watch your speed."

He glanced at me and slowed down. "God," he said, "maybe I should start drinking."

It felt like a slap. I couldn't think of a snappy comeback.

Nonni used to tell me that a boy "lost respect for a girl if she let him press his advantage." She meant sex, of course, though she would never use the word *sex*. Did Luke hate me now? Had I just imagined how sweet he'd been last night?

I had never told anyone about my last visit with Nonni. Not Natalie, not Devon, not Mallory. Why had I told Luke?

He scowled at the road, obviously irritated with the other drivers for slowing him down.

"Forever," Nonni had said. I felt tears threatening. I shut them off before they could start. The word *Kwahnesum* meant forever in Chinook jargon. Dad had told us how Kwahnesum was founded in 1850 by a fur trader called Joseph LaRonge and his Native wife, Izusa. They wanted Native people and white settlers to live together peacefully, so they called the town "Kwahnesum," hoping it would last forever. But within five years Governor Isaac Stevens had persuaded the Native tribes in Washington to sign treaties that banished them all to reservations.

Did anything last forever? I wanted to believe there was something outside myself that I could count on—some kind of spirit or higher power. And sometimes I felt something—a connection. I'd felt it during the Shabbat service and when I was bowing to the ferns. I'd felt it when Nonni used to pray with me. It had always been there at Cherrywood.

But maybe it wasn't anything at all—just a chemical reaction in my brain. That's what Mallory would say. It's what Dad had always said before he went off the deep end and began painting himself and communing with animal spirits.

My last summer at Cherrywood I had pestered Nonni about this all the time. "Is there really such a thing as God?" I'd asked her while we peeled potatoes or hung laundry out on the line or dug in the garden. "Is there really?"

Nonni had never said yes or no. She'd simply replied, "Is there such a thing as love?"

And now I wasn't even sure I believed in love. At least not the way Nonni meant. Maybe love is just hormones or endorphins—not some great force all around us. Maybe that's just nonsense. It's always seemed to me that love is about being found—the way you might find your missing cat because you knew he had a notch on his left ear and came to the sound of pebbles rattling in a can. But maybe that isn't the way things work. Maybe you can only be "found" for a little while. Just like Joseph and Isuza LaRonge discovered, "forever" isn't really forever. Everything ends. Everything is lost eventually.

I stared out at the highway and the fields rolling by. We came into a town called Montesano, and Luke pulled the Jeep into a mini-mart. He handed me a ten-dollar bill. "Can you just get us something to eat in there?"

I took the ten without answering and went into the store. I got strawberry Pop-Tarts, doughnuts, two reasonable-looking bananas out of a basket, and two coffees. Not much of a meal. But at this point, it wasn't much of a date. Mom would choke if she saw me eating stuff like that, but oh, well. I grabbed a bag of Cheetos at the register and added it to the stash.

I tried to give Luke his change, and he waved it off so I stuck it in the well by his gearshift. He pulled around to an empty park across the street and opened the doughnuts. He offered me one, but I shook my head. "Not hungry," I said.

He shrugged and went on eating, getting powdered sugar all over the upholstery of his fancy Jeep. I turned away.

"So," I said to the passenger window, "did I go to bed with Jekyll and wake up with Hyde?"

I heard him sigh behind me. "Am I being that much of an asshole?"

"Yes," I said. "You are."

He was quiet again, and this time it didn't feel like mad-at-Brigitta quiet. I shifted in my seat and looked at him sideways. "Do I really make you want to start drinking?"

He gave a short laugh. "Not hardly." He threw the garbage away and started up the car again. This time he took my hand. "Thanks for doing this," he said. "Coming with me, I mean."

I was so relieved I wanted to lift up his hand and kiss it. Instead I put my other hand on top of it. "Are you going to tell me anything?" I said. "So far you're one big secret."

And then he was back inside himself again. He took his hand away and pulled out onto the highway, not talking.

He made a left turn, and his eyes darted over to me and then back to the road. What did I have to do to lure him out and keep him there? Every time I got brave, I said the wrong thing.

But I was a secret, too—I had worked my hiddenness into an art form for almost everybody. The more time that went on, the more secrets I kept.

Luke punched a button on his stereo and searched for a track. Metallica. "The Unforgiven." He turned it up loud.

*   *   *

Luke's mother was standing in the driveway with her arms folded when we pulled in. She was barefoot and had on black slacks and a white blouse, untucked. Her arms were thin, and her eyes had deep wells underneath, accentuated by her dark hair.

"Crap," said Luke. "I should have dropped you off at your place."

His mother's eyebrows went up a little when she saw me get out of the car.

"Mum, this is Brigitta. She lives next door."

She shook my hand without a word. He didn't tell me her name.

My jeans and shirt were still in the back of the Jeep, but Luke didn't make a move to open it. He stuffed his hands in his pockets, suddenly younger. "I'll, um, see you around, Brigitta," he said. He didn't even look at me.

chapter twenty-six

I skirted the main trail and took the deer path past the well. I had to get to Felix and Kalimar before I did anything else. The junk food was sitting like a rock in my stomach. I wanted to be mad at Luke because it would stop me from being as sad as I was. I had felt so close to him and then he had shut down. Had I been stupid to share as much as I had? Like maybe I'd been stupid to let him touch as much of me as he had?

What's that Greek myth where the woman's immortal lover vanishes at sunrise? Cupid and Psyche?

I stepped over a tangle of roots from a downed cedar. Luke's mom had shaken my hand so icily. Did she think I was a slut? It was obvious Luke and I had spent the night together. Maybe she didn't want her son with "that" kind of girl. The thought almost made me laugh—that anybody could take me for worldly and experienced.

A wet maple branch thwacked my cheek, and I rubbed my face on the sleeve of Luke's hoodie. Maybe he'd come and find me once his mom wasn't watching him. Was she taking her anger out on him now? He'd said he could "handle himself," and I'm sure he'd be insulted if I thought differently. It wasn't like his tiny mother could overpower all that muscle. But there are other ways someone can make your life hell.

He seemed to feel responsible for taking care of her, hanging her pictures and going wherever she wanted to go at a moment's notice because she "wanted some sun." Didn't she have any friends?

Was Luke's grandmother who died his mother's mom? Had she gotten weird after her mom died like Dad had after Nonni died? Luke and I might have a lot in common, if only he'd talk about it.

I came to a spot where the afternoon sun hit the trunks of the Doug firs. Once a buck had come into this clearing while I was here "listening." I'd spent half an hour moving toward him, toe-heel, toe-heel, until he was an arm's length from me. I'd remained motionless another fifteen minutes, and he'd stayed near me, nibbling berries, as if I was a doe. Finally, I had reached out and put my hand on his warm neck. For a brief, suspended moment the energy coursing through him had flowed up my arm and into my chest. Then he'd turned with a swift motion and leaped away, flashing into the trees. I hadn't seen him again.

Would it be that way with Luke?

I came around the back of Adam and was about to cross under the tree house when two little boys ran by whapping each other with light sabers. Three women came behind them across the bridge, chatting and sipping tea. I walked past them and saw that The Center was swarming. Parents strolled along the paths while their children jumped, spun, and tumbled between the trees. How could this be? It was only 4:00. How would I get to the kittens' den? I'd have to wait until they all went inside. Whenever that was. I dodged the light sabers and was attempting a sprint to our apartment when the Fire-Breathing Shaman stepped onto the front porch.

"Brigitta, in here, right now." He swept me into his office and closed the door.

"Welcome home," I said hopefully. "You're earlier than I thought."

"Clearly," he said without smiling, "you haven't been paying attention. Your mother and I have been here since noon. Nothing had been cleaned, swept, or prepped in our absence. We had to scramble through the tasks we thought we'd delegated, so that we could greet our guests when they began arriving at two."

"Two? I thought this didn't start until seven."

"No," snarled Dad. "It started at two. Your mother called Natalie's at twelve fifteen and asked that you come home. That was four hours ago."

Natalie? Sweet Natalie had covered for me again!

"What happened to Mallory?"

"I have no idea what happened to Mallory." Dad pitched a stack of flyers into the recycle bin. "I just know we have forty-two people here that need taking care of, and you're off watching TV."

The phone rang. He picked it up, and I took my opportunity to get out of there.

Mom was on the porch passing out muffins to twelve or thirteen grubby-fingered kids.

I heard snatches of conversation: "Come to believe Benji is an avatar."

"And his teacher will not understand…"

"She had a dream about it three months before it happened…"

"I'm so tired all the time…"

I threaded my way through them before I could be nabbed by Mom. If I could slip into the trees from the hidden side of the tree house, I might be able to get to the kittens without attracting attention.

Where was Mallory? Had she checked on the kittens at all since last night? Would they still be there?

I'd reached the bridge before I realized I was being followed. A boy and a girl about seven and nine came into the clearing. "Who are you?" said the girl.

Usually I like kids, but I was not in the mood for this. "I live here," I said. "Who are you? Hansel and Gretel?"

"I'm Skylar," said the girl. "I can read auras. You didn't tell me your name."

"Why don't you tell me?"

The girl sighed irritably. "I'm clairvoyant, not telepathic," she said. "Jeremy, what's her name?"

Jeremy squinted. "I think it's Beth or Rita or something. I can't concentrate here."

"Forget it," said Skylar. "Come on!" She took off running. Right in the direction of the kittens.

Jeremy followed her, climbing over logs and under branches like he knew the route already. I went after them. Surely they wouldn't think to look in a dead tree.

"Hey!"

I arrived in time to see Skylar holding Kalimar aloft. "Sweet!" said Jeremy. He dragged Felix out into the open.

"Stop!" I said. "Put them down. They're wild animals!"

Skylar was cooing and rocking Kalimar like a baby. Felix struggled and scratched at Jeremy, who dropped him.

"Ow!" Jeremy looked at the blood on his arm with surprise as Felix scampered away.

I reached for Kalimar and sucked in my breath. Diarrhea covered her back legs and tail.

"Gross!" said Skylar, thrusting the kitten at me. Kalimar didn't resist, just lay there.

Felix reappeared from behind the cougar tree, looking wobbly on his legs. I felt sick. "You guys get back to The Center and wash your hands," I said. "We need to leave these animals alone."

I rubbed Kalimar between her ears. She didn't even purr.

"*You're* not leaving them alone," said Jeremy.

"Let's go!" Skylar pulled on Jeremy's shirt. "I want to show Brendan and Tom!"

"You guys—no."

But they were already scrambling toward The Center.

I had no time. I stuffed Kalimar in the pocket of Luke's hoodie and scooped up Felix. Kalimar's head drooped out, and I pushed it back in gently. Where would I take them? The tree house? Another snag?

It was already too late. Skylar and Jeremy reappeared with a crowd behind them, looking like they were about to cross the Red Sea.

"There they are!" Jeremy sang out. "Brigitta's got the other one in her pocket!"

Utter chaos broke out at that moment with two dozen psychically gifted moppets all reaching out to touch and hold the kittens, their parents calling out nondirective instructions, my parents shocked and amazed. All this was followed by the kittens being cleaned with a damp cloth by Mom and going into a towel-lined box in a warm corner of the dining hall, and then an impromptu forty-person discussion of why I'd been so tired the past week, the legality or illegality of keeping wild animals, the ethics of disrupting ecosystems, and whether a cougar can roar (it can't).

I knelt by the cardboard box, feeling the kittens' breath while the adults gathered in their Indigo Child circle. Felix draped himself limply across Kalimar. His eyes were closed. I felt the awfulness of what I'd done, leaving them like that. I should have known Mallory couldn't understand anything wild. When we were little and used to listen in the woods, Mallory had usually fallen asleep. She might think the kittens were cute and cuddly, but she couldn't "hear" them. She'd have given them their cat food, checked on them once or twice, and then marched off with her psychology god—the one named after a dictionary. Mallory wouldn't feel Onawa's presence from the spirit world. She lived in the world of neurons. Mallory loved provable facts. Mallory drew logical conclusions. Mallory had gotten Onawa a state execution.

Jeremy appeared beside me, surprisingly quiet, and put his hand on Felix's head. "We were too rough with them," he whispered. "This one told me."

Dad looked haggard and Mom drawn. I wished they'd shoo all those people down the stairs, but the energy of the Indigo Experience seemed to have taken everyone over. I was now the center of an Indigo family discussion, even though I'd never met any of these people. And the pre-vailing wind was that the kittens had to go—to someone more expert, capable, and trustworthy than me.

chapter twenty-seven

Kalimar's ear flicked, and she yawned a wide, pink yawn. Beside me, Jeremy dangled his hand in the cardboard box, but neither kitten batted it. I wanted to gather them up and run back to their den with them. I could make them better. I'd just start over with the Pedialyte. A little more research and I'd know what to do.

But would I? When Ophelia got sick I took her to the vet. There were people trained to care for wild animals. Even Luke had argued for that. Now that my own stupidity had put the kittens in jeopardy, it seemed silly to think Buck Harper was a danger. Maybe they should go to a wildlife rehab center. What were rehab centers for? The kittens hadn't menaced or attacked anyone. A rehab center could get them well and then release them. They could grow up in the wild the way they were supposed to.

I felt tears threatening. No way would I cry in front of strangers. Jeremy put his hand on my arm. "They want to stay here," he said.

"It's not practical," I snapped, wondering why I was arguing with a seven-year-old.

And then, from some deep-space wormhole, Mallory-of-the-superior-intellect swept in to have her usual final word.

"Why not?" she said. "Why not keep them here?"

I stopped arguing. Had aliens taken my sister and sent this one in her place?

Mallory set a bag of groceries on the counter. "Those cougars were born on this land. They belong here. If you want to talk about ecosystems, cougars have been roaming this area more millennia than you and I. Why shouldn't they stay and why shouldn't Brigitta feed them? She found them. She encountered their mother."

Mom stared at her. She didn't ask, "Where have you been all day?" because I suppose the answer was obvious.

Somehow the manifestation of Mallory woke Dad up, and he handed the Indigoes and their parents over to their retreat leader for their evening session. Jeremy unfolded himself from the floor, nodded at me slowly, and went with them.

Mom began boiling baby bottles I'd brought in from the tree house. Dad paced the tile floor. "A refuge is the best place for them. They're set up for animals like this."

"We could get set up ourselves." Mallory knelt by the cardboard box. "Don't most refuges start with some animal lover nursing squirrels back to health on her patio? It's probably just some license fee you have to pay."

Mom handed me two of the bottles, and I snapped off a Pedialyte cap and began filling them. Felix opened his cobalt eyes. Did I even dare to hope? I lifted Felix carefully out of the box.

Dad rubbed his temples. "I don't know that it's legal."

Mallory took six boxes of rice milk out of the grocery bag and lined them up on the shelf. "People keep exotic pets," she said. "That's legal with the proper permits. Webster had a student who raises ocelots."

Mom poured the boiled water into a jar for watering the plants later. "Clyde's ex-wife has a bobcat. We could get in touch with her and find out how it's done."

Without much energy, Felix licked at the nipple of the baby bottle. I squirted some Pedialyte into his mouth, and he began to suck. He did a turned-down rendition of his usual purr. Dad paused and gazed at him, seemingly lost in thought. He fingered the medicine bag around his neck. A tiny flame of possibility sparked in my chest.

Dad shook his head. "There are retreatants to be concerned about. It's not safe to have big cats here. No." He dropped the bag so that it bumped against his shirt on its cord. "We need to take them to an established facility." He gave a short laugh, as if he couldn't believe he'd considered keeping the cougars.

Felix rubbed his head under my fingers, wanting a good scratch. Dad dragged the phonebook across the counter.

"Wait!" I said. "Onawa!"

"What?" Dad stopped midpage.

"Onawa. Their mother. You did a ritual and called her."

He looked at me sharply.

"You did," I said breathlessly. "You called her, and this was the answer you got. She sent you her children. She gave them to us to take care of."

Mom sat down carefully in the chair next to where Dad was standing. She put his hand on her shoulder and stroked his fingers. Mallory took the other bottle and began quietly nursing Kalimar. She didn't say a word about the stupidity of spirit guides.

Dad ran his other hand absently through Mom's hair. "You say Wanda Redd keeps a bobcat?"

"It's just the logical response," said Mallory, nuzzling Kalimar. "They have to stay here."

"Or not." When had Webster come in? He crossed the room and peered down at Felix and Kalimar in our laps. "These animals are sick, Mally. Look at them. I'm not an animal specialist, but they need to be in the hands of someone who is."

Mallory raised her eyes to him more slowly than I'd have expected. "This is Brigitta's decision," she said.

"I have a former student," continued Webster as if Mallory hadn't spoken. "Her name is Dr. Helene Jackson. Dr. Jackson is a behavioral veterinarian who specializes in wildlife. This"—he wrote on a piece of paper—"is her number."

Mallory narrowed her eyes ever so slightly.

Webster went on. "I believe she is employed with a wild animal rescue outside of Seattle. I'd recommend strongly that you call her." He gave the paper to Dad, who nodded curtly, and then turned to Mallory. "Alas, my love," he said in that way that made me want to kick him hard, "I must depart." He bent to kiss Mallory, but she twitched away so that he missed. He pulled his Greek fisherman's hat out of his pocket, put it on his head, and walked out the kitchen door.

We brought the kittens up into the apartment. We were awake all night—Dad pacing the floor with his drum, Mom scurrying up and down the stairs to take care of Indigoes, while Mallory and I fed and watched the kittens. No one talked much about how we were going to raise two cougars to adulthood. It was as if that topic was off-limits.

The diarrhea didn't come back, but the kittens didn't pee, either, which seemed wrong. Mallory brought out a thick biology textbook to see if it had anything useful in it. She was quiet, running her hand over Felix's back and tail while she flipped the pages. Felix's motor revved up louder than it had been, as if he forgave her for not understanding him.

Mom went to bed around 7:30 Friday morning, but Dad stayed up and did the breakfast shift by himself, not talking much when he returned to the apartment. I curled in a beanbag chair with Kalimar against my belly. Mallory brought out her laptop and Googled more animal care instructions.

Officer Mark showed up at 11:30, shook Dad's hand, and took away Felix and Kalimar. Mack wasn't with him this time.

"They'll be in good hands," said Officer Mark. He put the cougars into a carry cage and walked out the door.

Why couldn't I move? Why didn't I run after him and wrestle the cage out of his hands? Instead I stood inside by the tomatoes, leaning against a support post while he loaded them into his truck.

Inside my pocket I found the gold scrap Kalimar had torn while she was still safe in her den. It made me think of Nonni's fabric scraps—of gathering them up from her feet that day at the nursing home, of taking them back to Cherrywood. I had brought them into the bunk room where I always slept. Under the top bunk Opa had made a secret panel where we used to hide things. I'd felt inside. The treasure was still there: two arrowheads and a rusty Boy Scout knife (Dad's), four seashells (Mallory's, from Nonni), a fluffy pink quill pen (mine). I had lined the hidden compartment with the scraps, adding layer after layer— Mallory's pink prom satin, my Winnie the Pooh plush, purple from a middle school shirt. Only when my hands were empty had I put the panel back in place.

As soon as Officer Mark drove away, Mallory rounded on Dad. "We could have done it!" she said. "We could have raised them. Why did you call that stupid number? Why do you always take the easy way out?"

Dad sat down heavily at the kitchen table. His shirt had a spot of pancake batter on it, and his hair was coming out of its hair tie. "Mallaboo, I didn't call any number."

"Well, then who did?"

Dad looked at Mallory for a long time and didn't answer.

twenty-eight

The door to Luke's house was dark green. I couldn't believe I was standing here. It was silly to avoid knocking on his door. What did I expect would happen? That a bodyguard would come out and say, "Go away"?

All the windows had blinds over them, so it was impossible to see inside. A few potted plants were set around the porch. Luke's Jeep was not in the driveway. Probably there was nobody home. I should go back. Luke was not here. I was sure of it. He'd have come if he was here. He'd have come to the cougar's den or the tree house by now. I'd have found his footprints on the bridge. No, he was definitely gone. On vacation or wherever it was he went for days at a time. Television interviews. Yeah, right.

I was halfway to the fountain when the door opened. I was afraid to turn around.

"Brigitta?"

I did turn then. He was standing barefoot in a slice of doorway wearing cargo pants and a beige shirt. His hair was messy. He smiled.

For some reason I was tongue-tied, rooted to the walkway.

"Hey," he said. "Aren't you even going to pass me a magazine and share a gospel message?"

"I didn't knock," I blurted.

"Yeah, I know. I saw you coming." He opened the door wider. "Come on," he said.

"Into your house?"

He laughed. "It seems only fair, seeing as how we've spent the night together twice."

My cheeks flushed, but I stepped back onto the porch. "Luke, they took the kittens!"

"What?"

"The Fish and Wildlife guy. Officer Mark. Mallory's boyfriend turned us in."

"Mallory's boyfriend?"

"The Psychic Children's Brigade found the kittens and the kittens are sick and we stayed up with them all night and this morning Officer Mark showed up with a cage and drove them away in his truck and where were you?!" The last three words came out strangled. My throat had that verge-of-tears soreness, and I swallowed hard. I wanted to hit him, not cry in front of him, but I managed not to do either.

Luke pulled me into his arms. "I'm sorry," he said. "I shouldn't have made you come with me."

"You didn't make me come anywhere." I took a deep breath. "I went with you because I wanted to. I stayed because I wanted to. For me. I should have thought of someone besides myself."

"Brigitta." He held me out from him. My face was probably all red blotches. "You did think of someone besides yourself. It's just that the someone doesn't deserve you. Come on." He led me inside.

The house was airier than I expected, with French doors opening into an enclosed garden off the living room. The living room was white: white couch and love seat, two small white armchairs, a soft white rug. A few books scattered the coffee table and couch: decorating, Renaissance art, and manga. The corner of the room was taken up with a white baby grand.

I pulled myself together while Luke gathered the manga off the couch. I glanced at the piano. "Do you play?" It gave me something to say.

"Mum does. Rachmaninoff's her favorite. She was a child prodigy."

"She performed in public?"

"Yeah. In France mostly. Her teacher was French. She performed at the Paris Opera House when she was ten."

"Wow. I've done state competitions, but nothing like that. And I was scared spitless. Wasn't it hard on her? Wasn't it a lot of pressure for a kid?"

Luke stopped stacking books. "Yeah," he said briefly. He sat down on the couch and patted the cushion beside him. "Where did they take them?"

It felt strange to be in his house. "Someplace called Cedar Haven Wildlife Center. Mallory's true love has some ex-student who works there."

"Where is it? Can we go see them?"

"Yes." An idea began to form in my mind. We could take them back! We'd go to the wildlife center, and we'd hide, the way we had in the lighthouse. We'd bring duffel bags lined with something soft and then we'd wait until nightfall. Felix and Kalimar would come. They knew us.

Luke touched my cheek. "What are you thinking about, Brigitta?"

I grabbed his hand impulsively. "We could sneak them out of that place. We could bring them back where they belong!"

"You mean catnap them?" He grinned at his pun.

"It wouldn't be like that! They're ours. We're their parents!"

"Brigitta." He was shaking his head, suddenly serious.

"Don't you feel like living dangerously?"

Luke sat back and folded his arms. "I already do."

With a pang, I thought about his mom. What was he living through that I didn't know about?

"Brigitta"—Luke took my hand and traced circles on the back of it—"it's a wildlife center. That's what they do. They'll take much better care of them than we could. Don't you want what's best for them?"

Suddenly I felt about ten years old. Ever since I'd reminded Dad about Onawa, I'd been nurturing a tiny spark of hope. Luke had just pinched it out at the wick.

"We could still go see them," he went on. "You could see how they're being cared for, talk to the people who work there. You'd feel better."

"Darling?" Luke's mother called down the hallway. She had a musical voice with a soft note to it.

"Coming, Mum!" he called back. He started readjusting the couch cushions. "I'm going to have to go," he said. "She's not in shape for company."

He peered down the hallway and then put his arm around me, led me outside, and closed the green door firmly behind him.

"We'll go see them then?" I pressed him, knowing that I was nagging.

"Tomorrow," he said. "You need to sleep first." He lifted up my chin. "I'll meet you by the tree house at noon tomorrow."

"And you'll really be there? You won't disappear again?"

"I'll really be there," he said. "I promise." He took hold of my shoulders and kissed me. I put my hands on his chest and felt like I was melting right onto the porch.

He stopped and wrapped his arms around me, resting his chin on my head the way he had right after Onawa walked back into the woods. "I don't want to lose you," he murmured.

twenty-nine

I slept the entire day and most of the night. No one woke me to do any retreat stuff. When I did wake up it was nearly 5:00 a.m. and I was still in my jeans. The sky was pink over the fir tops.

The kittens! How long since I'd fed them? I swung my legs out of the bed and had my shoes on before I remembered: Felix and Kalimar weren't out there anymore.

Mallory's bed was empty. Even now she couldn't stand a night without Webster.

As soon as I thought this, I felt bad. I'd seen her wiping away tears when Officer Mark drove off with the cougars. I'd even considered hugging her then.

I pulled my knees up and leaned back against the tires in the wall. Luke hadn't been as upset about the kittens as I'd wanted him to be. I'd wanted him to be outraged, to storm the gates of Cedar Haven Wildlife Center, to draw his sword—oh, God: I wanted him to be Prince Felix of Imlandria!

I couldn't stay in bed any longer, and I didn't want to get nabbed for Indigo duty, so I brushed my teeth, pulled on my ripped-up Nonni coat, and went out to the tree house.

Mallory was already there.

A single sleeping bag was stretched out on the floor, but Mallory was standing in her jeans and an oversized shirt in front of my Onawa shrine, scrutinizing the clipping. She touched the unblinking eyes in the picture. "Sad," she said.

"Yeah." I couldn't think of anything else to say. I sat on the window seat with my Nonni coat wrapped around me.

"How long did you take care of them?"

"A week."

She nodded. "Was Devon helping you?"

"Not Devon."

She didn't ask. Last night I'd dreamed I was with Luke on his porch. He was holding my hands as water rose around our ankles and up to our knees. "Don't let go, Brigitta," he said. "I'm in over my head."

I didn't know what it meant.

Mallory began rolling up her sleeping bag. I was grateful that she didn't pry about Westport. She sat back on her heels, frowning. Then she looked up at me. "I only left them for the afternoon, Gita, I swear to you. They were sleepy when I left, but they weren't sick."

"Don't blame yourself."

Neither of us spoke for a while. I watched a spider taking her web apart under one of the rafters. Mallory stacked the pillows in the corner.

I picked at the frayed patchwork of my coat. "I miss Nonni." I surprised myself by saying this, not knowing what it had to do with the kittens or Luke or Onawa.

Mallory sat down beside me. "Me too, sometimes," she said. "You were closer to her. I was always jealous of that."

"You were?"

"Yeah." Mallory looked at her lap. "She and you had this magic circle. I didn't think I could ever get in."

"We would have let you in."

Mallory brushed a strand of hair out of her eyes. "Sure you would," she said.

"I wasn't ready for her to die." I had to blink when I said this.

"It was sad," said Mallory. She picked up the cardinal feather, which I'd placed on my altar to Onawa.

"On the week of the funeral I saw more cardinals than I've ever seen," I said.

"Could be," said Mallory. "Or maybe it was that mostly you sat in Aunt Julia's kitchen and looked out the window."

She stood suddenly and looked out the window herself. Her face changed.

A man's thin voice was calling her name from below.

"Webster," she whispered.

I looked down and could see the top of his Greek fisherman's hat. He was gazing up at each tree in turn. Even with the hat, he looked like a banker lost in the jungle.

"Please don't let him up here," I said.

Mallory rubbed her temples. "I'll go down."

She did.

I watched them from above: Webster with his hands on Mallory's shoulders, grinning at her, Mallory smiling back, seeming to get smaller and smaller under his gaze. I felt sorry for her for the first time. What could have made her fall in love with Professor Smugbottom?

He put his arm around her finally and led her away like a tamed mustang.

★ ★ ★

I sat myself down across from my altar. Mallory was right about me staring at birds for a week. Aunt Julia the always efficient had already cleared out Cherrywood by the time we got to Indiana. Nonni's death had come at an "inconvenient" time for Aunt Julia. She made us stay at her house, which was way bigger than Cherrywood. She wouldn't unlock Cherrywood for us—"Too much of a mess in there"—and she had the only key. Dad didn't bother to argue with her.

In Aunt Julia's dining room she and Dad were signing papers. Dad looked up when I came in. "I have an idea," I said. "You don't have to go to all this trouble. I can take care of Cherrywood."

Aunt Julia smiled her thin smile. "That's sweet, honey. I don't think they let fifteen-year-olds live all by themselves."

"So Mallory could live there, too. She's eighteen. She could go to college here. It would give Mom and Dad extra room in the mobile." It would work. I could go on homeschooling, only I'd get my assignments from Mom by email. Mallory would go to school, and I would cook and take long walks in the woods. Someday I'd get married and my kids would live at Cherrywood, too.

Aunt Julia's smile didn't waver. "That's sweet, honey," she said again. She shifted her eyes to Dad.

He put his pen down. "We have a buyer, Brigitta."

"You can't!" I put my hand over my mouth and ran from the room. I spent the next two days curled in the guest bedroom pretending to read. I didn't even come out for meals. At night I rocked myself to sleep.

Our last day was the only time I saw Cherrywood. Dad had to make a "quick stop" there on our way to the airport. We still couldn't go inside. "There's no time," Dad said. "We have to catch a plane."

From the backseat my eyes traced the chimney and the line of roof I had loved. Dad stood in the front yard with the realtor who was attaching a "sold" placard to the lawn sign.

I stepped out of the car and walked along the driveway to the back. There was the brick walkway. There was the birdbath and Nonni's mint in the garden. And there, in front of the garage, sat a Dumpster the size of a swimming pool. I backed up to the raspberry bushes and craned my neck. Heaped inside were garbage bags, moldy cartons, the clock from the kitchen wall, a broken chair from the screened-in porch, a vacuum cleaner. And at the very top, a cardboard box, piled high with Nonni's sewing scraps.

I wanted to tie Aunt Julia to some railroad tracks.

A month after we came back to Kwahnesum, Dad had enough money to finish The Center.

* * *

After I finished the Indigo breakfast dishes it was 10:30. Ninety minutes until I'd see Luke at the tree house. I spent an hour picking out what to wear. I wished a little that I'd listened to Natalie's fashion advice. After pulling everything out of my dresser and trying on five outfits, I settled on layers, with my red shirt on top. Thirty minutes to go. I played with my hair for fifteen before putting it up in a clip. I probably ruined the whole effect by throwing my Nonni coat on, just for luck, before heading out the door.

He wasn't there.

I waited for ten minutes and then fifteen more before there was a rustling in the leaves. A rabbit darted out from under an elderberry bush. I waited another ten minutes. I checked the cougar den. My stomach felt heavy seeing it empty of cats. I walked back to Adam. No Luke. He had promised not to pull his disappearing act again. Had he forgotten? Or had he only made the promise to get me out of his house? Was that it? Had I become too clingy, begging him to steal the kittens back? Was that why he'd never given me his email or his cell phone number? So he could escape when it became necessary?

But just yesterday, on the porch, he'd said he didn't want to lose me. What did he mean by that?

It was 1:00 now. I hiked out to the property line. In Luke's driveway, on the other side of the fountain, was a silver Lexus. Cautiously, I moved toward the fountain. Droplets of water landed on my arms. The Lexus had a Cornish School of the Arts license plate holder. A wooden pendant on a green silk ribbon dangled from the rearview mirror— some kind of Celtic knot pattern was carved in it. On the seat was a copy of *Jane Eyre*. *Jane Eyre?* Not exactly guy reading.

Who was visiting Luke?

I was being silly. It was probably his mom's car. Or someone visiting his mom. Slowly, I climbed the steps until I was standing in front of

the green door. Not a sound came from inside the house. I raised my
hand to knock.

I turned back to the Lexus. Cornish School of the Arts? Weren't his
mom and her friends a little old to be going there? Did the car belong
to an art student? Someone older and more sophisticated than me? Was
she right now showing Luke her portfolio? Was he telling her every
painting was exquisite and he couldn't believe how talented she was?
Was she shrugging carelessly while Luke insisted? Was she asking to
paint him nude? Aak! Cancel that!

I walked back down the steps, past the fountain, out the driveway,
and through the line of maples. I wouldn't beg. If he wanted to see me,
he could come find me himself.

Natalie came to the door of the Inner Sanctum in pajama bottoms and a Hello Kitty T-shirt.

The Inner Sanctum is the entire basement of the Shapiro's split-level. A neon Hard Rock Cafe sign blinks over a wet bar filled with Italian syrups and a pretty decent espresso machine where Cheryl stood making lattes.

Natalie turned on the TV. "You look a little shell-shocked, Brigitta."

I sat on the couch and pulled a throw pillow into my lap. "Just some long nights."

"Long nights, huh?" She raised her eyebrows and shot Cheryl a look.

I was not in the mood for this. Not after Luke's desertion. And Mom had been on the phone with the wildlife refuge all day. The kittens were not doing well. They wouldn't take any nourishment, and they were listless. I wanted to go see them, but the rehabber thought it wasn't a good idea. They'd had too much human contact already, she said.

"How was Wednesday night?" Natalie clicked on a lamp with a fringy purple shade.

Wednesday? Luke? The Sea Star? What did she know about that? Guiltily, I remembered. Dad had called her house. She had told him I was with her. I couldn't even keep track of my lies, much less the lies told on my behalf.

"Can we just get to the show?" I found a spot on the couch.

"Fine." Natalie increased the volume on a Mazda commercial and brought up the TiVo menu.

Cheryl handed me a latte. "Irish cream," she said.

I took it, even though I hate Irish cream. Cheryl was trying.

I couldn't tell Natalie about the kittens—especially with Cheryl there. It felt too personal. Besides, the cougars were completely connected to Luke in my mind.

Natalie clicked on the saved *Letterman* show. "Get ready, girls."

Letterman's Top Ten was the Top Ten Secrets You Should Keep from Your Girlfriend. Number one was something about Viagra. (I didn't get it, but Cheryl laughed.)

It went downhill from there.

"Our first guest," said Letterman, "can not only sword fight standing on a moving horse, he is a force to be reckoned with in a dark alley. From Prince of Imlandria to Prince of Bad Boys, please welcome Trent Yves!"

The band began the *Rocket* theme. Out from the back in a red T-shirt and black leather jacket strutted Trent. My stomach gave a lurch. His face! For a moment the boy on the stage looked so much like Luke I didn't even have to squint. The audience went crazy. His dark hair was in a spike. He did a little spin on his heel.

I attempted a casual sip of my latte, which was a bad idea. It *was* just Trent, wasn't it? The same one I'd looked at a million times now online and on screen. I'd even seen him in interviews before.

"Trent," said Dave, "it's good to see you again."

Natalie poked me. "Look at him, Brigitta. I am telling you."

"Oh, Natalie." I rolled my eyes unconvincingly and set my coffee cup on the end table.

The camera zoomed close, taking in Trent's blue eyes, his strong chin. He grinned. "Looking good, Dave." He had a British accent—the one he'd brought with him from England when he was little. He hadn't used it in *Rocket* or *Presto!* because he played Americans. "I mean, you're looking good, Dave," he went on. "Everyone knows I'm looking good."

The audience whistled.

I had a strong desire to throw something.

"And I hear *Rocket*'s looking good," said Dave. "Cannes Film Festival, talk of an Oscar. But the women are complaining that you didn't take your shirt off."

Why did he look so much like Luke this time? After all the photos I'd seen online? And all the *Celeb'* magazines I'd paged through? Was my brain playing tricks because I was stressed about the kittens? Because Luke had disappeared again?

Trent grinned wider. "Well, you know I got sunburned in *Imlandria*. I mean second-degree burns. We were out on Kauai."

The British accent sounded so strange coming out of his mouth, even though I'd heard it in *Imlandria*.

He went on about his sunburn. "It's an insurance thing. They've got to protect the Trent bod. But I feel bad about it. I really do. You hate to disappoint people."

"You do," said Dave.

"But, you know, I can fix that." Trent stood and peeled off his leather jacket.

No, I thought. Don't do this.

The band began a "striptease" theme. The audience started cheering. I wanted to hide behind the throw pillow.

Cheryl's and Natalie's eyes were fixed on the TV.

"Take it off, Trent," hooted Natalie.

Trent pulled the shirt over his head, twirled it around a couple of times, and sailed it out to the audience. The camera panned to a couple of thirtysomething women, who were fighting over it. I felt physically sick.

The camera panned back to Trent's manly six-pack. My eyes moved involuntarily to his stomach. Had I seen those abs before?

"Mmm," said Cheryl, licking her lips.

I wanted to leave. This guy on the screen was so not Luke. He didn't have Luke's gentleness, and he didn't have his class. But he had Luke's body and face.

Trent put his jacket on over his bare torso and sat down.

Dave leaned forward confidentially. "Now, Trent," he said, "you and Gwen Melier…Is there any truth to the rumors?"

"What rumors, Dave?"

My stomach took another tilt.

"Well, that you and Gwen are…that you have a French connection."

"Gwen speaks fluent French. Her father is French."

"And your father is French. And we all know what a lovely lady Gwen is."

"Lovely, yes," said Trent.

A video clip came on the screen behind them: the rebuilt "Trentmobile" was parked in front of a Malibu grocery store. Its license plate said "HOTTBOD." Trent's driver emerged. Gwen stood on the sidewalk screaming with laughter, trying to pull Trent from the backseat. His muscly arms, head, and shoulders appeared briefly. He was wearing sunglasses and a red shirt. He rocked her back into the car on top of him. Their legs kicked for a moment, then disappeared. An arm reached out and closed the door as the driver hopped back in and took off.

The audience whooped.

"Now what conclusions can we draw from this, Trent?"

Trent never stopped smiling that horrible smile. "What conclusions would you like to draw, Dave?"

Seeing Starzz ★ Celebrities Find Their Deep Space
Hollywood's Hidden Spiritual Quest

July 14

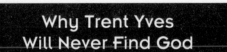

Why Trent Yves Will Never Find God

Let us throw up together on our knees. If anyone saw the cheap display on *Letterman* of Mr. Cannes Film Festival, you will be nauseated with me.

Starlet, however, has found the True Faith. The more naked Trent became, the more she and a fellow devotee fell into worshipful ecstasies. Too bad for them, because Trent's only interested in Gwendolyn Melier's cute little French butt—and himself. Some actors have vision and a hunger for God. Not Trent. He won't find God because he thinks he *is* God.

Xombiemistress responds:

He's not my favorite either, Mystic, but give him a break. They expect stuff like that from the "25 Under 25."

Namaste.

Aquarius0210 responds:

Mystic, he really does have a beautiful body, uv got 2 admit. I thought it was funny. Lighten up. He's had such a hard year with his dad going back to France. And that freak-out his mom had at the Emmys? She threw a chair at a reporter. And it nearly hit him. She only had a kid so she could make money off him. He's cute with

Gwen. They're a perfect couple. Gwen's an Aries, which is exactly
right for a Libra.

Trentsbabe responds:
   i thought u were in luv w/him???

chapter thirty-one

"Close your eyes." Natalie brushed something against my eyelid. I was allowing this out of pure, unadulterated guilt. "Open," she said.

I scooted my stool closer to the bathroom mirror. My hair was in a ponytail on top of my head to get it out of the way. I had on foundation. Red lipstick. So far I looked like the bride of Frankenstein. Downstairs there were still Indigo Children. We should have done this at Natalie's house, where the light was better in the bathroom, but Bekah was sick.

"It's pink," I said tentatively.

"This is just the undercoat." Natalie plucked a few of my eyebrow hairs.

"Ow!"

"Sorry." She patted my brow with a cotton pad. "We suffer to be beautiful."

"You mean you suffer. I was happy being plain."

Out at the dining room table we could hear snatches of Mom and Dad's powwow with Mallory.

"Old enough to make up my own mind…"

"Paying for your college…"

A raised voice ending in, "You and Mom had already moved in together in college. And your parents didn't like it, either!"

"Close." Natalie drew liquid eyeliner carefully above my lashes. More eye shadow swept across my lid and out to my temple.

"What are you doing?"

"Art!" said Natalie happily.

I sighed.

"So," she said, dotting something onto my cheekbones, "I read that no one has seen Trent Yves' mother since she had that meltdown at the Emmys."

"Mmm," I said. I had been trying to put Trent out of my mind, which was hard because I'd lain awake last night in the Inner Sanctum running the *Letterman* show over and over in my head while Cheryl snored in the next sleeping bag.

Natalie rubbed off one of the dots. "People think she's been institutionalized. She's, like, crazy or something."

"Well, that would explain a lot," I said. "He was pretty sick last night." I laughed, though it wasn't funny. The makeup session was doing nothing to distract me from my troubles. All morning my mind had bounced from the thought of Felix and Kalimar with strangers and unable to eat, to the image of an oh-so-Luke Trent Yves, peeling off his shirt and rolling around with Gwen in the backseat of his car.

"Brigitta, don't be so bothered at the sight of a little boy flesh." She giggled. "Hold still." She painted a black curve from my eyelid to my cheekbone that looked like a giant question mark.

"That's…dramatic, Natalie."

"Boy flesh is dramatic." She did the other eye.

"No, I mean the makeup."

She blew the lines dry. "Dramatic is what we're after, Brigitta. Live a little."

I was beginning to look catlike.

"Anyway," said Natalie, "as I was saying—that Luke Geoffrey? And his mother? Wouldn't this be a perfect place to bring your demented mother?"

"She's not demented."

"Oh?" said Natalie. "You know this? You've seen him since he went incognito to the arcade?"

I hesitated. "I've seen them…from a distance, Natalie," I lied. "She looks perfectly normal to me."

"But he's always wearing sunglasses, right?"

Luke had worn sunglasses on our road trip. And a hat pulled down over his head. But there was reason for sunglasses at the beach. And he didn't wear them when he was out in the woods with me. "No," I said. "He's just a normal guy, Natalie."

A normal guy. With a mom who drinks and who he has to take care of. Who disappears for days at a time and won't tell me where he's been. Who can check into a motel room on a debit card like he knows what he's doing. Who looks like that IDIOT on *Letterman*.

"Okay, Brigitta. Normal it is." Natalie put the brush into a pot of blue glitter and applied it thickly to my lids and temples. "Voilà!" she said. "Now the hair!"

I looked like a circus performer.

Out in the kitchen, Dad yelled, "Think about your future!" and Mallory shot back, "MY life, MY body, MY future!"

There was a knock at the apartment door. Probably someone from the Indigo retreat. Mom and Dad would be mortified if retreatants had overheard their fight.

Natalie dusted powder over the top of her work. "This is perfect, Brigitta. I'm going to take some photos. I could use this in my portfolio."

I could hear the Indigo guy saying, "Good afternoon, Mr. Schopenhauer."

Only it wasn't an Indigo guy. I felt the blood drain out of my face. "Just a minute." I got down off the stool and peered out the bathroom door. Luke was standing in the entryway shaking Dad's hand. In his other hand was my violin.

"What?" said Natalie. "What is it?" She peeked over the top of my head. "Oh, my God, Brigitta!"

I pulled back and closed the door. "You have to take this off my face, Natalie!"

Natalie started scrambling with curling irons and brushes. "What's he doing here?" She ran a brush through her own hair. "Just take your hair down, Brigitta. It'll be fine."

"No! I look like a tropical fish!" What was Luke doing here?

Natalie grabbed the lipstick and applied it to her own lips. "Damn!" She used a Q-tip hurriedly to erase her mistake, blotted with a tissue, and smiled. "Better. Don't just sit there, Brigitta." She squirted some perfume on both of us. I was frozen. My feet had grown into the floor.

"Gita." Mallory poked her head in the bathroom, scowling. "Ooh!" she said when she saw me. "That's something. Gita, you're wanted in the living room."

Natalie stared at me.

I had no time to fix my face. Natalie pushed me out the bathroom door and somehow kept herself from barreling toward the living room.

Luke sat sipping a mug of tea (I hoped it wasn't oolong). His hair had curled a little from the heat. He wore a white T-shirt that accentuated his biceps. My mouth went dry.

He was Trent.

Mom hovered nearby, giving me a "What's up?" look with her eyebrows. Dad sat across from Luke/Trent, nodding at something he had said. Mallory retreated to our room.

I felt like the room must be crashing down around me. I stepped around the pillar by the indoor garden. "Brigitta," Luke/Trent said when he saw me. "Wow."

I couldn't meet his eyes.

Natalie gaped when he said my name and then quickly regained her composure. "Do you like it?" She pulled up next to me. "I'm working on different designs. For my portfolio, you know. I think if I could get on with a major studio as a makeup artist, then I could pursue my acting at the same time. You know, I'd already have my foot in the door."

"Ah," he said.

The glitter was making my skin itch.

"Do you think that's a good idea?" Natalie went on. "I mean, is it unrealistic? I know I have to start with things like shampoo commercials. But if I already have my foot in the door…"

"You're very talented," he said earnestly. "We've met before, right? At the arcade in town? I'm Luke. Luke Geoffrey."

"Right," said Natalie, winking. "I'm Natalie Portman. Only here I'm known as Natalie Shapiro."

He stood and shook her hand. "I'm glad to see you again, Natalie." I thought she'd faint.

"Mr. Schopenhauer?" He turned to Dad. "Would it be all right if I spoke with Brigitta privately?"

My heart began to pound.

Dad nodded approvingly, which was kind of surprising, considering that the risk to his other daughter's virtue was suddenly an issue. "That would be fine, Luke. We have an interesting tree house on the property. Maybe you'd like to show him that, Brigitta."

"Yeah," I said. My stomach hurt.

Natalie followed us out the door with her eyes.

chapter thirty-two

Outside it was hot again. Jeremy, telepathic-discoverer-of-cougars, was throwing a Nerf football around with a group of other little boys. "Hey!" he called. "It's Felix!"

We were quickly surrounded by five of them. "Felix, Prince and Wanderer," Jeremy said soberly, quoting the movie poster.

Luke ruffled Jeremy's hair with a strong, tanned hand. "Well met, fair sir," he said.

My heart gave a jolt.

"That's not how Felix talks," said one of the other boys. "He says, 'Well met, feh suh.'" He swept his arm out in a grand bow.

Luke chuckled. "Not bad," he said.

"Where are the scrolls?" Jeremy persisted.

"In the back of my closet. In a shoe box." Luke winked. "Gotta go, guys."

The boys tried to follow, but the front door opened and two of the moms came out, calling them in.

He tried to take my hand, but I pulled it out of his reach and started down the path and across the bridge ahead of him. He jogged up beside me, but I kept going until we got to Felix and Kalimar's tree.

He stopped when he got there. He crouched and looked into the den, pulled out the carving, and turned it over in his hands. He stood slowly. "Brigitta," he began.

I swallowed a lump in my throat and faced him. "Why do you go along with them like that?" I said.

"Go along with who?" He wound the laces absently around the carving.

"Kids with Nerf balls and girls in shopping malls? Is this just an ego trip for you—'looking like a movie star'?"

Luke surveyed the blackberry bushes. He sighed. "Do you know how many times a day I would have to say, 'No, I am not Trent Yves,' if I didn't do that? And I'm not going to disappoint little kids."

"So you just lie to them? Or was that really you taking your clothes off on *Letterman*?"

Luke raised an eyebrow. "You're not making this any easier." His blue eyes were doing their magic on me. He put one hand on the tree trunk above me so that our faces were only a foot apart.

A butterfly of joy began to flit around in my chest. I swept it aside by thinking of the silver Lexus. Gwen?

He took a step closer so that his leg was brushing mine. "Brigitta, I screwed up. I know I promised to meet you yesterday, but something came up."

I folded my arms so that I could contain my heart before it did a swan dive. "Was it something or someone?"

"What?"

His bicep coming out from his sleeve looked like Michelangelo had sculpted it just for me. But I knew it was really some Hollywood trainer. "You seemed to have someone over yesterday."

Luke scrutinized the carving. "Yeah, I did."

"Did she speak French?"

He raised his head. "What are you talking about?"

"I'm talking about whatever black hole it is you drop into every few days." The tree was scratching my back. "Does she have a name?"

"Brigitta, it's not like that."

"Okay. What is it like?"

"It's not nearly as exciting as you think."

"Why should I find it exciting?"

He leaned over and tossed the toy lightly into the cougar den. Then he put his hands above me on either side so that I was trapped between him and the tree.

"Look," he said, "my parents have a software business together—previously a successful one—and I help them run it."

He smelled so good. Focus, Brigitta. "Software? This is about software?" My eyes traced the hollow of his neck, his Adam's apple, up to his chin, his lips. His lips. I looked away. "You said your dad was in telecommunications."

"Okay, I lied then. It's software."

My eyes went back to his lips, and my fickle little joy butterfly opened and closed its wings. Luke was so beautiful. Even when he was acting.

"I have to travel," he went on. "A lot."

"Right." I tucked my hands tighter into my arms so they wouldn't pop out and grab him.

"I know that seems weird to you, but Mum and Papa are barely speaking. They count on me for some of their client presentations."

"Uh-huh." I kept my tone sarcastic.

Luke dropped one hand onto my shoulder. "Really, Brigitta." His blue eyes searched mine. I ducked under his arm and moved away.

Luke leaned back and put one foot against the tree, hanging his thumbs on the pockets of his jeans. "I'm not making this up."

"What? Do you, like, wear a suit and tie when you do this?"

"As a matter of fact, I do. It makes me look at least nineteen."

I pictured him in a suit. A dark one with a burgundy tie and a crisp white shirt. I saw that I had moved closer without realizing it. If only he was telling the truth! "Okay, Mr. Software." I picked a salal leaf and folded it in half and then in half again. "What's the name of this company?"

"Is this so hard for you to believe?" He reached out and brushed a bit of spiderweb out of my hair.

"Yes." I could feel the heat of his skin. If he kissed me, I'd lose my resolve. I thought of him—oh, did it have to be him?—kissing Gwen Melier in his Mini. I took a step back. "It's called…?"

He was waiting too long.

"Schrödinger's Cat," he said finally.

"What?"

"Schrödinger's Cat. Schrödinger was an Austrian physicist. He won the Nobel Prize in 1933. Schrödinger's cat is a thought experiment he came up with to illustrate a point of quantum mechanics."

"Uh-huh. And Schopenhauer was a German philosopher who proposed that the 'will to be' is reality. I'm glad we both read Wikipedia. Did you just search on my name and then go to the next entry?"

He shook his head. His shirt was really too tight. It was distracting.

"What does Schrödinger's cat have to do with software?"

"Brigitta…"

I looked him in the face. The strong jawline, the blue, blue eyes. "Who are you?" I said.

His eyes widened. "I'm Luke. I'm me. Brigitta, what are you talking about?"

"Are you Trent Yves?" I'd said it. It knocked the breath out of me.

He was silent a moment, gazing at me. Then he shook his head. "Brigitta, you don't really think that."

I didn't answer.

We stood, staring at each other, ankle deep in ferns. Finally he reached out and traced my jaw with his fingertips.

I almost weakened then. I wanted to wrap my arms around him and listen to his heartbeat again, but I made myself stay still.

He stepped back. "You know where to find me," he said. He turned away and disappeared down the trail.

I didn't watch him go. I crushed the salal leaf into green pulp. If I let myself love Luke, I was in love with a character—a role played by an actor. And I couldn't love a lie anymore.

thirty-three

I wanted to sit in the tree house for a while, but I forced myself to go back to The Center. Natalie was on the bench out front, her purple hair care and makeup boxes on either side of her. "Oh, hi, Brigitta." She fiddled with her makeup kit.

"Are you leaving already?"

"I have to get back. Promised Bekah I'd stop in town and get her a movie." She rearranged a couple of nail polishes in their compartments. "So?" she said. She looked up and waited. A breeze blew her hair in her eyes, and she pushed it away.

"Nothing much to tell." I picked up a couple of cups the Indigo kids had left on the railing. "Just neighbor stuff."

"Neighbor stuff? Like he borrowed your lawn mower? He's wondering if you want some of the apples off his tree? Neighbor stuff?"

I picked up a Frisbee and stuck it under my arm. I wanted to go hide somewhere and cry.

"That was him up in the tree house with you that night, wasn't it? It wasn't Devon at all."

"Natalie—"

"I just don't get it, Brigitta. I thought we were best friends." She put a stray brush back into its proper compartment.

I added a plate to the collection in my arms, letting the comment stand in the air.

Natalie went on. "When I saw him, I was just—wow! I mean, that was a lot closer up than with Kirsten Dunst. That was as close as I have ever been!" She closed the lid to the makeup box. "But you've been… Brigitta, you've been with Trent all this time, haven't you? And you never told me." She didn't smile like she usually does.

I shifted all the stuff I was holding. "He's…he's Luke, Natalie. My neighbor. I got to know him a little is all. You were with your aunt in New York."

"Luke? You don't really expect me to believe that, Brigitta. Not after I've had a look at his eyes. Maybe it was a fantasy before, but now that I've seen him again, it's so obvious."

"He just looks like him. People sometimes look like other people."

Natalie played with a purple handle. "He told you to keep it a secret, didn't he?"

I couldn't answer. I couldn't tell her that Luke hadn't asked me to keep any secrets—because he didn't even trust me with his name. For a moment I wanted to tell her everything—how we'd hidden in the lighthouse, how he'd fed cougars in the middle of the night, how it felt when he held me, how he was looking for Eden.

Natalie leaned forward. "Does he have a bad temper, like they say? Does he boss his staff around? Does he have photos of himself everywhere?"

I clutched the Frisbee and plate to my chest. "Luke is nothing, *nothing* like Trent." I was surprised at the vehemence with which I said this.

Mallory stepped out onto the porch. She had her phone in her hand. "Brigitta, I just talked to Webster. He says the cougars are doing worse."

It felt like a punch. "Webster? What does Webster have to do with it?"

"He's been talking with his friend, Dr. Jackson. He's keeping us posted, Brigitta. He wants to help." Her brightness was completely fake.

"You believe that."

"Yes, I believe it!" she snapped, all cheeriness gone.

Natalie set her makeup box next to her on the bench. "Cougars?" she said.

"Cougar cubs." Mallory turned to her. "You know, the ones Brigitta found on our property. After—" She broke off, apparently unable to say, "After their mother was shot."

"Here," she said, taking the cups, plate, and Frisbee out of my arms. "I'll take those in."

Natalie got up and started walking all her gear to her car. I picked up her hair care box. "You don't have to go, Natalie. I thought you wanted to shoot pictures."

"The light's not good now," she said, even though we were standing in full sun. She reached into the backseat and pulled out her digital camera. "Here, Gita," she said. "Maybe you can get a couple of Trent pics for me? I'll call you later." She smiled a half smile and climbed into the car.

✦ ✦ ✦

By Tuesday night my bedroom was spotless, my closet wall was re-adobed, the skylights were clean inside and out, and I had removed all the whiteflies from the upstairs plants. Dad was at a drum workshop at another retreat center. Mallory and Webster hadn't been seen since Sunday. Mom had been worried enough about me Monday to take me to an energy healer in Carnation.

I called Cedar Haven five or six times and always got the same answer from Dr. Jackson: I was too dangerous to come see them. Only she didn't say it that way. She said, "A hands-off protocol is the best policy for them at the moment." She said they were "improving" and that I could see them "soon." She wouldn't tell me anything about their future, just that "the options were being explored."

And Luke? Well, that wasn't even his name, was it?

Part of me wanted him to come by again, to try and talk me back into his life. There were girls who would have killed to be in my position. But I wasn't those girls. And the whole thing just felt humiliating.

At least I had the bedroom to myself, which was where I wanted to be. I didn't want to be in the tree house. I thought about blogging, but what would I blog? That I really had spent two nights with Trent Yves and had fallen in love with him and that now I had dumped him because he was Trent Yves and not the boy I loved?

I wanted to tell him about Felix and Kalimar so that he would change his mind about catnapping them. We would drive into the wilderness, where we would find a stump to live in. We would teach our babies to hunt and hide, and they would be fine, just fine.

But I couldn't live in a stump with Trent Yves. Trent Yves would have better things to do than disappear into the wilderness with me. And what would he do there, anyway? Look at his reflection in a pond all day?

I picked up the phone to call Natalie. She hadn't called or come over since Sunday. What would I tell her when anything I could say was just a reminder of the secrets I'd kept from her? I was about to put the phone down when it rang in my hand.

"Natalie?"

"Brigitta! Get online."

"Why?"

"Just do it. Go to www.trentwatch.com. And look!"

I did what she said. The entry was almost all photos. Trent and Gwen photos. Trent in his pool at his Malibu ranch. Gwen flouncing up his driveway with Chinese takeout. The two of them kissing on his balcony in matching terry cloth robes. I felt like taking a hammer to the computer.

"Okay. I see it," I said. "Why do I want to see it?"

"Because…" she trailed off. "Okay, I feel really stupid now, but, Brigitta, look at the date on that entry. Read what it says under the pictures."

Sunday. "Trent and Gwen share an early-morning lip-lock at his ranch house Sunday."

"Do you see it, Brigitta? Sunday was when Luke Geoffrey came over to your house and I—oh, I made such an ass of myself! But he can't be two places at once, can he?"

I scrolled down the page. Other dates and other pictures. Trent at the LA Equestrian Center, Trent at The Grove at Farmers Market, Trent and Gwen whizzing down Santa Monica Boulevard in the Trentmobile. That one was taken last Wednesday, when Luke had been with me in Westport. "No," I said, feeling light-headed. "He can't be two places at once."

"Well, so," she fumbled around. "I admit it, Brigitta. I was jealous. I mean, I knew I was being silly after only seeing Luke at the arcade, but then when I saw him again I thought I *wasn't* being silly. He just had, you know, the eyes, everything. I thought, 'How could it *not* be him?' I thought this time I was right. And I really did see Kirsten Dunst at MoMA. For sure. Because I Googled it, and she really *was* there that day."

"I believe you, Natalie."

"Anyway, I feel really stupid."

Even with my own head spinning, I had a rush of sympathy for her. "Don't feel stupid, Natty. He does look like Trent. I can see why you were fooled." I couldn't tell her I'd been fooled myself. My mouth wouldn't say it. "We should go shopping," I said instead. "Or to a movie. Are you doing anything tomorrow?"

"Yes! I'm shopping with you! Redmond Town Center? How about nine thirty? We could catch the new Whitley Sandstone movie, too!"

After we hung up I sat, looking at the books on the shelf—John Donne's poetry, the Jewish festivals book, *Hinduism for Dummies*—they were supposed to unlock the Great Cosmic Mystery. I couldn't even unlock the small earthly ones.

Why had Trent seemed so much like Luke in his *Letterman* appearance? Except for the swaggering, the British accent, and the completely obnoxious attitude. I hauled all the *Celeb'* magazines out from under my bed and looked up everything Trent Yves. He both looked like Luke and did not look like Luke. But Natalie was right. Luke couldn't be two places at once.

chapter thirty-four

At 10:00 in the morning, Natalie still hadn't shown up. Something wasn't right. Natalie never forgot an appointment, especially if it involved shopping or a movie.

Her mom answered at her house. "Natalie's not here, Brigitta. I think she went out with Cheryl. Can I write her a note for you?"

"That's okay. I'll just call her cell."

There was no answer on Natalie's cell, so I left a message. Around 10:30 it occurred to me to check my email. A mail from Natalie was at the top of the list:

> B,
> Can't make it shopping. Something came up. Yeah. Something
>   really came up.
> www.seeingstarzz.bloggapalooza.net
> N

I clicked the link with a sinking heart. I hadn't posted to my blog since *Letterman*. But there was a reply. Was there ever.

Nattycat responds:
Mystic,
Now I know why you've been avoiding me all summer. If I had a friend as stupid and annoying as "Starlet" I'd avoid her, too. If this is

the way you treat your best friend, I'm not sure what good all your "trying to find God" is. In Judaism (which you've already studied and gotten bored with) we have a saying that goes, "Whatever is hateful to you, do not do to your neighbor. That is the entire Torah; the rest is commentary." Bet you didn't know I thought about anything that "spiritual," but I do—in between "worshiping" movie stars.

I printed out your blog this morning. It was thirty pages long, including your fan fic, which I printed, too. I thought your secret boyfriend would enjoy reading it, which is probably what he's doing now. He was surprised to see me. Sorry about that, but the truth has a way of coming out, doesn't it?

Nat

I shut down the computer and sat there, too numb to cry. Luke! Luke was reading my blog. And that awful fan fic. I wanted to die. Now that I knew he was Luke, just Luke and not somebody else, I'd wanted to go back to him. I'd wanted him to hold me again. I still wanted it, but I could never face him after what I'd written.

I spent the day reorganizing my side of the room. I put all my religion books in order, arranged the poetry by author, cleaned the violin trophies, and sorted my paper clips and thumbtacks. Then I took all the *Celeb'* magazines and *National Enquirer*s out from under the bed and burned them in the fire pit. I'd hoped to feel better, but I didn't. A voice in my head kept saying, "It's all about love, Brigitta-Lamb. It's all in how we treat each other." Nonni's voice. Even Nonni was condemning me.

chapter thirty-five

I woke up to a houseful of nuns. Mom, who'd already done all the baking, had asked Mallory and me to do the breakfast shift. I'd much rather have slept all day and not faced anybody. Luke would be home with his mom this morning. He'd have the blog printout in front of him. Maybe he'd be reading it aloud to her, appalled at what a terrible friend I was.

I dragged myself downstairs expecting black habits and—what are those headscarf things? Instead I found thirteen grandmas in jeans and tie-dye shirts chatting and reading newspapers. An ancient dark-haired sister with a face like a raisin sat a little apart from them, her hands held limply in her lap. Her narrowed eyes followed me across the room, making me uneasy. Were they really the eyes of God reproving me for my lies and meanness?

Mallory was in the kitchen making eggs. "I don't get these women," she said. "They say they're feminists. But...celibacy? I mean—no sex at all? Sister Susannah said she thinks of it as an act of civil disobedience."

"You asked one of them that? Mom will kill you. You're not supposed to ask retreatants those kinds of questions—especially not nuns."

Mallory looked affronted. "It was sociological research," she said. "I was professional. You know I'm always professional." She transferred the eggs to plates. "Grab the muffins," she said. "We're an hour behind schedule."

Ready or not, it was showtime. I gathered up bowls of blueberry and cinnamon pecan muffins, along with pats of butter. I even managed a pitcher of orange juice. I skirted the downstairs vegetable garden and set everything on the table like a pro. The nuns took hands around the table. "Our Father, who art in Heaven," they began, "hallowed be Thy name."

It was a prayer I remembered from Nonni and Opa's church. Hearing it again gave me a twinge.

I moved discreetly back toward the tomato plants just as Dad came briskly in the side door. His face was painted up again, and he was wearing what looked like a deer pelt over his bare shoulders. Apparently shamans need to do this—even if they're vegetarians.

"Thy Kingdom come, Thy will be done…" Thirteen silver crosses glinted around the sisters' necks.

Dad stopped. His mouth tightened, and he became suddenly interested in the tomatoes. He stayed still until the sisters said "Amen" and crossed themselves. Then he snagged one of his drums off the wall and moved swiftly out the other door.

Back in the kitchen, Mallory heated water. "Dad's been making himself scarce," she said in a low voice. "This Catholic thing's hard for him—you know, because of Nonni and Opa."

"Nonni and Opa weren't Catholic," I said, feeling unexpected heat creep into my face.

"Well, they were something like Catholic." She slid some jasmine tea out of the cupboard. "It's basically the same thing, Brigitta," her voice went even lower. "A religion that won't tolerate independent thinking." She took the honey drizzler out of a drawer.

"Nonni and Opa weren't like that!" I hissed.

"Calm down," she said, barely audible. "I'm not talking about Nonni and Opa, Brigitta, only their religion." She loaded three teapots and the honey on a large tray and headed for the dining room.

Out at the table I could see Mom talking with a tiny nun in gold-rimmed glasses. The sister's hand was on Mom's, and both of them were laughing at some joke I hadn't heard. Obviously Mom wasn't having "a hard time" with the nuns—even though her parents (who died before I was born) had been ex-Catholics.

Why did I feel so defensive of Catholics suddenly? I wasn't planning to be one. But it seemed like a lot of people, who claimed to be open-minded, had a lot of opinions about other people's spirituality.

I opened the fridge for goat milk. What were Felix and Kalimar eating this morning at Cedar Haven? My goat milk formula had worked. Maybe I needed to make some more and take it to them. Maybe Cedar Haven didn't know what the kittens really needed. Maybe that's why they were still sick.

Thinking of the kittens made me think of Luke again. And the blog. Luke would have come to the door, and Natalie would have handed him the envelope. He'd have stood in the doorway and read it all right there. Then he'd say, "Is this for real? Did Brigitta really write this?" Natalie would tell him yes, and then he'd look at her with his blue, blue eyes and say gratefully, "I'm so glad you told me. Please, come with me. I need someone to help me process this." And then he'd take her hand and lead her to his Jeep. They would drive out to the ocean together where maybe Natalie would be a little less freaked out than I was at the Sea Star Motel. "Stop!" I told my brain. "Stop this movie right now!"

I brought the goat milk into the dining room. Mom was picking tomatoes out of the garden. One of the nuns, a roundish woman with curly white hair, had scooted her chair out to include the wrinkly dark-haired nun. The round nun had a name tag that said "Sister Susannah." She winked, which startled me. Did my thoughts show on my face? For an odd moment she reminded me of Nonni.

I set the goat milk on the table. Sister Susannah nodded and said, "Thank you, dear."

The dark-haired sister scowled at me. "What's the matter?" she snapped. "Never seen a nun before?"

Was I staring? "You don't wear those black robes and scarves," I said stupidly, while Sister Susannah patted the older nun's back, saying, "She doesn't mean any harm, Sister John Marie."

Sister John Marie scowled deeper, and Sister Susannah winked at me again. "Sister Agnes"—she leaned back in her chair, turning to the tiny nun on her right—"do you remember what happened to my veil?"

"I believe you lost it." Sister Agnes sighed. "Sister Susannah was at the Trident Nuclear Base in 1979, protesting with the archbishop. She climbed the fence, and her veil was caught on the barbed wire. Pulled it right off her head. She managed to climb down, but the veil stayed, like a black flag. It made the *Seattle Times*." She chuckled.

"Yes," said Sister Susannah. "We were about done with veils by then."

Even Sister John Marie smiled a little at this. She tried to pick up a muffin with shaking hands, but fumbled, and it bounced onto the floor. Sister Susannah chose another muffin from the bowl and cut it smoothly into manageable pieces. She placed one in Sister John Marie's hand and helped her lift it to her mouth.

I had to look away. I gathered the other muffin pieces quickly from the floor with a rag and took them to the compost bin. My throat hurt. Where had I been when Nonni couldn't feed herself? Not at Cherrywood. I'd been at Kwahnesum High School mourning the fact that I didn't have any friends—even though I'd never really lost Natalie. And now I had turned Natalie into some freakish winged specimen to observe through field glasses: the *Starletta Ditzus*. I had treated her no better than Kwahnesum High School had treated me. So now Natalie was gone and Luke was gone and the kittens were gone and I was back to being alone and completely useless.

"Gita?" Mom's hand was on my shoulder. In her other hand she held a canvas bag of tomatoes. She set it down and put her arms around me and hugged me tight. She kissed my cheek. "Looked like you needed that," she said.

I nodded, my throat tight again. "Thanks," I mouthed. If I started talking, I would completely lose it. I wasn't going to do that. Not with Mom. Not with thirteen nuns sitting just around the corner. Not with Mallory ready to do sociological research at a moment's notice. Mom looked into my face but didn't demand to know my thoughts. I kissed her cheek. I had too many thoughts, anyway. I wouldn't know where to start.

* * *

When the dishes were done, I wandered down the deer trail until I was at the edge of Luke's property. I stepped out into his driveway and started around the fountain. I would do it. I would knock on his door and apologize for my bad behavior when he came to my house. Even if he thought I was a loser, I had to face him. If I could do that, then I could face Natalie, too. I stepped up onto the porch. The door opened and a woman came out. She was about Mom's age, stocky, with short auburn hair and gold highlights. She wore a black silk tank top. She closed the door behind her and then saw me. "Oh!" she said, and like an idiot, I turned and ran back into the woods. I watched her get into a Prius and motor off, looking in her rearview mirror. I had lost all nerve for knocking.

I searched my pockets for paper, and all I could find was an old movie ticket (figured). It was to a Timothy Castle movie, and I wondered if Luke would be insulted. I shook my head to clear it. Why was I still thinking as if he was Trent?

I found a pen in my other pocket. "Luke," I wrote in tiny letters. "I'm sorry. Please come back."

I ran up the porch and stuck it between the door and the jamb before I could lose my nerve.

On the way home I almost turned around. "Please come back." What kind of strong, independent woman thing was that to say? Mallory would never do that. Unless it was Webster.

thirty-six

There were places I'd have rather spent a Thursday afternoon than in the rear seat of Mallory's Mazda with Webster Lampson at the wheel. But he knew where the rehab center was.

"Now, I don't want you to be disappointed, Brigitta," Webster was saying. "They're doing the best they can, but of course, it's too late to put them back where you found them."

Mallory lifted her head from his shoulder. "It *is* a rehab center, Webster. Isn't rehab what they do?"

"Yes, yes," said Webster impatiently. "Just don't expect too much."

Cedar Haven Wildlife Refuge was spread out on ten acres. A large central building was surrounded by outdoor enclosures. We walked by eagles, raccoons, a swan. A large cage with a pool inside held two seals.

Outside the main building Webster took his jacket off and adjusted his hat. He unbuttoned the third button on his polo shirt, exposing a tuft of chest hair.

From around the side of the building, a woman in a lab coat came toward us. She looked to be in her late twenties. Her dark hair was caught up in a clip. "Helene," said Webster.

"Web." She appraised him with a slight smile. "You're looking well."

Mallory stood up a little straighter.

"Girls, this is Dr. Jackson." Webster put a hand on the doctor's shoulder. "Helene, this is Brigitta, who found the cubs, and her sister Mallory."

Dr. Jackson shook my hand and then Mallory's. Mallory took Webster's arm and smiled stiffly.

Dr. Jackson's eyes went from Mallory to Webster and back. "Well," she said, "shall we go see these kittens?"

Felix and Kalimar were in a brick-walled enclosure filled with cedar boughs. Kalimar was biting Felix's neck while Felix batted at chunks of bark. My heart leaped. I wanted to climb in there and scoop them into my lap. "They look good," I said. "Better than ever."

"Yes," Helene said. "They've rallied nicely. Kalimar ate a pound of hamburger this morning, and Felix ate almost that much. It's hard not to fall in love with them."

Hearing her use their names made me smile. And then it made me ache because Luke wasn't here. Why hadn't I just knocked on his door? How hard would that have been? "Then they're going to be okay?" I said a little too pleadingly. "They can go back to the wild?"

Dr. Jackson looked directly at me. "We don't know," she said. "They're very young. Too young to have learned the survival skills they needed from their mother. And they've been handled." She paused, gazing into the enclosure. Kalimar was now climbing in and out of the cement "den" where I could see a carrying crate and a cake pan full of water.

My stomach tightened. Yes, they had been handled. What were Luke and I supposed to have done? Leave them to starve? Invite Officer Mark to come shoot them?

"Perhaps a zoo, Helene." Webster put a hand on Dr. Jackson's back and moved closer to her.

"Yes." Dr. Jackson colored. She hesitated before going on. "A female like Kalimar is designed to roam fifty to sixty square miles. Felix would need one hundred and fifty to two hundred square miles by the time he's an adult. They won't get that here—or in a zoo."

Felix chewed at a cedar branch. Webster was still touching Dr. Jackson, and she'd made no attempt to remove herself.

Mallory narrowed her eyes. "They seem to be healthy now," she said. "Isn't there a remote area where they could be released? Radio-collared?"

Dr. Jackson looked down. "They wouldn't survive," she said softly. "We'd be sending them out to die." She sighed. "Believe me, there's been a lot of discussion here. We love these animals. You get attached to them so quickly. I understand why you wanted to handle them and feed them like that." She turned to me once again. "We may have to make…a more merciful choice."

"You mean kill them?!" I said it louder than I intended to, but now I couldn't stop. "It's more merciful to kill them than to put them in a zoo?"

Mallory opened her mouth and then closed it.

Felix sat in the sun cleaning himself. He looked up with his blue, blue eyes. Right at me.

"I know it's hard to understand," Dr. Jackson went on. "They're so adorable. We think they're like pets. But they're not pets."

"You can't kill them!"

"Now, Brigitta, let's talk about this rationally," said Webster.

"You stay out of it!" I shot back. Mallory took a step toward me, then moved instead to Webster's side. Dr. Jackson dropped her pen and crouched to retrieve it, and Mallory steered Webster toward the enclosure where they looked in at the kittens.

"What's wrong with a zoo?" I said to the top of Dr. Jackson's head. "A zoo isn't perfect, but it's better than shooting them."

Dr. Jackson stood. "We wouldn't shoot them," she said. "I know it's hard to understand," she repeated. "Zoos are a hard placement for cougars, especially two of them." She put her hand on the railing and tried again. "These are wild animals. They weren't meant to be confined. I don't believe they could live a full life in a zoo, even if we could find one that would take them." She shook her head. "I'm sorry to say it, but you really should have left them where they were."

Mallory turned away from the kittens, her arm around Webster's waist. Webster gave her a squeeze, and Mallory lifted her chin in the direction of Dr. Jackson.

Behind her in the enclosure, Felix jumped on Kalimar, pinning her to the ground. Kalimar kicked at him with her back legs. They looked strong, vibrant even.

"If I'd left them where they were they would have died," I said.

"Yes," said Dr. Jackson. "Yes, they would have."

chapter thirty-seven

We didn't talk at all on the hour drive home. Mallory kept her head erect, apparently not needing to nap on Webster's shoulder. My stomach tied itself in bows and then in granny knots. In my heart of hearts I had thought I was overreacting by telling Luke the kittens would die if we didn't keep them secret. But then I had left them to go running off with him. Now they were going to die. Because of me.

Webster dropped us off at The Center and didn't come in, claiming an errand. At the door I stopped Mallory before she could go in. "We have to do something."

Mallory shook her head. She looked defeated already. "What can we do?" she said.

I pulled out my phone. "Do you have a number for Felicity Bowen?"

★ ★ ★

Felicity was at The Center in twenty minutes, digital recorder in hand, smartphone at the ready. She had a Nikon slung around her neck and the ever-present pencil tucked behind her ear. At nineteen years old, I think Felicity was the most whiz-bang journalist ever to hit the Kwahnesum Valley. I'd thought Mallory was driven.

"Cougar babies! Cougar babies are a story!"

She still made me nervous, but she was the best hope we had.

Mallory came with us to the cougar den. I told Felicity about the Pedialyte and the goat milk and the all-night feedings. "We worked in shifts," I said. "Only sometimes I slept through mine and Luke took two shifts."

"Luke?" Felicity adjusted her recorder. "Who's Luke?"

What in the name of everything sacred had made *that* come out of my mouth?

Mallory's mouth opened. She turned to me. "It wasn't Devon, was it?" she said slowly. "It was that boy who moved into the Hansen place—the one who was here Sunday." She met my eyes as everything fell into place.

I looked away. A robin took off from the ground with something in its beak. Fur?

Felicity jabbered on, oblivious. "Oh! The boy at the Hansen place? Zach Thompson's little sister Cheryl has been going on about him. The one who's supposed to look like Trent Yves?" Felicity licked the end of her pencil and scribbled something on her pad.

"And is not Trent Yves," I said. "I think we should focus on the kittens." Cheryl the sophisticated had been going on about Luke?

Felicity took a step closer. "But Trent Yves is an angle—a hook. It could be what sells the story."

"But he only looks like him." I knocked a bit of moss off the cougar tree.

"That's what makes him interesting. I could get a few photos of the two of you by this empty stump. It would look like something out of *Imlandria*."

"Not that I'm Gwen Melier." I tried to laugh but felt sick instead.

Felicity grinned. "You're much cuter than her, Brigitta." She snapped a picture of me. "Look," she said. "I'll start making some calls—the *Times*, the news stations. Do you have a number for Luke?"

I shook my head, feeling a pang that I didn't have to lie about this.

"I'll just go and see him. Trust me, Brigitta. Most people love to have their picture in the paper. And if we get him in there, it'll bring just the publicity you want for these cougar babies."

*   *   *

Mom did breakfast duty with the nuns in the morning (Dad had some early-morning ritual he had to complete at the stream, and it was simply too difficult for him to help). Mallory and I had the upstairs to ourselves. I went to get the paper while she sectioned grapefruit.

The headline was on the second page of the entertainment section, above the fold. I set my spoon down.

Trent Yves Hides Out in Kwahnesum Valley.

Below the fold was a photo: an auburn-haired woman with groceries in her arms. The one I'd seen. Beside her was Luke. The caption said, "Former manager Donna Reardon spotted with her protégé, Trent Yves."

chapter
thirty-eight

TRENT YVES HIDES OUT IN KWAHNESUM VALLEY
Felicity Bowen—Special to the *Times*

Rumors of teen actor Trent Yves escaping to the sleepy town of Kwahnesum were confirmed yesterday by sightings of both Trent and his former manager, Donna Reardon. Yves, who recently won Best Actor at the Cannes Film Festival for his portrayal of a young runaway in *Rocket*, was unavailable for comment.

Yves has been using the name "Luke Geoffrey," apparently after his grandmother, Anne Geoffrey Burke, a professor of music at Nottingham Trent University in Great Britain until her death three years ago.

Yves' father, Valéry Boeglin, is reportedly living in Paris following a contentious divorce. His mother, former child prodigy pianist Wendy Burke, has been seen as increasingly volatile and unstable since a chair-throwing incident at the Daytime Emmy Awards last month. Reports of her entering the Betty Ford Center in Rancho Mirage, California, are unconfirmed.

"I talked with him last week, and he's so sweet," beams Kwahnesum resident Natalie Shapiro, 16. "He said I was very talented. I was shaking like crazy," she adds. "He's unbelievable."

Neighbor Buck Harper has noticed the young man in the black Jeep several times. "I didn't know he was famous," he says. "All I know is he drives too fast."

No. Please no. I squeezed my eyes shut. It couldn't be true. After all this, it couldn't really be true. But the details: the bitter divorce, his alcoholic mom being a child prodigy—Luke had told me that himself. I put my head in my palms. I was so stupid. How could I have been so gullible?

Mallory stopped picking mint out of the garden. "Brigitta, what is it?" She crossed the room. I pointed to the article. The kitchen was going in circles.

Mallory's eyes lingered on the photo. "So this Trent person really is quite well-known," she said.

"Eight million Google results," I said miserably.

"That's a lot." She put the paper down.

I traced the photo with my finger. I had seen him in that shirt— the black one with the zippers. I wanted to cry. Trent had stolen Luke from me. I couldn't hate one and love the other. Because they were the same person.

Mallory put her arms around me. "It'll be okay, Gita."

"She didn't mention the kittens—not even once!"

"Yeah, I know," said Mallory grimly. "The movie star is a better story."

I broke away from her and got my Nonni coat from the bedroom. "I'm going out," I said.

"Are you sure?" Mallory ran a kitchen towel over the counter. "It may be a media circle out there."

I almost smiled. "Don't you mean circus?"

Mallory frowned. "Sharks circle," she said.

* * *

I made my way through the woods. Dad was in the clearing in front of Eve. A man with a camera was climbing down the ladder from the tree house.

"This is private property," Dad was saying, none too patiently. "And the property next door is also private. You have exactly two minutes to remove yourself."

The man jumped to the ground and complied, but he only went toward Luke's house.

I took the deer trail past the cougar tree. I thought of Luke holding the kittens in his lap, smiling that lazy smile at me, saying my name. Had he only been acting?

I remembered how he'd looked on the beach when he began to tell me about his mother. Was that acting? Had he ever told those things to anyone else? Or was there no one in his world that he could tell?

Kwahnesum *was* a hideaway for Luke. But I was not the goddess in the woods with the golden hair.

What if he thought *I'd* sicced Felicity on him? What if he thought I'd shared his secrets with some reporter?

I had to talk to him—to let him know I hadn't betrayed him. And I had to tell him about the kittens before it was too late.

The scene on Luke's property was worse than circling sharks. People with cameras crowded in front of the house. They were shooting pictures through the windows, sitting in trees, standing on the edge of the fountain. There must have been forty of them—mostly men—all with microphones or gigantic cameras. The driveway was full of their SUVs. When the front door opened they jockeyed for position, pushing and shoving. "Trent!" they called. "Come on out, Trent! Don't be shy!"

I pressed my cheek against the bark of an alder and held my breath. I didn't want to see Luke swaggering for the press the way I'd seen Trent do on celebrity websites. At the same time, I wanted to see his face again—to see if Trent had erased him completely. The door opened wider.

Donna Reardon stepped onto the porch.

"Where's Trent?" voices shouted. "Bring Trent out!" You could barely hear them because the cameras were flashing and clicking like a horde of locusts. Some of them aimed their lenses into the entryway, but Donna pulled the door shut behind her. She looked better than I had seen her before. Hair perfectly styled, makeup even. She wore a short blue jacket with a blue silk shirt.

"Trent has returned to LA," she called as the din diminished. "He begins shooting on *The Lamplighter* in two weeks."

He was gone again! Only this time I knew where.

More shouts: "You sure he's not hiding in the house?" "Where's Wendy?" "You got Crazy Mum locked up in there?" "How does Trent feel about her getting a DUI in Seattle?" "Is Trent okay? Just tell us Trent's okay."

"Trent has had a difficult year," said Donna. "He would like to be left alone."

A balding paparazzo with a ponytail called out, "Is it true Wendy Burke was committed to the Betty Ford Center for a psych eval?"

Donna pressed her lips together. "You are all on private property. You need to leave now."

"But is she in the psych ward?" he persisted.

Behind Donna, the door opened. Three paparazzi tried to move in closer, but from inside the house, a burly man appeared and whisked Donna back to safety.

A bearded paparazzo with a video camera caught sight of me. Before I could get away he had crossed the distance between us. "Do you live here?" he said. "Do you know Trent?" I didn't answer, but I felt myself redden.

He grinned as if he'd won a prize. "You do know him, don't you, sweetheart?" He smelled of garlic. Out of his pocket, he pulled a hundred-dollar bill. "Can you answer a few questions?"

Several other paparazzi turned in our direction. Bearded Guy spoke quickly. "Has Gwen been here? Did you see her?" He thrust the hundred dollars at me.

I ran. Into the foliage and down a deer trail, switched back around the twin maples and charged through tangles of snowberry where there was no trail at all. At least three of them followed me into the woods. I could see their jackets through the trees. I stayed low and out of sight and moved only when they moved away. I kept moving until I got to the cougar tree. I climbed inside just as Bearded Guy stumbled over a rock and landed, sprawled, ten yards from me. I could hear a siren coming up Luke's driveway.

I pressed my back against the mossy interior of the cedar. The smell of Felix and Kalimar was growing faint. Beside me was the toy Luke had made, carved with their faces. I took it into my lap.

Bearded Guy picked himself up and began pacing down the trail, stopping every now and again to peer into the Indian plum bushes. My heart was beating fast. I ran my thumb over Luke's carvings. I slowed my breathing and grounded myself. I was a cougar, resting in my den. I could see a human, but he couldn't see me.

More voices. "Police! That's private property! Get out of there!" Running feet. The sound of a car door and an engine starting. More engines. And finally, silence.

I let the earth sing to me, the heartbeat of the earth steady me. The smell of damp cedar calmed my senses. A song sparrow began chattering with its mate. Finally, I crawled out of the den, leaving the toy with the odd thought that Felix and Kalimar would come back for it.

*　*　*

Mallory was doing yoga when I slipped into the apartment. She was in downward facing dog. "There were three reporters at the door," she said with her butt in the air. "Dad said he'd call the cops if they didn't leave. We've turned off the phone. It's like being under siege." She shifted to plank, then cobra—flat on her stomach with her head and chest raised. "The nuns are all praying for you."

"For me?"

"Yeah. Sister Susannah thought you needed it. She knows who Trent

Yves is, and they're praying for him, too. They're sweet, really." She went into child's pose, kneeling, with her arms stretched on the floor in front of her, as if she were praying, too.

I remembered Luke asking "Do you pray, Brigitta?" and I remembered that I used to. I'd even prayed once or twice this month, but never for him, and definitely never for a celebrity. In fact, I'd never really prayed for anyone but me.

chapter thirty-nine

I convinced Mallory that now was the time to drive back out to Cedar Haven. Natalie would have driven me if I'd asked her. In fact, she'd have been preparing speeches for Dr. Jackson. But now that she hated me it was no use calling her.

"Where's Webster?" I asked Mallory as we drove up I-5.

"He's working on some research," she said vaguely.

"I thought you were helping him."

"I was…I mean, I am, but he's at a juncture where he has to work alone for a few days."

I wondered how you'd study the impact of sex on coastal environments—or whatever the heck he told Mallory he was researching—by yourself. I wasn't mean enough to say this. Suddenly Mallory was the only friend I had.

I pressed my forehead against the window glass. I was relieved to be away from the reporters. How long would they lay siege to Luke's house? Had he really escaped or was he in there hiding?

"Look!" Mallory pointed. A peregrine falcon dove from the sky to a field just ahead.

"What do you think she saw?" I said as the field gave way to a shopping center.

"Oh, a rabbit or a vole or a mole. Dad says a peregrine shifts its shape to slip through the air's molecules."

"You mean they're shape-shifters?"

Mallory laughed. "Not exactly." It was good to hear her laugh—a change from the cynical poke-holes-in-everything Mallory who had come home from college three weeks ago.

"Are you still mad at Dad?" I rubbed at a speck of dirt on the window.

Mallory was quiet. "I thought you were the one who was mad at Dad," she said finally. She took the next exit, and we began passing farms, forest, an old lumber mill.

I studied the latch on the car door. "Why would I be mad at Dad?"

"Do you think I can't see it, Brigitta? Just because you never open your mouth and tell him? I don't know why you're mad at him, but you're fake around him. It was really obvious when I came home from school because things didn't used to be that way between you. It's like you're walking on eggshells all the time."

Now it was my turn to be quiet.

She was wrong. I wasn't mad at Dad. I was embarrassed by him leaping around in the woods with feathers stuck in his hair. I was annoyed that he was too busy planning retreats and hosting sweat lodges to take me hiking like he'd promised. But I wasn't angry, I was just…indifferent, I suppose. He had his thing to do, and I had mine.

As soon as I thought this, I knew I was lying to myself.

Dad wouldn't be able to understand me if he tried, but I did understand him. I understood him walking the perimeter of our property stepping toe-heel, toe-heel, listening for the voices with his feet. I understood him wanting to find the heartbeat of the forest. I understood how he heard the animals speak to him through tracks they left in the dirt, a piece of fur caught on a fallen log. I understood all that. Because I did it myself.

Mallory and I talked more than we had in a long time. She wouldn't say anything else about Webster, so I didn't push her. But I finally told her a little about Luke—not everything, but about going to the coast and how he'd kissed me in the lighthouse and how I didn't want him to be Trent.

"Love is complicated," she said.

"Yeah. And now Natalie won't talk to me."

"Why?" She turned. "Because of Luke? Is she jealous?"

"Maybe." I stared at the telephone poles flying by. "Actually," I began. "It's something I did."

It seemed easier to confess in the car with no nuns around. I told her about the blog. I couldn't bring myself to tell that I'd been just as nasty to "Dr. Freuda" as I'd been to Natalie.

"You've been so hidden, Brigitta." Mallory spoke quietly. "You've been hiding yourself away since that public school year. Do you think Natalie was just getting too close?"

"I don't know." It came out a squeak. Unexpected tears gathered at the corners of my eyes. "And I don't know how to tell her I'm sorry."

★　★　★

Dr. Jackson gave Mallory a long look before leading us to the kittens' enclosure. "Web's not with you?"

"He's busy." Mallory smiled frostily. "I'll tell him hello for you."

A young guy with a Cedar Haven Volunteer shirt was sweeping scat into a scooper while Felix and Kalimar followed each other from one log to another.

"I've enjoyed observing these two." Dr. Jackson smiled sadly.

Kalimar was busy tearing up a piece of steak with her teeth.

Mallory put her hand on my arm, as I absorbed Dr. Jackson's past tense "enjoyed."

"Are they going somewhere?" I asked.

"They're already restless." She sidestepped the question. "They're already beginning to pace. They can't be released because they're not prepared to fend for themselves. And because they've had human contact"—she looked at me pointedly—"they'd be a danger to any nearby community."

"But a zoo…" I ignored her guilt trip.

"Is a prison for animals like these," finished Dr. Jackson.

"So you prefer the death penalty to a life sentence?" I didn't care if she was some fancy animal doctor. She had no business playing God.

Dr. Jackson put her hand on the chain-link fence that separated us from the kittens. "Death is not always a penalty. These creatures pay the penalty when we move into their territory and prevent them from living normally. I'm sorry, girls," she said. "This breaks my heart, too."

"No," said Mallory. "I don't think it breaks your heart at all." She drew herself up. "Dr. Lampson feels they should be in a zoo. He told me so privately." She paused as a barely perceptible shadow flickered across Dr. Jackson's face. "Surely you'd take his opinion into account."

Dr. Jackson tightened her grip on the chain-link fence. "Dr. Lampson is a fine behaviorist," she said stiffly. "He does not, however, specialize in animals."

Mallory stared her down.

"Well," said Dr. Jackson finally. "We've one or two calls out yet. No final decision has been made."

★　★　★

Felicity met us back at The Center, which was now clear of all other reporters. I really didn't want to talk to her after what she'd done, but she was our only hope. She snapped pictures of us crouched by the empty cougar den and interviewed us both about what Dr. Jackson had said.

"There's not much more I can do," she said.

That was easy for her to say. She hadn't been up nights caring for Felix and Kalimar. She hadn't held them and looked in their faces. To her it was all a story.

"You could have mentioned them in your article," I snapped. "That was what you *said* you were after."

Felicity looked away. "I tried, Brigitta. I really did. I called my mentor at the *Times* and sent her the pics of Trent and his manager. She knows an entertainment reporter in LA and forwarded them to her. Turns out the paparazzi have been looking for Wendy Burke ever since she threw the chair at that reporter. This is as close as they've gotten. I figured out her mother's maiden name was Geoffrey and that was all it took."

"Well, that's very exciting." My voice was sharp. "But this was supposed to be a story about cougars. You said you'd help us."

"Like I said, Brigitta, I tried. I put the cougars in the original article. But Cedar Haven wouldn't let any reporters in, and there aren't even pictures of the cubs. We couldn't get a statement from Trent. The paper edited the cougars out."

"But Luke doesn't want a story about him. That's why he came out here. To get away from stories. He would want Felix and Kalimar to be saved. He put so much time into them. Can't you just try it for Luke's sake if you're so interested in him?"

Felicity looked at me curiously. "How close are you to Trent?"

"He's a friend. We're just friends." I said it a little too quickly.

"Felix and Kalimar? Sounds like you've gotten to know him pretty well." Felicity rubbed her thumb across the top of her Nikon.

"Felicity." Mallory stood, brushing dirt off her jeans. "Brigitta doesn't need this."

"Don't you see?" said Felicity. "Brigitta does need this! This is what can awaken this story. Think." She swung her camera around to her hip so she could talk with her hands. "The kittens were cared for and tended by Trent in the middle of the night. Didn't you say something about him taking two feeding shifts in a row? 'Trent was dedicated to the task by his love for the beautiful Brigitta Schopenhauer.'"

"No!"

"Yes!" said Felicity. "Really, hon. You're his Mystery Gal Pal. It's perfect." I felt sick.

Felicity arched her eyebrows at me. "It could work."

Could it? If I told the story, would it bring the press to Cedar Haven in such great numbers that they'd have to let them in? Could they save Felix and Kalimar from execution? What would I say? That Trent Yves had found the cougars? That he'd almost been killed by their mother? That he was sad a lot of the time and wanted to find Eden? That he was kissing me when he wasn't kissing Gwendolyn Melier? And if I did tell the story, what would be the difference between me and every crazed fan or paparazzo he'd ever come across?

"No," I said finally. "He asked for privacy. It would be a betrayal not to leave him be."

Mallory had been silent for several minutes. "He's already a public figure, Brigitta," she said gently.

I looked at her. Did she think this was Felix and Kalimar's last chance? It couldn't be. There had to be another way.

"No," I said. "And no."

Felicity shrugged. "Okay," she said. "I can respect that."

* * *

Mom wasn't home when I went in, and I suddenly wanted her to be. I was ready to curl up in her lap, like when I was six, and tell her everything. Instead I climbed into her hammock chair and let its multicolored folds envelop me. This was where Mom sat and wrote in her journal every morning, with the sun splashing across her feet. The hammock swung comfortingly. A tumble of books lay at arm's reach on a small table—one on angels, another on aromatherapy, a copy of *Mansfield Park*, and a packet of stapled pages, probably downloaded from somewhere. I picked it up: "How to Become a Wildlife Rehabilitator." My throat tightened. Mom must have printed these the night we stayed up with Kalimar and Felix. We had been so close to keeping them with us!

I skimmed through the pages, stopping at "An animal that is too severely injured or sick to return to the wild has a right to euthanasia." I cringed at the irony of having a "right" to be killed. If the kittens were in pain and couldn't get better, maybe putting them to sleep would be a kindness. But Felix and Kalimar weren't sick anymore. Surely the other vets at Cedar Haven would talk sense into Dr. Jackson. They wouldn't let her kill the kittens just because she didn't like zoos.

The Trentwatch blog had six new photos dated today, Friday. Four of them were Trent riding a horse on his ranch. They were taken from a distance, so I couldn't distinguish any of his features. The other two were of him by his pool with Gwen wrapped around him like a koala. And I'd thought today couldn't get any worse.

If these had been taken this afternoon, Luke had made tracks to get there. He'd have been on a plane yesterday. Or early this morning. I looked back at the other pictures, supposedly taken when Luke was with me. How could he have been with me and in California at the same time? I clicked through again. The pictures themselves didn't have dates on them, only the blog entries. And while the captions said things like "Tuesday" or "yesterday," there was no way of verifying pictures that were simply sent in by people snooping around LA. These photographers weren't even sophisticated enough to be real paparazzi.

I thought of Luke saying he'd been to a horse show in LA—probably at the Equestrian Center, where he'd crashed his Mini. It was so obvious. Why hadn't I seen it? Because every time I'd looked at Luke, I'd so not wanted him to be Trent that I'd seen someone else.

* * *

I got up at 6:00 Saturday morning, too restless to sleep any longer.

Dad was already in the kitchen eating granola. On the table was a vase of roses. "Are those for Mom? Your anniversary isn't until next month."

"They arrived an hour ago," he said. "Look at the envelope."

It said, "Brigitta."

In the vase were twelve roses, pink with red tips. Their fragrance filled the kitchen. I unsealed the card and took it to the sofa to read.

B,

I let it go too far. Forgive me. I never meant to hurt you.

—LG aka TY aka MLB

At the bottom was a small hand drawing of a cat.

chapter forty

I read the card over and over. Let what go too far? What did he mean? Had he never wanted to be with me in the first place? Did he mean good-bye forever? Did he think I'd told the press he was Trent?

"Brigitta?" Dad came up behind me. "Do you want some granola?"

I shook my head, annoyed to be wet-eyed.

"Girls aren't supposed to cry when boys send them flowers," he teased, like the old Dad would have.

"What if they're the roses of consolation?"

Dad perched on the edge of the sofa and gave me a quick hug. "Don't worry, sweetheart, he'll be back."

"If he's Trent Yves I don't know if I want him back."

Dad cocked his head to one side. "Who is Trent Yves?" he said. "And why wouldn't you want him?"

Only Dad or Mallory would not know who Trent Yves is.

"He's an actor," I said. "And that's why."

"Well," said Dad, "it explains the reporters. I'm glad to know he's not an ax murderer." He plopped onto the sofa next to me. "Or is this almost as bad?"

"Almost," I said. I slid Luke's card into my pocket.

"These are the gods we worship," Dad mused softly.

"You mean Hollywood actors?"

"The American pantheon," said Dad. "Better than Zeus and the boys."

"If that was my pantheon, I'd be an atheist."

Dad clapped me on the back with a burst of laughter. "That's my girl," he said.

I put my head on his shoulder. It felt good there. He sat with me for a long time.

✦   ✦   ✦

At eight o'clock I was spreading compost around the potatoes in the upstairs garden when there was a knock at the door. I checked to see whether it was a reporter. It was Devon.

His hair was longer and uncombed. He had three zits on his chin. He stepped into the apartment tentatively, as if he wasn't sure he still belonged here.

"How have you been?" he started.

"Good," I said. I wiped my hands on my jeans. "It's been interesting here."

"Yeah," he said but didn't elaborate. He ran his hand along the tops of the kitchen chairs and stared out the window at the maples. I leaned back against the pillar.

"So, I've been thinking," he said. "It's been a long time since we discussed philosophy."

"You want to discuss philosophy?" I remembered that this was a typical Devon conversation.

"Well, we could discuss religion if you'd rather." He fiddled with the lid of Mom's teapot.

"No, no. Philosophy's fine."

"I've been reading Spinoza," he said. "The difference between mode and substance." He picked up some postcards of Dad's drums and riffled through them.

"Hmm," I said.

"You and I are modes," he went on. "At least in our bodies we are. Because they're temporary. But according to Spinoza, the substance of us is what's underneath the mode. The thing that stays forever." The postcards whirred as he flipped them with his thumb.

"I thought you didn't believe in forever," I said. "Wouldn't that mean believing in God?"

"Almost," he said. "Well, maybe I do believe in God now." He said it shyly, and it reminded me of the Devon I had always known—the one I'd eaten raspberry sandwiches with and who had doctored my bee stings with mud.

"Why are you here?" I asked him, not unkindly.

"It's just been a while, Brigitta." He set the postcards down and put his hands in his pockets. "I thought maybe we could spend some more time together. Pick up where we left off."

"Where did we leave off?"

He looked across at the stained glass medicine wheel with the morning light coming through it. "We left off at…well, I thought maybe we should just *be*. You know, be together."

"In mode or in substance?" I shot back.

"Both," he said. "Maybe."

In the silence he took in the room: yesterday's paper still on the sofa where I'd left it, spread open to page two of the entertainment section, the roses in their vase on the table.

For a whole year I had wanted to be his girlfriend. Now everything had changed. But he was reaching out to me when everyone else had turned away, and the sweetness of this caught me off guard. "Devon," I said. "I'd have loved to hear you say that a month ago. But—"

"But," he said.

I caught his eye. "Yeah," I said.

He held my gaze. "I understand."

Mallory came up from downstairs with a basket of laundry. Devon and I walked outside. "I've just had a rough year," I told him. Two brown rabbits appeared from the foliage and tipped their ears to the wind.

Devon put one foot up on the bench. "I know," he said. "It was your grandparents, wasn't it? Them dying?"

I nodded slowly.

He sat down, straddling the bench. "Where was that place you used to go? In Indiana? Didn't it have a name?"

"Cherrywood," I said. "Nonni named it that." It caught in my throat.

"You should go back there, Brigitta."

"Can't." The rabbits bounded away. "It's been sold."

"Yeah, that's right," said Devon. "Just an idea. You always came back from there in a good mood."

I had a rush of warm feeling for him and surprised both of us by kissing the top of his head. "You're a good friend, Devon."

He stood up and gave me a quick hug. "You are, too, Brigitta. See you around?"

"Yeah," I said. "You will."

* * *

When I got back, Mallory was holding the phone. She covered the mouthpiece. "Dr. Jackson," she whispered. "She won't talk to me."

I took the phone from her. "Brigitta, I'm sorry," Dr. Jackson said after a few preliminaries. "We can't find a placement for those cubs. It's really looking like euthanasia is the best option for them."

I couldn't answer her.

"Are you there?"

"Yes," I finally said. "You can't do this."

"We've had to make a professional assessment of the situation. It's unfortunate. Nobody wants to see this happen. But they just don't have any future under the circumstances. It's for them that we make this decision and…well, we wondered if you and your sister would like to come say good-bye to them."

"When?" I croaked.

"Any time between now and noon," said Dr. Jackson.

chapter forty-one

Felicity arrived at 8:30, looking contrite. "We still have time, Brigitta. I have a list of all the TV contacts, and I have seven newspapers I haven't even tried yet.

"That's a good thing," said Mallory, "because you owe us, Felicity."

Mallory drove between seventy and eighty while Felicity and I sat in the backseat calling every television station and newspaper within a hundred miles. The answer was always the same: they'd get someone out there if they could; it might make the evening edition; did we have pictures we could send?

At 9:30 one of the volunteers let us in at Cedar Haven. Staff members smiled and waved, but nobody talked much. Even the kingfisher and the seals seemed glum today.

The volunteer unlocked the gate to the enclosure and handed each of us a pair of leather gloves. I pulled them over my scratched and bitten hands, wondering why I hadn't thought of that before. Kalimar climbed right into my legs and began to purr when I sat down. She began kneading my thigh with her claws. I disconnected her gently and ran my gloves over her sleek fur. I wanted to touch her with my bare hands, but when she grabbed the glove with her teeth, I thought better of it.

Mallory picked up Felix and let him sniff her neck. She touched his big paws. Luke should be here. The thought was a lead weight. He was the one who had found them, and he needed to be here now. Only he wasn't.

Kalimar went after an interesting bug, and Felix jumped in my lap. He rubbed his mouth against my chin. I've heard cats do that as a way of marking what's theirs. I took the leather gloves off. Let them scratch me. I plunged my hands into his rough fur and rubbed him all over. His ears were cold. His ribs vibrated. He curled up on my belly. Mallory scooped up Kalimar and nestled her against her brother. For a few moments, they both stayed there, purring, letting me caress their backs. Then they scrambled up, digging their claws into my legs, and ran off to play. Felicity took plenty of pictures of them tussling together, drinking water, pouncing on a small red ball.

We left reluctantly. I wanted to stay all morning, but we were going to save them and we had work to do.

Dr. Jackson passed us on the way out. She nodded and went back to her clipboard. Was that a guilty look I saw?

✱　✱　✱

At The Morning Buzz coffee shop, we imported the photos to my laptop and sent them to every contact we had. It was 10:00. I uploaded the best picture onto my blog.

Seeing Starzz

Celebrities Find Their Deep Space
Hollywood's Hidden Spiritual Quest

Can You Save These Cubs?

At exactly noon today, Felix and Kalimar will be killed by the very wildlife center that is supposed to be helping them. Here is the number for Cedar Haven. Ask for Dr. Jackson. Tell her you want the kittens to live.

I'm not much of a friend, but if I can do one good thing this year, it will be this. Let them live!!!

I posted Dr. Jackson's number.

Felicity's phone began to ring. But every call was the same. They'd have a crew out at 2:00. Or 4:00 or 4:30. It would make the news tonight at eleven or tomorrow morning. A few of them posted Felicity's "Save the Cougars" article on their websites.

"We need a better plan," said Mallory.

"We'd better find it fast." I glanced at the clock. It was well after 11:00.

Felicity took a swallow of her latte. "Maybe there's some rule Dr. Jackson is breaking. I have connections with the county for stuff like that."

Mallory fished around in her backpack until she came up with "How to Become a Wildlife Rehabilitator" from Mom's journaling corner.

"You've been carrying that around?" I asked.

Mallory laughed sheepishly. "Wishful thinking," she said.

I felt a pang of tenderness for her.

"I haven't actually read it through." She ran a finger down the table of contents. "Euthanasia guidelines," she said. "That should give us something."

Felicity and I followed the words over Mallory's shoulder:

A wild animal must be euthanized if:
1. It is unable to recover from injuries or illness.
2. It has a terminal illness.

"There you go," said Felicity. "Your cubs don't meet either requirement. She tapped the contact list on her phone as Mallory flipped to the next page:

3. It is imprinted on humans.
4. It is tamed due to improper care during the rehabilitation process.

My eyes stopped at the words "improper care."

"*Must be euthanized*," said Mallory. "That can't be."

My mouth tasted acid. Felix and Kalimar loved us *because* we'd given them "improper care." And now, without a zoo to take them, they'd pay with their lives.

"I really think you should call your boyfriend, Brigitta," said Felicity. "We could use some celebrity help right about now."

The thought of talking to Luke again was so sweet I almost cried. He would help, wouldn't he? He had sent me flowers.

I shoved Gwen Melier out of my brain and got onto Whitepages.com. I looked up "Michael Boeglin," "Wendy Burke," "Ann Geoffrey," and even, "Trent Yves." I checked the Malibu listings, feeling stupid. Nothing. I hadn't expected there would be. It dawned on me that he was out of my life, just when I needed him most.

"This is a waste of time," said Felicity.

"You have a better idea?" Mallory snapped.

"I know," I said. "We go back there. We blockade the vet office with our bodies. We wrestle with Dr. Jackson for syringes." I winced. It made it sound too real.

Mallory pulled her car keys out of her pocket. "Let's go," she said.

* * *

We arrived at 11:30, ready to do battle. No one followed us as we marched to Felix and Kalimar's enclosure.

It was empty.

My eyes swept over the logs and branches, the sheltered room with their crate. Only their crate was gone. And so were Felix and Kalimar.

"I'm sorry." Dr. Jackson stood behind us. "I thought you'd already said your good-byes."

"You've done it already?" I grabbed the rail around the enclosure to steady myself. "It's only 11:30."

Felicity put her hand over her mouth.

"I'm sorry," Dr. Jackson said again. Her eyes were a little red. "They're in a better place."

Mallory took a step forward. "Don't you dare give us that kind of sanctimonious bullshit," she said. "You killed healthy animals."

"I'm afraid you'll have to leave," said Dr. Jackson.

chapter
forty-two

Webster's red Porsche was waiting when we pulled back onto The Center grounds. "Oh, God," said Mallory. "Not today."

"What?" said Felicity. "Is that your boyfriend?"

Mallory composed herself and got out of the car. I stayed where I was. I didn't need to see Webster. My whole brain was numb. I thought I might curl up and go to sleep right there in the backseat.

Webster walked across the gravel and greeted Mallory with a kiss, like they were an old married couple. I saw her introduce him to Felicity. She had that sophisticated Mallory mask back on. She swept her hand across the air, as if brushing away a fly. Webster beamed down at her, as if he'd just sculpted her in his very own studio.

Felicity took a picture of the two of them, arm in arm in front of the Porsche. Then she waved and got into her car.

It was like watching a movie. I couldn't think what I was supposed to be doing next.

Mallory came over and knocked on the window. I rolled it down.

"Webster and I are going for a drive," she said. "It's a nice day. Mom's off at her herbalist meeting. Dad must be at the co-op buying supplies. His car's gone. Do you want to come with us?" She smiled a little too brightly, and I wondered if this was a plea.

Spending the day with Webster was too awful to imagine. "I can't," I told her. "I just need to be alone for a while, okay?"

For a moment, she was Mallory again. "Okay," she said. "Do you want us to bring you anything?"

I shook my head no.

★ ★ ★

After they left I really did fall asleep in Mallory's car for a while. I wasn't sure how long. Finally, I got out and wandered across the foot-bridge to the tree house. I climbed up and stood at my Onawa shrine, my mind full of nothing. In the photo, the kittens' mother lay frozen, her wound hidden by fur. I lit the candle. Then I took the clipping down and burned it to ash. I pinched out the candle and tossed it into a drawer. I folded my mother's scarf. All that was left was the metal box—Dad's flute. I lifted it up and took it to a patch of sun in the window seat.

The flute lay snug in the red velvet. It was real silver—an expensive instrument—and I knew he'd had it since high school. Nonni said he used to play on some kind of church worship team. It was hard to imagine.

The light glinted off the tarnished mouthpiece. Dad had always kept it polished—that is, until he decided to throw it away. I closed the case and climbed down out of the tree house with it, barely knowing what I was doing.

In the kitchen I squirted a tiny bit of organic ketchup onto a rag. Strange, I know, but it really does remove tarnish—and it isn't as nasty as silver polish. I took it to the meditation room, where I sat cross-legged on the wide expanse of rug in front of the windows. The mouthpiece warmed in my hands as I turned it, rubbing at each little crevice. Dad and I had played together since I first started violin lessons at seven. He'd helped me through "Twinkle, Twinkle, Little Star," and made my halting squeaks sound musical with his airy accompaniment. I'd never gone through an "I hate to practice" phase, because practice time was always Dad time. Even when I was up to four hours a day, I could usually count on him to pick up the flute for fifteen minutes when I hit a hard patch. I was sure hitting a hard patch now.

I put the flute together and rolled it across my palms. Dad had been sweet this morning. Comforting. It was the first I'd felt connected with him in a long time.

I got to my feet and raised the flute to my lips. I found the first few notes of the *Pleni* and blew: E-F-G-A-E-A-G. They came out clear. I played them again, louder, lengthening the G and letting it hang as I lowered the instrument.

A sharp voice cut the air. "What are you doing?!"

I whirled. Dad stood in the doorway with his drum, his face the mask of an angry god. The instrument slipped out of my hand and tumbled across the floor.

"Dad, I—"

He blazed into the room and snatched the flute up. "You had no right, Brigitta, no right! You should have left it where it was!"

The words slammed against my body. I felt the blood drain from my face. Dad didn't even notice. He spun around and out, flute and drum clutched in his hands, leaving the front door of The Center hanging open.

I watched the stranger he'd become disappear down the path.

The kittens' den was a damp refuge. I leaned my head against the soft bark and set my hands flat on the leaf-cushioned floor. For a while I could hear Dad drumming out by the half-completed hermitage. Then the drumming stopped, and I heard his car rumble out the driveway. I should feel something, shouldn't I?

Luke's kitten toy was still nestled against the bark wall, untouched. Had he really learned to carve at Scout camp? Had he ever done anything that ordinary? I wrapped the beaded leather laces around my hand. Trent Yves had a shirt with beaded leather laces in *Imlandria*. Were these them? Had he been trying to tell me who he was all along?

I traced the bite marks on the wooden handle. Kalimar's? She loved to chew. I ran my thumb over the indentations. It would probably be good to cry, but it took too much energy. I wanted Luke here holding me. I wanted Nonni. I wanted things that couldn't be.

Back at Cherrywood I'd had a secret grove—a place in the woods where the ground was curved like a bowl and surrounded by a screen of gum trees, beeches, and sugar maples. "You should go back to Cherrywood," Devon had said. It was a sweet thing to say. I imagined myself there now—the smell of warm Indiana earth. I'd called my grove secret, but many days I'd find things there—a tin of gingersnaps, a jar of iced lemonade. And Nonni would be singing when I came back to the house.

A sharp longing to be there knifed into my numbness. Cherrywood was my true home, not here. I loved where I lived, but it was not a haven, the way Cherrywood had been. I'd thought Cherrywood would be there always, and now it was gone.

But it wasn't gone! I sat up. I could go there! I had some money. I could buy a plane ticket and just go, just take off, the way I had with Luke. I'd flown back and forth to Indiana by myself since I was nine. It wouldn't be any big deal. I could go and sit in my woods and breathe the humid air one more time. Maybe then I would finally be real.

grabbed my laptop out of Mallory's trunk and hauled it to my room. I had $857.02 in my savings account. Most of it was from working for Mom and Dad at The Center. The rest was from a violin competition I had won. I transferred $850 into my checking account.

It took $762 to buy a plane ticket on Travelocity, but I didn't care. It was worth it.

I printed out bus routes and maps of Indianapolis and Westfield. My heart was pounding. I was really going to do this.

It was after 2:00. How long had Mom and Dad been gone? I packed quickly: two pairs of jeans, two T-shirts, underwear and socks, a toothbrush and flashlight. I dropped a candle stub and matches into the backpack for good measure, and shoved my laptop in as well.

I scrawled a note: "Went bike riding. Back late. B."

That should buy me some time. I didn't want to worry Mom and Dad, but I had to, had to do this. They would sit me down and try to make me think logically. I couldn't go to Cherrywood, they'd say; Cherrywood belongs to someone else now.

But this wasn't logical. It wasn't something I could explain. I just knew that I had to go there if I was ever going to find the Brigitta I had lost.

*   *   *

At the bus stop, I wheeled my bike into a grove of trees out of sight and locked it to one of the trunks.

When I finally boarded the plane at 7:30 it seemed a natural thing to do, as if I was a returning salmon. It was strange, though, to be doing this without permission. The tight feeling in my stomach was part dread, part excitement.

I had a window seat, but I barely noticed the view outside. I had always loved the moment of ascent, so full of possibilities. Tonight it seemed to take too long, as if each leg of the journey was an impediment to the destination. Had Mom begun to wonder about my absence? Had Dad? How late would they expect "home late" to be? I should have told them I was spending the night at Natalie's. But that would have been even more unbelievable now.

I kept having the nagging feeling that the kittens needed food. Then I'd remember Felix at the rehab center, his blue, blue eyes pleading with me to save him. Only I hadn't saved him. Had he been scared when Dr. Jackson came with her needles? Had Kalimar?

I couldn't eat the airplane snacks.

I leaned my forehead against the window and tried to pray.

★ ★ ★

It was 2:30 in the morning when I arrived in Indianapolis. I pulled out my map and bus information. The warm air hit me like a walk-through wall when I stepped out onto the sidewalk. Even at a bus stop, the atmosphere had a familiar and exotic quality to it, a smell I never smelled at home, sounds I never heard there.

At 3:30, I got off the bus in Westfield. The streets were empty, and I walked, putting one foot in front of the other, heel-toe, heel-toe. On the left was the Kroger where Nonni always shopped; on the right the ice cream place where Opa let me get a triple scoop cone when I was eight and didn't know any better. Stores gave way to neighborhood—sturdy sandstone houses with arched entryways—many of them built by Opa.

And then, there it was: the porthole window of Opa's study, the white-painted bricks, the long curved driveway sweeping around to raspberry bushes. Cherrywood. My heart felt suspended in midair.

Six oaks lined the front yard. The porch light illuminated Opa's stone frogs.

I walked the driveway quietly to the backyard. I was the only one awake in the world. A soaker hose was running. I skirted the spray, making my way down the grass hill and out to the rail fence that divided the yard from the woods. At the fence I turned back. The house was there, sleeping. The screened-in porch, the attic window—all as it had been. Maybe Nonni and Opa would be inside. Maybe they had left the porch light on for me.

I stopped at the edge of the sweet gum trees and inhaled the green scent of their spiny fruit. Home. I was home.

The curtain of branches parted as I pushed through and walked down, down. My secret grove was so dark it was as if I was hanging in space. I crouched to gather beech leaves in my hands. Gradually I could make out the shapes of honeysuckle bushes, rocks, and roots. And through the branches I could see the house with the blue Dutch kitchen door Opa had made that opened at the top. Nonni would stand there and call, "Hoo-hoo!" when she wanted me, and I would climb up out of my secret space and take a little side path to the house so I could pretend she didn't know where I'd been hiding.

Where had I been hiding? All this past year and a half, where had I been hiding? I remembered Nonni reading to me from Genesis how Adam hid from God in the Garden of Eden. "Adam," God called, "where are you?"

I felt tears rush to my eyes, and I couldn't stop them this time. There was something I needed to do here, and I wasn't sure exactly what it was. In my backpack my fingers found the wooden kitten toy and brought it out. I touched the faces: Felix with one ear bigger than the other, Kalimar with her extra-long whiskers. The beads clicked at the ends of the leather laces, and I saw Luke wearing them in *Imlandria*, climbing a sheer rock wall to save Gwen Melier—his Kalimar. And being too late.

Where was he now? Back in LA—maybe at some party with Gwen. I had this floor-dropping-away feeling when I thought of this. All the times he'd been calling me beautiful, touching my hair, kissing me, he had flown off to LA the very next day to do the same things with Gwen. I wanted to be furious with him. Instead it just hurt, which was worse.

Without stopping to think about it, I cleared a circle in the leaves and began to move handfuls of earth. When I couldn't dig down any farther with my hands, I used the toy to dig until I had a hole that went up to my elbow. My eyes were so blurred I could barely see. My throat hurt. I realized that I was clenching my jaw.

I sat back on my heels and let the cougar stick rest on my palms with the laces dangling between my fingers. I imagined Luke sitting by the kittens in the middle of the night and carving it, Kalimar climbing Luke's shirt, and Felix in my lap with goat milk dribbling down his catly beard. Luke gazing at me with his blue, blue eyes.

I wrapped Luke's *Imlandria* laces around the wood and laid the toy gently in the hole. My mind could barely form the word *good-bye*.

My hands swept the earth back in until the hole was filled to the top. I pressed it down, leaving my imprints. Only then did I notice that my shoulders were shaking.

A sound came out of my throat that I didn't recognize. It was wild and fierce like an animal, and it went on and on and on. I couldn't stop. I didn't want to stop. I pressed my face to the grave I had made and let the feral yowl rip out of me. And then I was pounding the earth, sobbing, "You left me—you promised—you said you didn't want to lose me—you lied. And they died—and we could have saved them—you could have saved them—I could have—I could have—I could have saved them. And I didn't—I didn't—I let them die!" I scratched at the ground. I had dirt in my mouth and in my eyes. I stayed inside the scream until the last shudder had passed through me.

Once I was still I curled my knees up to my chest and listened, sure someone would come out with a flashlight or yell sleep-disturbed curses from their window, but there was nothing.

A swarm of cicadas began their whirring chorus. I wrapped the patchwork coat around me and pulled some sweet gum branches over myself as a blanket.

When I was little and didn't know what cicadas were, I'd always thought their sound was angel's wings surrounding the house. "Sleep," the angels told me now. "Sleep and find your heart."

chapter forty-four

When I woke up, my head felt stuffed with straw. Somewhere I could hear a bird call: *Chip, chip, chip, chip. Burbury, burbury, burbury.* For a moment I was in the bunk room, Opa rustling around in the kitchen on the other side of the door. I opened my eyes. A flash of red and two cardinals alighted on a beech tree. I sat up as my location veered into focus.

Several little bugs had crawled off the sweet gum branches and onto me. Leaves were tangled in my hair. My stomach was tight. I scanned the curved ground for a tin of Nonni's gingersnaps. Scattered sweet gum pods mixed with beech leaves around the knees of roots. A chickadee hopped between them: No tin. No jar of lemonade. No Nonni.

I ran my hand along the round place where I had buried the cougar toy. I thought I had cried everything out, but there was another, deeper sea inside me, still untapped.

I shook my head. I was ravenous. I rummaged in my pack and found a bottle of water and a packet of airplane snacks, which I devoured. There. Almost human.

I climbed the sloped ground and parted the curtain of leaves just a little. Nonni's garden was gone! So was most of the rolling lawn. Instead, a series of dirt islands dotted the yard with little shrubs sticking out of them. A soaker hose snaked its way through these, squirting haphazardly.

The house gazed at me surreally. It was no longer white, but gray.

Opa's Dutch door was brown. Inside me a slumbering current stirred, dark and cold.

The door opened, and a man came out—pale, with red hair and a beer gut. He wore a bathrobe and no shoes. He made his way down the walk and turned off the soaker hose. I pulled some fern fronds and began stripping the leaves off. I remembered that the buyer was a vending machine salesman and lived alone. He was by himself rattling around in all those rooms. My rooms.

I had to get into the house. Here behind the sweet gum branches I knew that the grove was not enough. Nonni was not here. But the house—she'd be there. Something of her would be lingering there. When we were twelve, Natalie and I had gone through a phase of reading real-life ghost stories. We'd known the locations of every haunted mansion, warehouse, or theater in Washington, though the idea of going to any of them was terrifying. But if I could see Nonni's ghost— just to talk to her one last time—that wouldn't be terrifying at all.

The beer-gut man stuck something in Nonni's milk box. Asking this squatter for permission to enter Cherrywood would be absurd. He went back into the house.

Before long the garage door opened and a white van came out. The lettering on the side said "Polzin Enterprises: Vending Solutions to Meet Every Need. Snacks, Soda, Candy, Coffee." Behind the wheel I could see the red-haired man in a jacket and tie. The garage door descended as he drove away, and I had a sudden thought to scoot underneath it. I didn't act fast enough before it hit the ground, sealing me out.

I covered my backpack in branches and approached the house cautiously. The mint Nonni had planted under the kitchen window was still here. I put a sprig my mouth, feeling the coolness spread across my tongue. I climbed the kitchen steps. The Dutch door was locked. Through its window I could see a new oven and refrigerator—shiny silver invaders in Nonni's kitchen. Gone was her spice-jar wallpaper, replaced with stark white paint. The cupboards Opa had built had been ripped out, in favor of some steel-knobbed Plexiglas thing filled with stacks of black plates. Through the bedroom door I could see the bunk beds, the only thing still intact, with a bunch of houseplants filling the top bunk under a grow light. A Coke machine glowed against the wall. The undersea current in me rose.

Turning away, my foot hit the milk box. Inside was a note: "Please stop delivery until Friday." He was gone!

I made my way around the house: the porthole window of Opa's study revealed a wide-screen TV, a wet bar, and a stationary bike. The living room window exposed leather couches strewn with laundry, the mantel stripped bare where Nonni's Hummels used to sit. It was all changed—every room. How could there be any of her left here?

I tried every door and window. Nothing would budge until I got to the screened-in porch, where the door opened easily. I stepped inside and smelled the warm bricks. I remembered the wonder of sitting on them in a great pool of soapy water when I was five, scrubbing for Nonni like I was Cinderella. No one had told me chores weren't supposed to be fun.

It was one place the furniture had stayed: the glass-and-iron table with chairs, the chaise lounge, the wicker love seat. All had new cushions. I used to curl up with Nonni's old books out here while she sewed and Opa read the newspaper. The sea in me surged. I took a deep breath. Not now; it couldn't come now.

Off the porch two sets of French doors led into what used to be the dining room. I rattled the handles. Locked. Against the window three gray birds perched in gold cages. Parrots? The middle one ruffled its feathers and blinked at me. I turned just in time to see a woman come around the corner of the house and walk up the kitchen steps. It was Virginia Riley from next door. I ducked below the brick wall. "Chuck!" she called out, peering in the window. "Are you home?" She knocked: one-two-three-four-five. "Chuck! I'm here about the trash can situation." Knock-two-three-four-five. I stayed low. I wouldn't have wanted to be caught by Virginia Riley even if I was supposed to be here. After another series of knocks, I could see her writing a note, which she taped to the window half of the Dutch door. (Who carries tape around with them?)

Once she was definitely gone, I began breathing again. The wall and floor cradled me, and outside the porch screen a junco began its circular trill. In my pocket the vine-patterned fabric patch Kalimar had torn was smooth, comforting. Inside that bunk bed my stash of Nonni scraps might still be there. The bed had been Dad's; Aunt Julia might not have known about the secret panel when she purged the house of Nonni. The scraps would be proof that this was still Cherrywood, that Nonni and Opa had lived here, that I had been part of them, too.

Before I could move, a car pulled into the driveway and a guy got out. He looked about Mallory's age, skinny with an angular face. He put a key in the kitchen lock and went inside the house. I froze. If I tried to run, he'd see me. But if I stayed where I was, I'd be doomed anyway. I could hear him running water, padding from room to room. The steps came closer, and I knew there was only a wall between us. I could hear the birdcages opening and the rattle of pellets in the feeders. "He shoots—he scores!" said a voice too old to be the college kid's. "Time to party!" said another. "He shoots—he scores!" announced the first voice. The parrots, I realized.

Suddenly, I could see him coming toward the French doors. As fast as I could, I slid under the wicker love seat. I had to flatten myself completely to do it, and I was afraid I'd knock the love seat over. I pulled my feet under just in time. I could see his feet as he walked from plant to plant with what must have been a watering can. He got to the love seat and paused. Did he notice something unusual? I held my breath. Finally, he turned and walked back into the house.

I pulled myself out from under the love seat, scuttled to the screen door, and dashed for the woods. College Kid came down the kitchen steps just as I darted behind the sweet gum trees.

He was met in the driveway by Virginia Riley, who was nothing if not persistent. I could hear her explaining something about "Chuck putting his can where mine has always been" and the kid nodding, reaching for his car door. Suddenly Virginia peered out in my direction. Her head moved from left to right, surveying. She kept stopping mid-arc. Did she see me?

Her conversation was cut short by a burst of rain. It flooded down, not like Pacific Northwest rain, which drips and drizzles, allowing one to dodge the drops. This was serious rain, and even under my canopy of trees, I was getting wet. Virginia put her hand on her head and tapped the college kid. She pointed out into the woods. She began walking toward me. I yanked up my pack from the ground and ran, out of the trees, down the trail, back toward the creek. My hair was soaked, my jacket was soaked, and I hoped my pack would keep its water resistance.

I had not yet done what I needed to do. I was leaving empty-handed, running away unfinished. For now, I couldn't risk going near the house. I'd need to figure out where to sleep, where to get some food. I was home, but I was not home at all.

forty-five

I took the first bus that came because it was dry inside. It smelled of wet shoes and body odor. I managed to get a seat to myself and put my pack next to me. We passed the elementary school, the hospital, the Westfield Heritage Village, where I had loved to go with Opa. Once a boy got on who looked like Luke. When he turned I could see he looked nothing like him at all. We passed a movie theater with a *Rocket* poster in the window. Luke's angry face stared out at me, daring me to come near. I shut my eyes. The bus rolled on and on like a great ship. I dreamed I was falling overboard, into the sea below.

When I woke up the bus driver was standing over me—a large man with a speckled beard. "This is as far as I go," he said. "You'll have to get off the bus."

Outside it had stopped raining. The streets were wet. I was in a neighborhood. I walked past houses, a grade school, a church advertising "free lunch for our blessed poor." Kids with skateboards and balls and iPods gave me a wide berth. A woman looked up from her garden and scowled, then went back to work. I wondered if I looked frightening with my hair awry and the big pack on my back. Did she think I was going to steal her china?

I found a diner where a grandmotherly woman, with a name tag reading "Sophia," served me vegetable soup, along with several packets of crackers. She refilled my bowl twice, and I realized I probably looked like a street urchin. I left her a large tip and asked her if there was a place nearby with Wi-Fi, so I could look something up. She shook her head. "I don't know what you're talking about, honey, but there is a library. Go two blocks and turn left."

The library, fortunately, was open. And it had Wi-Fi. As soon as I opened my blog, the anger hit me like a searchlight beam. How hard would it have been for Luke to post, "RU OK?"

Like a slave to some sick addiction I clicked over to Trentwatch. Why did I miss him so much? He had lied to me, betrayed me. And roses or not, he obviously had more important people to be with than me.

There were new photos: two grainy shots of him with Gwen in the garden of his ranch house. In one she was kissing his cheek. In another, he was feeding her something. She was giggling and her breasts were spilling out of her top. Stupid me for even thinking he could care about a boring backwoods freak who hung out in a tree house.

As soon the thought came to me I was even more furious. Why couldn't he care about me? I wasn't giggling and jiggling and covered in makeup. I could even feed myself. I may not know any more French than I'd learned at Kwahnesum High School, but I had at least as much to offer as Gwendolyn Melier.

"I don't want to lose you," he'd said. What did he mean by that? That I should be okay sharing him with Gwen?

How could I believe anything he'd ever said? The last time I'd seen him he'd stood there calmly denying he was Trent. But I remembered how he'd traced my jaw with his fingertips, the resignation in his eyes as he'd walked away.

Schrödinger's cat was the kind of thing Devon would have rattling around in his brain. Maybe Luke was secretly Devon's most loyal friend. They had cooked this whole romance up together so that I could be utterly crushed and the lovelorn Devon could catch me on the rebound. But it hadn't worked.

I leaned back in the library chair and squeezed my eyes shut. Even my silly stories didn't make me laugh today. Near me, in the children's section, a librarian began reading *The Owl and the Pussycat* to a clump of preschoolers. Idly, I typed "Schrödinger's Cat Software" into Google.

The very first link was a company webpage—"Security Solutions for Here and Then…by Schrödinger's Cat." I sat up so noisily the librarian paused at "the land where the Bong-tree grows" and shook her head at me.

Hurriedly, I clicked to the site: up in the left-hand corner was the company name, along with its logo: a cat. What was familiar about that cat?

I reached into my pocket and pulled out Luke's note. The cat he'd drawn—a jagged black circle with triangle ears, slashes for eyes, a dot nose, and no mouth—the same as the one on the screen. My breath caught in my throat.

The U.S. Headquarters was in Paris, Illinois. *Paris?* I entered the address into Google Earth. I clicked "satellite" and moved the map closer and closer in. Not an office building, but a house. Trees. A pond. Something that might have been a stable with a corral outside it. It was what Luke had described.

Was he trying to tell me he was in Illinois? But he had to be in LA. Donna Reardon had said so. And there were pictures—taken by fake paparazzi who couldn't read a calendar? None of it made sense.

I put my head down on my arms. Every single thing in my life was in suspended animation: Natalie, Nonni, Luke. If I had even a remote chance of seeing Luke one more time, I had to take it. I couldn't leave it all unfinished. I lifted my head. What did I have to lose?

I printed a map on the library printer and got a bus to the Greyhound station. It was nearly fifty dollars to buy a ticket, but I didn't even think about it. After Sophia's soup I wouldn't need to eat for a while. And I wouldn't be eating because I was saving the rest for cab fare.

I settled against the bus seat and let the highway fly by. I thought I was calm, but for some reason my inward sea was leaking silently out my eyes. It seemed a normal condition, as if I'd been crying for years. I passed a bandana over my face, but it just got wet again.

Kalimar and Felix romped through my imagination. Nonni and Opa sailed by together on Opa's rider mower. I ran my finger over Luke's words: "Forgive me. I never meant to hurt you." I had buried him with his carvings in that hole in the grove. Why was I on my way to Illinois?

It was three hours later when the cab driver pulled up in front of the address I had given him. Once I paid him, I had four dollars and four-teen cents. A long driveway arced up to a rambling colonial whose roof was obscured by oak trees. To the right a horse barn was surrounded by a white rail fence, to the left a pond with weeping willows drooping over it. Several other buildings dotted the property. A carriage house? Who knew? I felt like I was walking into a Jane Austen book. The sun was setting over the pond, and the sky was rosy orange.

At the door I hesitated. What was I thinking? What would I say? What if I had this completely and inescapably wrong? But every time I had stood on Luke's doorstep, I had wussed out before knocking on the door. This time I would knock, even if I wussed out afterward. I could always run.

A man came to the door. He was tall and sandy haired and had blue, blue eyes. When he saw me he narrowed the opening of the door. "Yes?" he said.

My mouth went dry. "I'm looking for, um…Michael."

"Who are you?" he said. He had a French accent.

My head felt light. I wondered if I would pass out. "Brigitta," I managed.

He stood for a moment, staring at me. Then he opened the door wider. "Follow me," he said.

The entryway was light and airy. A spiral staircase swept up to the left. A crystal chandelier hung down where the stairs curved. To the right was a sitting room with red velvet furniture and a fireplace.

"Michel-Luc!" the man called up the stairs. *"Viens ici!"*

Michel-Luc? Michael Luke?

Then he was there on the landing, pounding down the stairs until he stood in front of me. "Brigitta!" He ran a hand through his hair. His voice sounded different. "I'm…oh, wow…Brigitta."

He threw his arms around me, and I hung on, crushed against his chest. I didn't want him to let go.

He held me away from him, finally, to get a look at me. "How did you get here?"

That strange voice again. It was a British accent. He'd had it in *Imlandria* and on *Letterman*. Trent and Luke crashed together in my brain.

"It's a long story."

His face was close to mine. His long lashes—Trent's lashes, his mouth—Trent's mouth. "The kittens!" I wanted to wail. But not to Trent Yves.

Luke's dad cleared his throat.

"Oh," said Luke. "Papa, this is Brigitta Schopenhauer, the girl I told you about. Brigitta, this is my dad, Valéry Boeglin."

"Enchanté," said Valéry. His eyes took in my pack, my disheveled hair. "You are a long way from home."

"Yes." I stared at my feet. A longer way than I had even realized.

"You are not with your parents."

"No."

"We will have to call them, Brigitta. Right now we will have to call them."

It was Mallory who answered the phone. "Gita!" she said. "Dear God, where are you?"

"Um, Illinois."

"Where? Are you okay? Has someone got you?"

I felt the blood drain out of my face. I'd never considered that they might think I was kidnapped. "No," I said. "I came on my own."

"Dad's on his way to Indiana."

"He is?"

"We traced you through your debit card. Only I was praying it was really you who made plane reservations and not that you were…Oh, God, Brigitta! What were you thinking?"

"You were praying?"

"Are you kidding? I even looked up the Hail Mary. Where exactly are you?"

"Can I talk to Mom?"

"Mom's out with the Shapiros and the Thompsons and Clyde Redd and Rainbow and Tarah. They found your bike in the woods, and they're doing another search."

"A search?"

From the stairs where he was sitting, Luke raised his eyebrows.

"Yes, a search. We've had the police out here. Everyone. I'd kill you if I wasn't so glad to hear from you."

By the time I was done and had talked to Mom on her cell phone (she was sobbing) and Valéry had given them the address and the phone numbers and offered to send a driver to the Indianapolis airport, I was exhausted.

Luke stood and took a few steps toward me, but his dad steered him into the study and then showed me to a second-floor guest room.

Once he went back downstairs, I could hear raised voices in French. I strained for my name. Was I only causing him more problems?

The attached bathroom was enormous with steps going up to a sunken tub that looked out over the dark pasture and pond. The trees looked like Japanese shadow puppets out there. I sank into the water and let myself float with my hair drifting out behind me. Over the tub a marble statue of a woman in Greek robes looked down at me. "What are you doing here?" she seemed to say.

When I was finished I put on a clean T-shirt and my spare pair of jeans. I wasn't sure whether I was supposed to go to sleep. It was nearly 10:00, but my mind was racing. Dad would be here by morning. Police had been looking for me. And then there was Luke: as glad as he seemed to see me, he was still Trent—a stranger who had come out of a television set. And I didn't even want to think about Gwen.

I trailed my hand along the window drape and the doors of an antique wardrobe. On the wall was a framed photo of a small Luke, maybe seven years old, sword fighting with Johnny Depp. Who are you? I asked the picture.

I nearly jumped out of my skin when I heard a tapping sound from behind the drape. I heard it again. Cautiously, I approached the window and pulled the drape back. Luke was perched in the branches of a sycamore just outside. He put his finger to his lips.

chapter forty-six

I opened the window and Luke reached out his hand. My mind flashed to the clothing rope he'd climbed down with Randi Marchietti on *Presto!* (Had he really gotten her pregnant?) I climbed out anyway, too weak-willed to resist his slow smile.

He guided me from branch to branch without a word. Once we reached the grass, he cocked his head in the direction of the pond. We walked there silently, not touching. The moonlight reflected off the water. The night was warm. Luke stepped around a wooden Adirondack chair and ducked under a weeping willow. I followed him in, the branches creating a curtained canopy over our heads.

Luke slid his hands around my waist and gazed at me. "I can't believe you're here," he said in that same out-of-place accent.

"I can't believe you're Trent Yves." I hadn't planned on saying that right off.

Luke lowered his head. He took a breath and let it out. Then he met my eyes. "Does it bother you?"

I took a step back from him. "You lied to me!"

He released me. "I did," he said quietly. The moonlight through the willow leaves made patterns on his face, his hair going dark and light.

"I don't want you to be Trent Yves."

"I know." Luke put his hands in his pockets and looked out at the water. His mouth was the same mouth I had loved, his chin the same chin. And it was the same face a million other girls had fallen in love with, taped in their lockers, used as a screensaver.

"How can I believe anything you say? You made promises to me. I counted on you. You said you'd be there." I took a ragged breath. "And then you come back with the excuse that *something suddenly came up*? Do you have any idea how lame that is?"

Luke turned slowly away from me, resting his hands on the wood of the Adirondack chair. He'd been with Gwen. The realization burned a hole in my hopes. He'd been with Gwen that day, and now he couldn't face me.

"I'm talking to you!" I shouted at his back. "For once you're going to stay and listen—not take off for Aruba or LA or wherever it is you go when I get boring."

He didn't move.

"You left, and they killed them. They killed the kittens, Luke. They're dead. And maybe it didn't mean anything to you, but it sure did to me."

His shoulders tightened. He didn't answer.

I pictured him with Gwen, her bikinied body wrapped around him by his pool. That had to be a lot more interesting than wildlife. "But why should you care?" I spat. "You've got important things to do. Why would you care about a couple of cats and some hippie-freak girl in a tree?"

He rounded on me. "Don't tell me what I do and do not care about!" His muscles were taut, his hands in fists.

I stood my ground. "It's obvious what you care about. Read your press, *Trent*."

He winced.

I barreled ahead. "You care about being beautiful. You care about being seen. You care about hooking up with the latest *Celeb'* poster girl—especially if she's got more boobs than brains!"

"You don't know anything about my life, Brigitta!" He had fire in his eyes.

"Well, you've got that right! Stupid me for thinking I knew you! Stupid me for trusting you! Stupid me for waiting when you said you'd be back. But you were never really there to begin with, were you, *Trent*?"

His face darkened. "Well, maybe I wasn't!" he shouted. "You want to know where I was? I was in New York, watching my mother get drunk in the green room in front of Cher. I was in LA, losing yet another role. I was at home, paying for my lack of talent by having to fight my mother for a bottle of painkillers. I wish I could save everyone's life, Brigitta. But this month I could only save one." He sagged against the trunk of the willow. "And don't call me Trent."

I was rooted to the ground. "Your mother tried to kill herself?"

He nodded.

"Where is she now?"

"Betty Ford." He slid to the base of the willow.

"Is she going to be okay?"

He shrugged. "She's alive."

All the gossip mag talk about Wendy Burke—plus the vague bits Luke had actually shared with me—and I'd been too preoccupied with my own sorrows to give a care.

I sat down beside him. "I'm sorry." I put my hand on his back. "I didn't know."

His shoulders relaxed. "Well, I don't exactly make it easy," he said to the ground. We sat for a while, listening to each other breathe. He let me pull his head into my lap. I ran my fingers through his hair and found the bird-beak scar behind his ear. "How did you do this?"

"*Laser Boy.* Pyrotechnics got a little out of hand. Nearly burned my hair off." He sat up. "Brigitta, you don't need to worry about me. I'll be all right."

I still wasn't used to his accent. "I'm sorry I called you Trent."

He flashed me an ironic smile.

I drew my knees up. "I don't know what to call you," I whispered. "You don't sound like Luke anymore."

He bowed his head, running his palms down his thighs. "This is how I talk," he said quietly. "But I won't if it…if it upsets you. I'll go back to American."

I opened my mouth to answer and found that tears were sliding down my face again.

"Hey," said Luke. "Hey. Shh." He wrapped his arms around me, and I let him rock me and rub my shoulders. Here he was taking care of me again, when maybe he was the one who needed taking care of. He put his chin on my hair, and we were back where we had started: hanging onto each other for dear life under a tree. Only now there were a few things about his life I'd rather not have known. He bent his head to kiss me, but I stopped him. "Why didn't you tell me who you were?"

Luke sighed and leaned back against the willow. "You were the only one…who didn't know."

My stomach tightened. "Am I that clueless?"

"No! That's not what I mean. And it's not a lie. I'm not him. I'm not Trent."

"Except when you're sword fighting on a moving horse."

He smiled. "Well, then I'm Felix."

I took a breath. "How about when you're kissing Gwen Melier?"

Luke looked me in the face. "Brigitta, I don't want you to worry about Gwen."

I drew circles in the dirt with my finger.

He put his hand on my knee. "I don't kiss her unless a camera's rolling."

I closed my eyes for a moment. My stomach hurt. "Luke, I've seen pictures."

He nodded. "Trentwatch, Perez Hilton, Celebitchy, and I think *National Enquirer*'s got a few. I try not to look, but Kenny, my manager, keeps sending them to me."

"Then what—?"

"They're not me, Brigitta."

"Like Trent's not you. Yeah, I get that, but if you think I'm willing to—"

"No. I mean it's really not me."

I raised my eyebrows in a question.

"Brigitta, you can't go to the press about this."

"You don't think I'd do that."

"Okay," said Luke. "His name is Bryan Kohler. We hired him as a decoy during the second season of *Presto!*"

I remembered how blurry some of the photos had been. And in the Trentmobile footage, there was only a flash of him before he'd pulled Gwen into the backseat.

"We can't send him out in public except in the car—and it's got tinted windows. He's pretty much holed up at my ranch right now. But the paparazzi'll come by the house in trucks with the cameras on these big turret things so they can shoot over the fence. It's crazy. They can never get a very good shot from that far away, but it's enough to keep the gossips in business."

"So he's kissing Gwen."

"She likes him. They got acquainted during *Imlandria*. And it helps her press to be seen with Trent. It's a win-win."

"Unless somebody finds out."

"Right," said Luke significantly.

"Was that him doing a striptease on *Letterman?*"

"That," said Luke, "was Trent."

"Luke, it's obnoxious when you do stuff like that. Stripping on *Letterman?* Telling that reporter you couldn't believe she could keep her hands off you?"

"Trent is a role I play."

"Then who are you?"

Luke stared at a floating log. "Did you see *Rocket*?"

"Yes," I admitted.

He shifted his gaze to the Adirondack chair, but he didn't continue.

I remembered that scene—the one he wouldn't talk about in interviews—where Theo died and Rocket went crazy and beat up his dad. And when he'd broken down sobbing I'd been bothered by how much it affected me.

I touched his arm lightly. "Was that you? Rocket? When Theo was shot?"

"I've never cried well on camera. But that time…" He trailed off.

"I believed you," I said. "And it scared me."

"Yeah," he said. "It scared me, too."

"Do you still hate your dad?"

He looked at me sharply. "You could tell?"

"You beat up Christopher Walken."

Luke ran his hands through his hair. "You know, I really hurt Chris. He had bruises afterward." He stared at the chair again, avoiding my eyes. "They had to pull me off him," he said, so quietly I almost couldn't hear him.

I didn't say anything, and finally he went on. "I won an award for that film," he said. "And there may be more coming. But there's something kind of wrong with that. Because it was just me, going crazy."

I squeezed his shoulder. "You're not crazy."

He laughed. "I'm glad you're here, Brigitta." I finally let him kiss me.

I leaned my head against his chest. A swarm of cicadas started their chorus.

"You know, I did try to save them," he said finally. "Felix and Kalimar. As soon as I saw your blog, I called Kenny. I wanted to get on Twitter and make some kind of a plea, but Kenny's got somebody else doing all my tweets, and he wouldn't pass on the message. He said it would backfire on us and create bad press. So I got on the phone and called Cedar Haven myself. I offered them a bunch of money, even."

"You did?"

"Yeah. But it was too late. They'd already done it." He was quiet. "Those cats were…otherworldly. Every time I held one it seemed like they could transport me somewhere. That night I sat up with them and carved, it was like they'd taken me Where the Wild Things Are." He laughed wonderingly.

I raised my head. "You too?"

He nodded. "Maybe that's where they are now, Brigitta."

I leaned my head back. Through the willow leaves I could see constellations. "I hope so."

Luke pulled me to my feet. We walked the edge of the pond as the moon rose, spotting frogs and a raccoon. Somehow it seemed that Felix and Kalimar were following right behind.

Out in the open field we lay on our backs, staring up at the Milky Way. I showed him the three brightest stars in the summer sky: Vega, Altair, and Deneb.

Luke rolled onto his side. "What were you doing in Indiana, Brigitta?"

"Cherrywood. I went back there."

"Yeah?"

I told him about circling the house and about almost getting caught. "All I want to do is go in there and walk through the rooms. Just once. I need to find whatever it was I lost there. It's like an angel with a flaming sword is barring the gate to Eden."

Luke sat up. "We could go."

"Go where?"

"To your Eden. To Cherrywood. You said the guy was going to be gone until Friday, right?"

"Yes, but I want to go inside the house."

"Brigitta, you know when I did *Rocket,* I did all kinds of research. They got me an interview with a class two felon. He taught me how to break into a house."

"You can't be serious." My heart was beating fast.

"We can do it with a credit card. We wouldn't damage or touch anything. And if all you want to do is walk around in there, I don't see what harm it would do. The guy's not even there."

It was crazy. And Dad would be coming here with a driver in a few hours.

"That is nuts," I said.

"Well," said Luke, "maybe that's who I really am."

chapter forty-seven

We made it to Cherrywood in half the time it had taken me by bus and cab. Luke parked his dad's car two blocks away, and we approached on foot. The house was dark, with not even a porch light. We went around to the back, and Luke slid his debit card out of his wallet. In the moonlight I could make out the name "Michael L. Boeglin." What would I have done if I'd read his real name on that card in Westport? Should I have looked then?

Luke put his hand on the door. He had done this in *Rocket*, only Rocket had been breaking into his own house. Now he was breaking into mine.

"Is this really going to work?" I whispered.

"Watch," he whispered back. He worked the card between the door and the frame and pushed. We were in!

Luke smiled at me in the dark and took my hand. "Here we go," he mouthed.

The garage smelled of grass clippings and gasoline. It made me think Opa was still in the house, dreaming of going out on his rider mower. We crept into the basement where Nonni used to hang clothes up on a line—even after she had a working dryer. The woodworking projects Opa had given me were gone, cleared out by Aunt Julia. All of them must have gone into the Dumpster.

We climbed the stairs cautiously, even though there was no one in the house. We emerged into the alien kitchen. Luke opened a window.

"Escape route," he mouthed. He crept to the living room and opened another one.

I paused by the stove, breathing in, trying to find Nonni's presence. I shook my head and walked toward the hallway. Opa's study was gone! The entryway, study, and living room had been opened into an enormous "entertainment area" with a pool table. There was no chance of sensing Nonni here.

But the bunk room! The scraps could still be there inside the secret panel. I took two steps and realized: the window in that room looked out on Virginia Riley's house. I'd have to work up my courage.

I led Luke to the attic where I used to play with Aunt Julia's old dollhouse, built by Opa. Once I'd found Opa's old love letters to Nonni in a trunk up here. "And now my love," he'd written, "I must to bed, kiss your picture, and go to sleep to dream only of you." Finding them hilarious, I'd taken them downstairs to read aloud to Nonni and Opa. Opa was not amused. The trunk was gone—at Aunt Julia's I supposed—and now the attic was crammed with boxes, a telescope, an artificial Christmas tree. Luke saw my face and took me to the window. "Look," he whispered. It was the same moon, the same woods that had always been here. But the attic was empty of Nonni.

We stole back down to the awful living room. Where was she? I felt panicky. Luke put a steadying hand on my back. I led him to the French doors. Out on the porch we'd be able to hear the cicadas and be draped in the warm air. I had forgotten about the parrots. The first one woke immediately. "He shoots—he scores!" it said. Another one woke. "Nevermore!" it croaked.

"At least the owner's got a sense of humor," said Luke.

"Shh!"

"Don't worry," said Luke. "The house is empty, right? No car in the garage. He's gone."

That was when we heard footsteps. "Who's there!" called a voice.

Lights were switched on in the hallway, in the living room. Luke pushed me ahead of him into the kitchen. Out to the window. The drop was fifteen feet. I balked. "I'll go then," whispered Luke. "And I can help you down."

He was hanging by his hands when the man appeared and flipped on the kitchen light. The man wore nothing but a green bathrobe. A fireplace poker was clutched in his fist. He stepped between me and the window. "What the hell are you doing?" he snarled.

I couldn't speak. The man took a step toward me. "Who are you?" he yelled. "Don't you move. You stay right there."

I couldn't have moved if I'd tried.

And then behind him, Luke hoisted himself back up through the window and climbed inside. The man whirled around with the poker, narrowly missing Luke's head. "We can explain," Luke said.

"Well, you damn sure better start now."

In the next room, one of the parrots said, "Fourscore and seven years ago!"

The man stared from one of us to the other, clinging more tightly to his poker. His eyes darted around, as if looking for the phone, but he stayed planted where he was. "What did you steal?" he barked. "Give it here, now!"

"I didn't steal anything!" I was shaking. "This is my house! You're in my house!"

"What the hell are you talking about?"

"Brigitta," said Luke in a warning tone.

I kept going. "It is my house. I didn't want to steal anything. I just wanted to be here."

The man lowered his poker a few inches, making sure he kept Luke in his line of sight as well as me.

"Who are you?"

"I'm Brigitta Schopenhauer. My dad sold you this house, but it was

a mistake. It was never supposed to be sold. I even left something here."
If it was still here.

Now he was eying me warily as if I might suddenly start tearing his hair and my own out in clumps.

"What did you leave?" he said.

"It's in the bunk room. In the secret compartment above the bed."

"What secret compartment?"

"I'll show you." I prayed Aunt Julia hadn't discovered it.

He made us go ahead of him into the bunk room so he could brandish his poker in our wake. This room was largely unchanged, except for the pop machine and the plants. The man's covers lay askew on the lower bunk. On the dresser was a picture of a young red-haired woman. His daughter?

I went to the bunk bed, and Luke moved carefully between me and the man. I pushed up the panel and put my hand inside the compartment. I came out with fabric scraps: red polka dots, plain navy blue, small purple flowers, green plaid.

"What's this?" the man said. "Have I got mice?"

"They're my grandmother's. She made me this coat." I took it off and held it out to him. Onawa's claw marks were fraying now.

He looked at the coat and at the scraps on the bed. "I'm calling the cops," he said.

And then the phone began to ring. "Is this a setup?" he challenged.

I shook my head.

The phone rang a second time, a third, a fourth. He picked it up. "Yes?" he listened. "Yes, who is this?" He narrowed his eyes at me. "Your daughter?" He shook his head. "Yes. Well, you'd better come get her." He hung up. "This is ridiculous." He punched three numbers into the phone and waited. "A burglary," he said. "In progress."

The man herded Luke and me to the couch and stood over us with his poker. In his other hand, he had the phone on speaker, the police dispatcher still on the line. Luke held my hand, his face white as beach sand. What would this do to him, if they found out who he was?

Dad arrived first. The man went to the door, never turning his back on us. When he saw Dad, he visibly relaxed. "Schopenhauer," he said, opening the door. "It is you."

"Chuck," said Dad. "Brigitta!" Dad ran to me. "Oh, thank God!"

Chuck set the poker back by the fireplace. "So this really is your daughter."

Dad held me so tight, I could hardly breathe. Luke sat with his hands in his lap, the color just beginning to come back into his face.

Dad let me go and put his hands on my shoulders. "Why would you do this, Brigitta? What a foolish, foolish thing to do." He looked at Luke. "And I'm not even ready to get started on you," he said.

"Mr. Schopenhauer, I'm—"

I moved out from under Dad's grasp and interrupted. Chuck sat down in an armchair and stared at us. I didn't care. "This was my place," I said to Dad. "My real place. Cherrywood. With Nonni and Opa. It was where I came to—to be me. Where there were no people running around with drums and no eco-workshops and no pounding dirt into tires. When I was here I belonged. Someone knew me. They had time for me. And you sold it! You sold Cherrywood! So that you could build your dream. No one even asked me about mine."

"Brigitta," Dad began, "things change. They died, honey. Nonni and Opa died."

"I know they died! Do you think I don't know that? And if it hadn't been so important to you to prove how brainless they were, then maybe we could all miss them!"

"Honey, Brigitta, I don't understand what you're saying."

"You were all freethinking then, and now you're all spiritually evolved and non-Eurocentric. But you never had any room for them. You were too busy being mad at them all your life. And they loved me! They really loved me! And I'm your daughter!" I couldn't stop crying.

Dad opened his arms. I walked into them. "Oh, love," he said. "I'm sorry. I'm so sorry." He was crying, too.

He held me tight. He smelled of wood smoke and cedar boughs. Once when I was very small I had gotten my foot wedged in the branches of a fallen pine at the edge of our property. I'd been stuck there nearly an hour before a frantic Dad had swooped in, freed my foot, and wrapped me in his arms, just like now. "I've found you!" I remember crying then. "Daddy, I've found you!"

chapter forty-eight

I had imagined my mug shot next to Luke's in the *Indianapolis Star*, but miraculously, Chuck Polzin did not press charges. Valéry, Luke's father, invited Dad and me to stay at his house for a few days until his pilot could fly us home—which, on a cosmic level, was really outrageous, considering what I, as a near-felon, deserved.

Dad was quiet—out of place in a house like this. Luke's dad showed him his art collection and gave him a book on the cave paintings of Lascaux. Gradually Dad began to relax.

It didn't seem to be going as easily for Luke, who would emerge sad but determined from Valéry's study, following regular bouts of shouting in French.

"Am I adding to your problems by being here?" I asked him after Luke had given me my third riding lesson on his horse, Olivier.

"It's not you, Brigitta. Papa's just making up for lost time." Luke ran a currycomb over his horse, Charlot. Both horses were Arabians—Olivier, pearl white, Charlot, the color of rich earth. "Watch his feet." Luke guided me to the safer end of the horse, and I picked up another comb. Charlot nosed Luke's pockets and came up with a hidden apple.

I ran the comb through Charlot's sleek hair. "Can you really sword fight on horseback, or was that a stunt double?"

"Hey, I'm hurt. Of course it was me. That's my trademark."

"But you're not going to show me in the arena?"

Luke combed Charlot's neck and moved closer. "The horses are tired," he said. He plucked the comb from my hand. "Besides," he whispered, "who would I fight?" He turned me around and wove his fingers through mine, pressing me against Charlot's shoulder. "I don't want to fight with you, Brigitta." His mouth swooped down on mine—a perfect capture. I reached up to touch his hair. Charlot swung his head. My feet came out from under me, landing me on my butt in the straw. Luke reached his hand down, laughing. "Are you okay?"

I took his hand, remembering how I'd refused it in the arcade. I'm sure I was a lovely shade of rose. I dusted myself off and tossed the currycombs into their bucket. "How about a Trent Yves film festival? I'll watch the movies, you do the commentary."

Luke looked surprised. "You sure? I thought you didn't like Trent."

I touched his cheek. "He's growing on me."

It took hours. We watched *Rocket*, *Le Petit Chose* (subtitled), *Imlandria*, *Sparrowtree*, and even *Spookville*.

"What about your first one? Wasn't it called *A Capella*?" I asked him as we did the dinner dishes. Dad and Valéry had cooked moussaka with lots of mushrooms and were now out drinking wine on the screened-in porch.

Luke handed me a plate to load. (Somehow it delighted me that he did his own dishes.) "I can't watch that one."

"Why?"

"Have you seen it?" He rinsed out four tumblers before setting them in the top rack. I bit my tongue to keep from chiding him about overuse of water.

"No. Weren't you about five?"

Luke nodded. "We were still in England then. It was about a priest who molests choirboys. I was the choirboy."

I blanched. "Do you mean they…I mean, how did they set that up?"

Luke chuckled at my horrified expression. "Well, nobody molested me if that's what you're asking. But they had to scare me enough to make me scream with terror."

"How?" I dropped the forks into the basket one by one.

Luke shook his head. "I can't believe I'm telling you this."

"You don't have to."

Luke grinned. "I think you're entitled to my private childhood nightmares."

I stuck the platter into the dishwasher.

Luke pulled it out again, scrubbed it within an inch of its life, and stuck it back in.

"Well, Alan Markham was the priest. I liked him when we started filming. He played with me, told me jokes. But they had to make me not trust him for the last half. So they shot this scene in a dark chapel—only enough light for the shot—stood me in the aisle, alone, and had him climb in a window wearing a clown mask. They got their terror." Luke closed the dishwasher.

I put my hand on his. "They didn't really do that! To a little kid?"

He lifted my hand up and kissed it. "Trust me, it gets worse." He began drying the counter, wiping under a bowl of pomegranates. "The film was released, and we began getting all these phone calls. Private number, you know, with someone just laughing. After the first one, Mum wouldn't let me near the phone. And then we're at a petrol station one day, and this guy in a clown mask sticks his face through the open car window. He knew who I was. I mean, he called me Michael. It completely panicked Mum."

"Didn't it completely panic you?"

Luke took a pomegranate, split it, and gave half to me. "Well, yeah." He put his foot on the rung of a stool and popped some red seeds out onto a spoon. "After we moved to LA, Mum never called me anything but Trent in public. She even tried to get my real name taken off IMDB—like you can do that! She started to build a fence around our identity. She made sure Papa kept this place hidden—which suited him fine—and for a while we even kept our place in Malibu under wraps. That didn't last long. It's impossible to do that in California."

I fingered my pomegranate. "I guess it would be, when you're so well-known."

Luke set his fruit down. "I'm not well-known, Brigitta."

"I don't know what you call eight million Google results."

He spun his spoon around on the countertop. "I call it fame."

I must have looked puzzled.

"Think about it." He gave the spoon another twirl. "Why do people pay for entertainment? Because they believe that's not a real human on the screen. Nobody wants to watch someone ordinary. So the industry takes ordinary people and decorates us. It makes us more than we really are."

"But you're an amazing actor." I burst some seeds open on my tongue.

"Sure I am. And you're an amazing violinist. What's the difference? Talent doesn't give either one of us superpowers."

"My dad says Hollywood is like the modern version of the Greek gods."

"He's spot-on, Brigitta. But I don't want to be anybody's god." He paused. "It's not the same as being known."

I thought of the little boy in the picture, crossing swords with Johnny Depp. I thought of him even younger, standing in a dark chapel. I stopped his spoon spinning. "Thank you for your nightmares."

This time I kissed him.

At Cherrywood, there was a crack in the front step that Opa never got around to fixing. I poked it with my foot as Dad rang the bell and waited for Chuck Polzin.

Dad had rented a car to make the drive back here. I knew what I was supposed to do—make a sincere and abject apology. And I had fully intended to deliver it, had mentally rehearsed it all the way here. But I wasn't sorry. How could I be sorry for trying to reclaim what was mine?

Chuck appeared with a pitcher of iced tea in one hand and ushered us onto the screened-in porch. Dad steered me as if I didn't know the way there.

A swallowtail butterfly clung to the screen, its dark blue wings dotted with orange. The yellow paint on the screen frames had been peeling at least five years.

Chuck set the pitcher on the glass tabletop. "Cookies?" He offered a box of flat, factory-baked gingersnaps.

I shook my head. I should feel bad that he was trying to be nice after what I'd done.

Dad pulled out one of the wrought iron chairs and took a few cookies. "Chuck, I'm sure this is an inconvenience," he began.

Obviously, my cue. I stayed standing, tracing the curlicues on the back of my chair. On the road, Dad had tried for the conversation we hadn't had at Luke's. I was so unused to him trying to talk to me—a thing we hadn't done much since he stopped driving me to Youth

Symphony. I couldn't think of anything to say. Instead I had found the classical radio station, and we'd listened to a Metropolitan Opera broadcast of *The Magic Flute.*

Now that I was actually standing here in Nonni and Opa's screened-in porch, I had a tidal wave of thoughts, but no way to say them.

Chuck poured some iced tea into my glass, even though I hadn't asked for any. "It's no inconvenience, Paul."

I moved to the brick sill where the screen attached and perched there awkwardly, with my backpack in my lap. No one said anything.

Opa's chaise lounge sat empty in the corner of the porch. He used to smoke a pipe out here in the evenings, until Nonni persuaded him to quit. Why could I bear it that Opa was gone? I loved Opa.

But Nonni had known the inside of me—sometimes before I even understood myself. And when Opa died, Nonni had told me where he was: he was dancing on the walls of heaven. I'd been so angry when she said that, but by saying it she'd offered me a map.

I had no map to her.

Dad had avoided this porch when we'd been here after Nonni's stroke. Did he remember the last time he'd been out here—how he'd shattered Nonni's heaven and stormed off into the night? Had he heard her crying?

I stood. "I need to, uh…"

Chuck gestured. "Down the hall and to the left."

"Yeah," I said. "I know." I escaped into the house.

I wandered through the living room with its interloper furniture, the former study with its pool table, the kitchen, stripped of Nonni's plates and kettles. She ought to be just through the next doorway—maybe ironing or at her sewing machine.

I heard the front door close and the slam of a car trunk. Dad? He'd better not try to drag me out of here now.

The bedroom Nonni had shared with Opa was a bathroom now.

I opened her ironing closet and found three vending machines—two for coffee and one for temporary tattoos. I slid down the wall to the carpet and put my head between my knees. How could she not be here? This was her place. There couldn't be a Cherrywood without Nonni. Couldn't she have haunted it, just long enough to say good-bye?

"Brigitta?" I looked up.

Dad was standing at the end of the hall. He opened his mouth as if he was about to say something, but instead held out his hand to me.

"We're not leaving already!" I stayed rooted to the floor.

Dad shook his head. "Chuck thought you might want to walk in the woods."

I brushed myself off and shouldered my pack. Maybe I wasn't expected to apologize. The thought filled me with relief. I followed Dad through the kitchen, out the back door, past the rail fence, straight to the line of sweet gum trees. Dad slipped between them and disappeared into the secret grove—*my* secret grove.

I stumbled momentarily, surprised to be surprised. Dad grew up here—why wouldn't he know about the grove? Wordlessly, I followed him in.

Sun filtered through the beech branches, dappling the ground. The smell of warm soil and sweet gum leaves rose up to meet me.

"This was my hideout," said Dad. "Back when I was ten or twelve. I'd forgotten about it."

"Yours?"

Dad nodded. "Once I discovered skateboarding I had no interest in the woods until I was about twenty." He settled himself between the roots of an oak tree.

I sat back on a pile of leaves, laying my pack beside me. "I cannot imagine you having no interest in the woods."

"Imagine it," he said. A vireo landed just above his head and gave a *seewee, seewit* before flitting away.

Unwittingly, my hand reached out to stroke the smooth circle of earth where I had buried Felix's and Kalimar's carved faces. Dad leaned his head back against the oak trunk. For the first time I noticed gray hair at his temples. For a moment, he looked like Opa.

"Why were you so mad at them?" I said.

Dad blew air out his cheeks. "I thought they'd taught me to believe a fantasy," he said. "And they were so…panicked all the time that I'd stopped believing in the fantasy and that meant the fantasy God was going to torture me for all eternity."

I gathered a few spiny sweet gum pods into my lap. "I don't remember them being panicked."

Dad raised his eyebrows wryly.

I lobbed one of the pods at the nearest tree trunk. "And I don't remember Nonni mentioning torture."

Dad didn't answer.

An ant crawled onto my knee. I let it climb onto an oak leaf and gave it a ride to the ground. My stomach was starting to hurt again. I pulled my pack into my lap and hugged it. "Do you still think God is a fantasy?"

Dad shook his head. "A shaman could hardly say that."

"Then why does it always feel like we're in a war over it?"

"A war?" Dad sat up. "Who says there's a war?"

"What if I ended up a Christian?" I shot at him.

"Well…" Dad shifted uncomfortably, as if I'd said, "What if I dumped toxic waste into the Olympic rain forest?"

"See?" I pushed harder. "But I like Nonni's Jesus. I talk to him every day." This wasn't strictly true.

Dad plucked a cardinal feather from the dirt beside him. "Well," he said slowly, "there's a lot to like."

I looked up, startled to hear him say this. It drained the fight out of me.

I traced the veins on my oak leaf and didn't look at him. "The thing is," I said, "when I'm in the woods, the animals talk to me." I glanced at him sideways. "At least they used to. Sometimes I feel like I'm right on the threshold of...somewhere else."

Dad leaned over and put the feather in my palm. "Maybe you are." He closed my fingers around it.

"But it doesn't matter." My voice was ragged. "Because I can't get there!" I brought up the fist with the feather in it and pressed it hard against my mouth. "I keep looking for her, and I can't find her!"

Dad wrapped me up in his arms. "I know," he said. "I know."

My shoulders were shaking again. It seemed like all I'd done since I got to Indiana was cry. I guess I was making up for lost time.

Finally, Dad let go of me. He stood and leaned around the back of the oak tree. He emerged with his hands full: my violin in his left, his flute in his right. He set the violin case in my lap.

I started to cry again. I leaned my cheek on the smooth leather and sobbed as Dad opened up his flute case and fit the pieces together. He played a tuning scale and then cupped my face with his hand. "Come on, Gidget." His voice cracked. "You know what to do."

We hit the *Pleni* straight on and wove around each other and on into the *Benedictus.* My bow remembered everything—even with so long away from the piece. A breeze swept through the trees, bringing the scent of honeysuckle. I had never heard Dad play with such power. He soared into the *Agnus Dei,* and I echoed him, our notes floating back and forth to the final phrase: *Dona nobis pacem*—Give us peace, give us peace, give us peace.

Dad's face was wet when we played the last notes. He gazed up through the trees for a long moment and then back at me. He put his hand on my shoulder. "I think they heard," he whispered.

chapter
fifty

Dad lifted the leather pouch from around his neck—his medicine bag. He took out a small frame and tapped clinging bits of tobacco back into the bag. He opened the frame. In each side was a picture. One of Opa, one of Nonni. He slid the Nonni photo out and laid it on my palm. Nonni smiled up at me—her brown eyes gazing through her glasses, her halo of white hair. Dad kissed my forehead and closed his flute back in its case. He climbed up the bowl-shaped ground and left me alone.

I drew my knees up and cupped the picture in my hands. I listened to my own breathing, to the squirrels chittering on the rail fence, to the rustle of rabbits. After a long while I unfolded myself.

I rummaged around in my pack until I found the candle stub and matches. I propped Nonni's picture on the sweet gum root, weighting it with the feather. I pushed the candle into the soil in front of it and lit the wick. "Nonni." I said her name into the air. "Where are you?" I took a breath. "Why didn't you tell me you were leaving? I'd have stayed with you. I'd have fed you ice cream. I'd have helped you get dressed. You know I would."

The smell of beeswax drifted up. "We could have walked through the woods one more time. We could have picked raspberries. I'd have brought you into the grove. We could have looked for cardinals."

Without thinking, I moved onto my knees. "Where did you go?" I said. "You talked about heaven, but I don't know where heaven is. And I've been searching and searching."

A zephyr set the oak leaves fluttering. The flame cast light on Nonni's face. For a moment it was as if I was the picture, and she was looking at me. Her eyes held me. The earth cradled me. And the air was filled with wings.

Suddenly, I was transparent, stretched thin like a veil. And Nonni and I were connected to roots and rocks and every constellation. And surging through me was something greater still—an energy that filled up every seed and leaf and also sang my name.

I don't know how long I was there on my knees before I blew out the candle, kissed Nonni's picture, and slid it into my pack. Gradually the weightless sensation dissipated and the veil that had been me withdrew to some invisible place. I wondered if that invisible place was Eden.

chapter
fifty-one

Someone was knocking on the door. I rolled over. "C'mon in," I said before I thought better of it.

Luke stepped into the room carrying a paper bag. "It's eleven in the morning, beautiful. Thought I'd see if you were still among the living." He sat down on the edge of the bed.

"Mmph." I rolled over, burying my face in the pillows. "I look awful, Luke. I haven't even brushed my teeth."

He took me by the shoulders and turned me around. "I don't care," he said, and kissed me full on the mouth.

I leaned back in his arms. "Agh," I said. "How can you stand me like this?"

He brushed the tangled hair back from my eyes and kissed me once more for good measure. "It must be love," he said lightly.

My heart did a triple axel. Had he just said what I thought?

He set me gently against the headboard before I could recover. "And now, perhaps mademoiselle is hungry?" His French accent was all the more fantastic because it was real. "Perhaps...*un pamplemousse?*" He stood, reached into the sack, and pulled out a grapefruit, waving it around like a magician.

I started to laugh.

"But *non*, perhaps mademoiselle would *préfère une orange?*" He withdrew an orange from the sack and began juggling it with the grapefruit. "Or better...*une banane?*" He added a banana to the circle. "*Une pomme? Un grenadier? Des raisins?*" An apple, a pomegranate, and a cluster of grapes joined the whirl. He caught them one at a time and set them on the bed.

"Show-off."

He grinned. "You know it. Took me two seasons of *Presto!* to get that down." He popped a few grapes in his mouth

I picked up the grapefruit and began peeling it, amazed that even with my puffy eyes the urge to dive for cover had passed.

Luke reached into the bag again. "There's something you need to see," he said, suddenly serious.

He handed me a copy of *Celeb'* magazine dated for this week. "Page forty-two," he said.

In the top corner of the page was a photo—blurry, but unmistakably of Luke. And me.

"Trent's Cheating Heart" blared the caption.

Caught on a lobby security cam, Trent and a mystery babe (who is definitely not Gwen), check in to a Washington coastal motel. "Must've been quite a night," says a source, "judging from all the champagne bottles and lingerie they left."

A sobbing Gwen had to be sedated when the photos became public.

My stomach gave a lurch. "Champagne and lingerie?"

"I was hoping it wouldn't start this soon." He smoothed the paper bag. "Brigitta, you may be about to get a lot of unwelcome attention. It's only a matter of time before these weasels find out who you are."

"How would they find that out?"

"Believe me, they have ways." He looked at his hands. "I didn't think...when I lied to you...what it might cost you. I told myself I was protecting you. But I was protecting me." He gave a short laugh. "I *am* a conceited slimeball."

I tickled the back of his hand. "No, you just play one on TV."

He caught my eye.

"Luke, I shouldn't have written things like that in my blog. I was just"—I blushed— "being a fan."

He winked. "With fans like that…"

"I know."

He rubbed my fingers. "I have to go back to LA."

My heart crashed. I'd known we were leaving. I'd even accepted that it was tomorrow. But somehow I'd thought Luke was coming back to Kwahnesum. "When?"

"I begin shooting on Wednesday."

"How long?"

"Two months. I may get a weekend here and there."

"Okay." I put on my "brave face." Obviously it wasn't very convincing.

Luke fell back on the bedspread, staring up at the ceiling. "I will be completely miserable." He pulled the banana out from behind his head. "Oops," he said. "Don't eat that."

I scooted my feet under his leg and wiggled my toes.

"Hey!" He rolled onto one elbow, laughing. "Maybe you could—do you think your dad would let you—no." He frowned. "It would be worse for you in LA."

"You're asking me to come to LA?" My heart started beating faster.

"I couldn't put you through that."

"Isn't it up to me what I volunteer to go through?"

He frowned. "It can be really brutal."

"Maybe I'm tougher than you think."

His blue, blue eyes gazed at me. That slow smile spread across his face. "Maybe you are."

Seeing Starzz ★

Celebrities Find Their Deep Space
Hollywood's Hidden Spiritual Quest

Exclusive Interview with Trent Yves

Mystic: Trent, do you think there is a spiritual aspect to your work?

Trent: Wow, you don't start with small talk, do you?

Mystic: Nope.

Trent: Spiritual. Well, we're all trying to live a good life, do good things in the world.

Mystic: That is such a cliché! You know you can do better than that.

Trent: I can, huh?

Mystic: Yes.

Trent: Okay, well, I do yoga for conditioning. That's kind of spiritual. And I think that whole Kabbalah thing is pretty fascinating. But no Scientology. I stay away from that.

Mystic: You are impossible!

Trent: What are you after?

Mystic: Life and death.

Trent: Life and death…Okay. Well, one thing I've figured out is that life works better when you don't think you're the only one on the planet. You're only here for a little while, so if it's just a giant grab for glory, you're going to be disappointed. We're here to take care of each other.

Mystic: Wow, Trent.

Trent: Not the Trent Yves you know and love, eh?

Mystic: Just keep your shirt on.

Trent: Have I made even the slightest mention of my beautiful abs?

Mystic: I'm sure your abs make the world a better place.

Trent: I like to think so.

Mystic: Okay. Spirituality. Is there anything spiritual about making movies?

Trent: Geez, you like to go for the jugular, don't you?

Mystic: Sorry.

Trent: 'sokay. Any good movie asks "big questions." Heck, even bad movies ask them. Things like, "Why is there evil?" and "What's my purpose?" I like to figure out what questions the movie is asking so I can try to answer them.

Mystic: You do? I mean, what have been some of the questions in your films?

Trent: Well, *Imlandria* was all about, "How do you find what is lost and restore it?" and *Rocket* was mostly about forgiveness.

Mystic: And how did you answer those questions?

Trent: Sorry. Something has to be sacred.

Mystic: So, is there a God?

Trent: Yes. I think so. See "something sacred."

Mystic: Where do you feel most spiritual?

Trent: I like to have some trees around. In the woods, I think.

Mystic: Why the woods?"

Trent: Well, it's amazing what you find there. In fact, a while back, I found a goddess.

Mystic: Thanks so much for your time today, Trent.

Trent: Don't mention it.

One more thing. You'll notice a lot of deleted entries in this blog. I've figured out a few things about spirituality, and one of them is you don't trash your friends.

N, you're smarter than I ever gave you credit for—and you are a true friend.

My sister, M, I don't know how to say how much you mean to me.

Trentsbabe responds:

mystic, u are so lucky! i hope u live haply ever after.

Malibu1 responds:

Thanks for what you wrote, Mystic. I haven't always been the best sister. I really love you, and we're so much alike. Let's spend more time together: "Birds of a feather move in mysterious ways."

M

Nattycat responds:

I miss U.

—Starlet

Discussion Questions

1. Why do you think Luke came to Kwahnesum?

2. What does Brigitta find so fascinating about celebrities? Why does she keep it a secret?

3. Why does Brigitta feel it is so important to find a religion? What do you think about this? Does Brigitta find a religion by the end of the book?

4. Brigitta's dad, Paul, has made some dramatic changes in his life. Why? How has this impacted his relationships?

5. Why is religion a source of conflict in Brigitta's family? Have you ever found it to be a source of conflict in your life?

6. Why is the image of the Garden of Eden used over and over? What does Luke mean when he says he wants to find Eden?

7. Was the wildlife center wrong to handle the situation with the cougar kittens as they did? Were Brigitta's actions wrong concerning the kittens? What "should" have been done? What would you have done?

8. Why is Cherrywood so important to Brigitta? Do you have a place that has strong emotional significance in your life?

9. If you were to ask several characters in the book what happens after we die, how would they reply? What would Brigitta say? Mallory? Nonni? Natalie? Paul? Luke? What do you think?

10. If you have ever lost someone close to you, how did it change the way you view life and death?

11. Why did Luke keep such an important secret from Brigitta? What would have happened if he had told her earlier?

12. Brigitta talks a lot about being "known." What does she mean by that? In what ways do you want to be "known?"

13. Brigitta says she loves Luke. Is it possible to love someone after knowing them such a short time?

14. Do you think Brigitta and Luke have a relationship that can "go the distance?" Why or why not? What does a romantic relationship need to survive?

Acknowledgments

Mom and Dad, for encouraging my writing from "A Cookie Named Gaggy" onward.

My amazing husband and soul mate, Fr. Andrew Bond, for your steady presence these last three decades.

For my kids, Sarah, Taelor, Aaron, and Tom Bond, for cheering me through all the many incarnations of this book.

My beautiful agent, Sara Crowe, who believed in the book.

My fabulous editor, Leah Hultenschmidt, and all the wonderful people at Sourcebooks, for taking a chance on me.

Artemis: Janet Lee Carey, Heidi Pettit, Jill Sahlstrom, Dawn Knight, and Lisa Sheets, for being my muses.

Dawn Pontious for keeping me organized in mind and body.

Bet Alef Meditative Synagogue, Bellevue, Washington, for welcoming me at your Shabbat service.

Paul Bokor, Sr., for Hollywood advice.

Mary Eliza Crane, for astrology advice.

The Diviners writing group: Peggy King Anderson, Molly Blaisdell, Judy Bodmer, Janet Lee Carey, Holly Cupala, Dawn Knight, Justina Chen, and Nancy White Carlstrom for holding my hand through eighteen years of the writing life.

Rabbi Mark Glickman, Congregation Kol Ami, Woodinville, WA, for advice on Hebrew and Jewish traditions.

Dr. Briggs Hall, Washington Department of Fish and Wildlife, for pointing me in the right direction.

Beth Harris, for insight on child actors and Hollywood culture.

Connie Hsu, for your paparazzi expertise and your support of this project.

Dr. John Huckabee, PAWS Wildlife Center, for advice on the behavior and needs of cougar cubs.

Paula Kinzer and family, for letting me stay in your Earthship.

My friends at Living Hope Ministries, for believing for me, even when I stopped believing.

Sheila MacDonald, for sharing your story about the cougar kittens who came to you, and for advocating for them.

Ahnday Meweh for shamanic advice.

Kalon Randall for Brigitta's Tarot reading.

My manuscript readers: Annika Browne, to whom I gave Luke as a present, Laura Hunter, who hugged the manuscript after reading it, Molly Blaisdell, who stayed up all night reading and decided the book wasn't lame after all.

My TEENWriters and all my students, for helping me hold on to my sixteen-year-old self.

Ted Willey, Guardian of Cherrywood, for putting your life on hold to care for Nana and Grampy in their final years.

The Wilderness Awareness School, Duvall, Washington, for inspiration.

Eric Kitching for seeing the eyes of the cougar.

Jenn Wolfe, for taking me tracking.

Rocky Spencer, 1952–2007, Carnivore Specialist and brother to cougars, Washington Department of Fish & Wildlife, for reading the "cat" sections, and even adding a few touches of your own to the text. RIP.

God, without Whom I would be impossible.

Any factual errors in the manuscript are mine, alone.

About the Author

Katherine Grace Bond often finds herself in the woods of Washington State escaping from giant cats and shadowy figures in cloaks. The founder of TEEN *Write*, a live action role-playing community where participants come as characters they create, she lives with her husband in a dimension populated by younger people, some of whom resemble her. Previous titles include *The Legend of the Valentine*, a children's story about the Civil Rights Movement.

www.KatherineGraceBond.com
www.TheSummerofNoRegrets.com